Loser's Town

Daniel Depp

**SIMON &
SCHUSTER**

London · New York · Sydney · Toronto

A CBS COMPANY

First published in Great Britain by Simon & Schuster UK Ltd, 2009
A CBS COMPANY

1 3 5 7 9 10 8 6 4 2

Simon & Schuster UK Ltd
1st Floor
222 Gray's Inn Road
London
WC1X 8HB

www.simonsays.co.uk

Simon & Schuster Australia
Sydney

A CIP catalogue record for this book is
available from the British Library

Trade Paperback ISBN 978-1-84737-407-3

Typeset by M Rules
Printed in the UK by CPI Mackays, Chatham ME5 8TD

Author's Note

They are not They.

He, She or It is not You.

Any resemblance in this book
to people living or deceased
is purely coincidental and will
merely be taken by the author
as a tribute to his genius.

To John

in memory of
the flying Scaramanga Brothers.

'I came out to Los Angeles in the 30s, during the Depression, because there was work here. LA is a loser's town. It always has been. You can make it here when you can't make it anywhere else.'

Robert Mitchum

'It's all very well going around thinking you're a cowboy, until you run into somebody who thinks he's an indian.'

Kinky Friedman

One

As the van turned off Laurel Canyon and up onto Wonderland, Potts said to Squiers, 'How many dead bodies have you seen?'

Squiers thought for a minute, his face squinted as if thought were painful to him. Potts figured it probably was. Finally Squiers said, 'You mean, like, in a funeral home or just laying around?'

This sort of thing never failed to drive Potts crazy. You ask him a simple question and he takes three fucking days and then gives you a stupid answer. This is why he hated working with him.

'Jesus, yeah, okay, just fucking laying around. Not your fucking grannie in her coffin.'

This sent Squiers into another round of thought and facial manipulation. I could go out for a freaking cup of coffee while he's thinking, Potts said to himself. Potts wanted to hit him with something. Instead he bit his lip and turned his head to watch the houses they passed.

The elderly van trudged up the steep, winding street that seemed to go on forever. Squiers drove, as always, because Squiers liked driving and Potts didn't. In Potts' opinion, you had to be an idiot or a maniac to enjoy driving in Los Angeles. Squiers qualified as both. Potts read somewhere that there were more than ten million people in LA, people who spent literally half their lives on the roads. In some places twelve lanes of traffic going eighty miles an hour, bumper to bumper, within inches of each other. Careening along in several tons of glass and metal, your knuckles white on the wheel. You go too slow they run over your ass. You go too fast you can't stop in time when some old fart brakes at a senile hallucination, standing a lane of a hundred cars on its nose. You got no choice but to do whatever everybody else is doing, no matter how stupid. Mainly you just do it and try not to think about the mathematical impossibility of it all; the sheer, mindless optimism that any of this could function for longer than fifteen seconds without getting you killed or mangled. On the other hand, every fifteen seconds somebody actually *was* getting killed or mangled on an LA freeway, so it was perfectly sane to stress about it. You had to have a fucking death wish to drive in LA.

What Potts hated mainly, though, was that you were forced to pretend people knew what they were doing when they clearly didn't. You look out the window at the faces hurtling past and they give you no reason for hope. Whizzing past goes a collection of drunks, hormonal teenagers, housewives fighting with their kids, hypertense execs screaming into cellphones, the ancient, the half-blind, the losers with no reason to keep living, the sleep-deprived but amphetamine-amped truck drivers swinging a gazillion-tonned rig of toilet supplies. Faces out of some goddamned horror movie. One false move and everybody dies. You had to lie to yourself in order to function. This is what got to Potts. Potts was no optimist. You spend five years in a Texas prison and it changes your view of what people are like. Jesus, so many fucking psychos loose in the world it's a wonder we manage to wake in our beds alive, much less navigate a fucking superhighway. Then you were forced to shove all this aside, cram it into some little cupboard in your brain and shut it away, whenever you walked out the fucking door in the morning. You had to make yourself forget everything you knew about life, everything you knew to be true, and pretend that people were somehow Good and not the collection of thieves and madmen and basic shits you knew them to be. This is what drove Potts crazy. It was exhausting, this burden of self-deception. The goddamn weight of it made him tired all the time.

Potts looked over at Squiers, who stared straight ahead over the wheel, brow creased, mimicking the act of human thought. Squiers was huge, pale and dumb, Potts' exact opposite, and Potts almost admired him. Potts hated being around him, of course, and felt the world would clearly be a much safer place if Squiers happened to get run over by a train. Squiers was slow and plodding and whatever happened in his head bore no resemblance to what happened in Potts'. Squiers never worried, never got nervous or frightened, could fall asleep standing up like a goddamn Holstein. Never questioned anything, never contributed an answer, never argued. He'd either do something or he wouldn't, and you could never be sure which way it would go, since there appeared to be no thought process behind it. Squiers was maybe the happiest person Potts had ever met. There were no conflicts in his life. You give Squiers a nice blood-soaked chainsaw movie or a pile of cheap porno mags and Squiers was as content as a child. Meanwhile Potts had a bad stomach and couldn't remember a time when the sky wasn't fixing to collapse on him. Potts had to envy him a little, while still hating his psychotic guts. Richie called them Mutt and Jeff, made jokes about their each being one half of the perfect employee, though utter fuck-ups individually. Potts didn't like Richie very much either, though Richie paid well and ex-cons couldn't be too choosy.

The van climbed up and up, out of this world and into the next, past fancy-ass places costing millions of bucks but still had their asses on stilts hanging a hundred feet over a goddamn canyon. For that kind of money you'd think you could get a backyard. Potts couldn't imagine life without a backyard, you had to have a backyard.

Someplace you could go out and drink a beer and barbecue a goddamn hamburger. Even the little shitpile he rented out in Redlands had a fucking backyard. The truth was, though, the whole Hollywood Hills scene was bullshit. For a couple of million bucks you got a dinky house with no yard at all and its ass hanging over a goddamn abyss. Well yeah, that was fucking Hollywood all over, wasn't it? The whole goddamn place was a con. Movie stars my ass. A bunch of suckers. Give me a house with a backyard anytime.

'A hundred and twenty-three,' said Squiers.

Potts looked at him. 'What?'

'Dead bodies I seen.'

'You lying sack of shit. A hundred and twenty-three? What kind of number is that? You a fucking guard at Auschwitz or something? Jesus.'

'No, no kidding. I saw a plane crash once. A hundred and fucking twenty-three people perished.'

Squiers saying that word, perished, really irritated the hell out of Potts. He was lying, he'd heard it somewhere on the news, and the newscaster had said perished. Squiers didn't even know what it meant, where the hell would he get off using a word like that. Potts decided to nail him on it.

'You saw a plane crash.'

'Yeah, that's right.'

'You actually saw it crash.'

'No, I didn't actually see it, like, hit the ground. But I

5

come along right after it did, when all the fire trucks were there and shit.'

'And you saw the bodies?'

'What?'

'You saw the bodies, right? A hundred and twenty-three fucking bodies, thrown all over the ground. And you counted them, right? One, two, three, a hundred and twenty-three?'

'Well, no, shit, I didn't actually see the bodies, but they were there. A hundred and twenty-three people on that plane and they all perished.'

Potts took a deep breath and sighed. 'What did I ask you?'

'When?'

'When I asked you how many bodies you've seen. I said seen. That's the word I used. I didn't say how many bodies have you heard about, how many the fucking bozo on the news said there were. Are you grasping this?'

'They were there, man. I didn't have to see them. It was a fucking planeload of people.'

'But the point is, you didn't actually see them, did you? You heard about them, but you didn't actually see them with your own little eyes. Am I correct?'

'Yeah but—'

'No, no fucking but. Did you actually, personally, with your own eyes, see a hundred and twenty-three bodies? Just yes or no. Yes or no?'

Squiers steamed for a minute, he wriggled his ass a little in the driver's seat, then he said curtly: 'No.'

'A ha!' said Potts. 'I rest my case.'

The van climbed slowly up the steep winding road. It was three o'clock in the morning and a goddamn fog coming in didn't help matters. They had to stop several times to check the streets. It was like a rat maze up here. It seemed to Potts that the climb was endless. He didn't like heights. He liked nice flat ground, that's why he lived in the desert.

'This is it,' Potts said.

They stopped at a large metal gate. Squiers edged the van up next to the keypad. Squiers looked at Potts, who was shuffling around the various pockets of the combat gear he liked to wear.

'You got the code?'

'Yeah, of course I've got the code.' Truth was, Richie had written the code on a little Post-it note and given it to him and now Potts couldn't find it. He'd taken it from Richie back at the club and hadn't thought about it and now he couldn't find the goddamn thing. He fought back a rising panic attack. Squiers, the bastard, was watching him with a barely hidden smirk on his face. He was hoping Potts couldn't find it, so they'd have to call Richie and Richie would rip Potts a new asshole. Squiers was pissed about the airplane thing and was too dumb to figure out how to get revenge on his own.

At last Potts found the Post-it note, stuck in one of the chest pockets on his camouflage jacket. He felt his bowels relax and Squiers looked disappointed. Potts tried to look

7

cool, as if it hadn't been any sweat, and read the code to Squiers, who reached through the window and punched it in. The gate shuddered a little then opened and they drove through.

The house was perched on a knoll right up at the very end of Wonderland Avenue. As the gate shut behind them, they climbed up the narrow drive to a level paved area where the garage was. There was a sharp right and the drive continued up at a steep angle to the house itself. Squiers parked the van in front of the garage. They got out and stared at the steep rise.

'Shit,' said Potts. 'How are the parking brakes on this fucker?'

'Hell, I dunno. It ain't my van.'

'We have to back it up and park the bastard there,' Potts said, motioning up the drive. 'And you better hope the sonofabitch don't roll downhill and go shooting off into outer space.'

'Shit,' said Squiers. He looked at the spot where they'd have to park, then followed the possible trajectory of the vehicle downhill and off the edge of the knoll and down onto a valley full of houses.

'Well, let's do it,' said Potts. 'Let's go have a look first.'

They trudged up the hill. Potts was small and wiry but he smoked. Squiers was a huge fucking buffoon. By the time they got to the top they were both out of breath. They sat for a moment, then Squiers tried the door. It was unlocked. He looked at Potts, waiting.

They entered the darkened house, stepping into a living room with a cathedral ceiling, enclosed on two sides by floor-to-ceiling walls of glass. Beyond was a patio that wrapped around most of the house and a panorama of the lights of Los Angeles far below.

Squiers reached over to flip on a light but Potts stopped him.

'What the hell are you doing? It's like a goddamn fishbowl in here. They could fucking see us from fucking Compton.'

Potts went over and pulled the heavy curtains closed. 'Now you can turn on the fucking light.'

They looked around the room.

'It's a fucking dump,' declared Potts. 'The fucker's got about a billion fucking dollars and not a lick of taste. Not a goddamn thing worth stealing.'

'Richie'd get pissed if we stole anything,' said Squiers. 'He said not to touch anything.'

'Fuck Richie,' said Potts. 'Anyway, there's nothing to steal. Look at this shit. Jesus.'

Potts started opening doors. 'Where the hell he say it was?'

'Upstairs, I think.'

They trudged up the steps. Potts opened a door. An office. He opened another one. A large messy bedroom. He pushed open another one.

The girl sat slumped on the toilet. She looked maybe sixteen or seventeen, very pretty, with long brown hair and a good figure. She was wearing a short, plaid skirt and a pair of colored tights were down around her ankles. A needle and a syringe stuck out of her left thigh, and the works for cooking up heroin sat on the sink next to her.

Potts and Squiers stared at her for a while.

'She's cute,' Squiers said after a while. 'You sure she's dead?'

'She fucking better be,' said Potts.

'Cute tits.'

'You're a fucking pervert,' said Potts distastefully, 'you know that?'

'All I'm saying is that I'd fuck her. If she was alive.'

Potts made a disgusted face. 'Where's the fucking camera?'

Squiers dug out a small, cheap 35mm tourist's camera.

'How come he didn't give us a digital?' asked Squiers, examining the camera. 'This is shit.'

'Because he wants the fucking film, that's why.'

'Yeah, but why's it got to be film?'

'Because he doesn't fucking trust us, okay? We could make copies before we got back. He wants the fucking roll of film.'

'Oh.'

'Can I have the fucking camera now, please?'

Potts took pictures of the girl from all angles, pausing only to let the flash recharge.

'Okay, go and get the van,' he told Squiers, 'and back it up as close as you can. I don't want to have to drag this bitch all the way down the hill.'

'How come you don't go and get the van?'

'Mainly because you're a fucking sick motherfucker and there's no way in hell I'm going to leave you alone with this bitch. Does that answer your fucking question?'

Squiers looked at him. He didn't move. For a moment Potts thought he was going to turn on him. But you could never tell what Squiers was thinking, if what he did could be called thinking. There was always just that sort of glassy look, as if he'd managed to focus through your eyes and onto the back of your head. Potts waited for a move, the flicker of a muscle before he struck, because you'd never see it in his eyes first. Squiers might be a fucking moron but you couldn't read him and you couldn't assume he'd even do what was in his own interest.

Finally Squiers just shrugged and turned and went downstairs. Potts took a deep breath and went into the bedroom to take a few shots. Richie wanted what he called 'establishing shots', photos that clearly identified the place. Richie thought of everything. Potts didn't like the miserable goombah shit anymore than he liked Squiers, but you had to hand it to him, he didn't miss a trick.

Squiers meanwhile was having a hell of a time getting the van backed up the hill. He'd borrowed the van from his brother-in-law, who'd told him it was reliable. Squiers imagined the weaselly little sonofabitch laughing at him and made up his mind to beat the shit out of him when he got back, sister or no sister. The gears were shit, first wasn't enough and second was too much. After a lot of grinding and rocking, Squiers finally just pulled all the way up to the garage, then backed up quick enough so that the bumper scraped the pavement before it rose up the hill. When he got to the top, Squiers left the van in first and locked the emergency brake. It lurched a few inches downhill but it caught. Squiers waited and the thing didn't go anywhere so he got out of the van and went back into the house.

'You think you made enough fucking noise?' Potts said to him when he walked in the door.

'I think we ought to hurry. I don't trust the brakes on that thing.'

'Shit.'

Potts went into the upstairs bedroom and pulled a duvet off the bed. He dragged it into the hallway outside the bathroom and spread it on the floor. Squiers started into the bathroom to pick the girl up but Potts pushed him aside. Squiers stood back and let Potts tend to her. Potts pulled out the syringe and laid it on the sink next to the works. He lifted her off the toilet and dragged her into the hallway and onto the blanket. The skirt had ridden up and she was naked underneath. Potts wrestled the pantyhose back up over her hips.

'Why bother to do that?' asked Squiers, who'd been watching all this appreciatively.

'I don't want anybody thinking we interfered with her.'

'What difference does it make?'

Potts didn't bother with a reply. It made Potts sick to

think of somebody finding the body and believing it had been interfered with. It was just the sort of filthy thing that the newspapers and TV loved, and it made Potts sick to imagine that somebody might think it was him, even if they had no idea who he actually was. When he'd made the girl decent he rolled her up in the blanket, like a Tootsie Roll.

'What about the works?' Squiers asked him.

'Richie said leave it, it'll give this fucker something to remind him when he comes home.'

They held opposite ends of the rolled blanket and awkwardly carried the body down the stairs, out of the house and to the van. Squiers reached with one hand to open the back door of the van when the vehicle lurched forward half a foot. Then again.

Panicked, Squiers let go of his end of the blanket. The end with the girl's head struck the ground with a dull thud. Squiers was dancing alongside the van, struggling with the door, as it began rolling downhill. The van was picking up speed as Squiers jumped inside. He pushed the brake and nothing much happened. The garage was looming up fast. He stood up on the goddamn brake, trying to push it through the floor, pushing his back against the seat and pulling hard at the wheel with his hands. There was an ugly grinding noise and Squiers thought the brakes had given way completely but the van slowed with a sound like a freight train stopping and came to rest a couple of feet from the bumper of the Porsche sitting in the garage.

13

Squiers slumped over the steering wheel. He got out and looked up the hill at Potts, who had sat down next to the girl, his mouth open.

Squiers came trudging up the hill. 'Fucking brakes, man,' he said happily, as if he'd just stepped off some ride at Magic Mountain.

There was nothing Potts could possibly say. They half-carried, half-dragged the girl down the hill and stuck her in the van. They were nearly to Ontario and Potts was still shaking inside and smoking another cigarette to calm himself down when Squiers said, out of the blue:

'At least her ass was clean.'

Two

The agent's office was nine floors above Wilshire Boulevard in a building that cost thirty million dollars and still looked like a cross between a cuckoo clock and a Forest Lawn mausoleum. It was owned by the largest and most powerful talent agency in the world, but with all that glass the air conditioning was useless and the windows didn't open in case somebody felt tempted to jump. The bigwigs had a west-facing view of the Pacific. This particular agent had a panorama of East LA and a layer of smog that reached all the way to Redlands. Even from here, you could practically hear them wheezing in San Bernardino.

'. . . not dealing here with some used-car dealer from Reseda who wants you to get pictures of his wife fucking around, and I told them how important it was that they send somebody with a little tact, not some fucking clown who doesn't understand a fucking thing about the business, or about dealing with talent of this caliber, someone who got a little sensitivity . . .'

She'd been going on like this for fifteen minutes and still hadn't told him a thing he could use. She wasn't a bad-looking woman, really, if you like over-compensating East Coast types. Sometimes he actually did. She had short auburn hair, full red lips, pale skin, and the overall demeanor of a Gila monster. He had a fantasy of her slashing flesh all day long, then going home to bill and coo at her cats.

'. . . With discretion, for fuck's sake, and not bounding in like some steer in a rose garden . . .'

She wore a simple black Balenciaga dress and he thought he caught a whiff of Opium as she walked behind him. She had excellent taste in clothing but the steer and rose garden analogy hit too close to home. His thumb ached and without the bandage it looked like a slightly bent eggplant.

'. . . can keep their mouth shut and not go running to the tabloids with material that could . . .'

Her office was small and the sort of cubicles they give middle-management at insurance companies, but without the family photos and the national park calendar. Anything that could give a clue to her personal life had been carefully removed. A floor-to-ceiling bookshelf full of scripts covered one entire wall. He counted six that had already won Academy Awards and four more that probably would. In Hollywood, you could easily admire such complete dedication, but he'd long ago decided he didn't care to.

His thumb was beginning to throb now and his back was hurting as well. He refused to take the painkillers but he badly wanted a cigarette and a hefty shot of Jack Daniel's. At a rodeo in Salinas the week before he'd gotten thrown from a horse named Tusker and pulled a muscle in his back. Then he'd managed to dislocate his thumb while trying to rope a calf. He'd looped it between the rope and the saddle horn – a truly greenhorn mistake that had gotten him much laughter but absolutely no sympathy from his peers. The Salinas rodeo had been a disaster, but there was another one at the end of the month in Bakersfield. He was wondering if he had enough vacation days to make that one when he noticed she had stopped talking.

'What the fuck are you doing?'

She was standing next to him with her hands on her hips and a look that made him wonder if he'd suddenly developed Tourette's syndrome. It took him a moment to realize he'd absent-mindedly pulled out his cigarettes and had started to light one.

'Jesus Christ,' she said, 'this is a non-smoking building, just like everywhere else in this state! How fucking observant are *we*?'

He put the cigarettes back into his jacket pocket. He was getting sleepy now, too. He'd driven all night from his sister's house in Flagstaff, cutting his vacation two days short because Walter, his boss, said he'd been expressly requested for this case, and that the client was an important one. It was now late-Thursday morning and he wasn't supposed to go back to work until Monday. He was betting that Walter, the chintzy bastard, hadn't even put him on the clock for this. It was just the sort of crap he'd pull. Spandau made a note to get this straightened out before Walter slipped out of the office and spent the rest of the day getting hammered somewhere.

'You haven't been listening to a fucking word I've said. Geary said you were supposed to be good, but frankly you don't look to me like you could handle a street crossing, much less a case like this.'

Paul Geary was a TV producer he'd done some work for, and was the one who'd given Spandau's name to the Allied Talent Group, the agency that had constructed this particular air-conditioned nightmare. They in turn had foisted Spandau off on her, and now she was sweetly telling him she wasn't happy about it. Annie Michaels was one of the best agents in the business, known for being intensely loyal and protective of her clients. She was also famous for having one of the nastiest mouths in Hollywood and Spandau was getting particularly tired of having it aimed at him.

David Spandau stood up and carefully closed a single button of his Armani jacket. She was about five feet three inches and now he towered nearly a foot above her. She stopped talking when she had to look up at a forty-five-degree angle. As Spandau's old mentor Beau McCaulay used to say, 'When all else fails, just be taller.'

'Thank you,' he said. 'It's been a pleasure meeting you.' He held out his hand. She simply stared at it.

'Where the fuck are you going?' she asked incredulously. Hollywood agents are so used to people trying to get in to see them, they forget people can also walk out.

'First,' he said, 'I thought I'd stand in front of your lovely new building and light a cigarette, provided nobody runs out and douses me with a fire extinguisher. Then,' he said, 'I thought I'd go over to Musso and Frank for the eggs and roast-beef hash. After that I don't know. Somebody told me there was a German Expressionist exhibit at the county museum. While I adore Emil Nolde's woodcuts, I'm not sure I could deal with all that angst on top of the roast-beef hash.'

It's hard to get the drop on a good agent. The trick is that they're so used to people caring, their motor-neurons lock up when confronted with someone who simply couldn't give a shit. She continued to give him a blank stare as she processed the fact that he was actually walking out on her. She looked him up and down, as if actually noticing him for the first time. A big, dark man with a broken nose and tired eyes. Something wrong with his thumb. Good suit, a real Armani, but what's with those fucking cowboy boots? He looked a little like Robert Mitchum but she thought Robert Mitchum was sexy as hell so she tried to ignore that part of it. Genuinely tough, she figured. Tough

19

enough that he could afford to downplay it. Maybe he even had a brain. Finally the program completed its loop, and she gave Spandau a nasty smile.

'A real smart-ass,' she said.

'No,' he said, 'it's just that I've got better things to do for the ass-end of my vacation than to sit around and be verbally abused by some Long Island neurotic in a two-thousand-dollar potato sack.'

'Look, *Tex*, you were hired—'

'No, I wasn't hired. Nobody's hired anybody. Your agency asked me to come here and see if I wanted to help them out with a problem. So far this is just a freebie, a pro-fessional courtesy among supposedly civilized people. Frankly, though, I'm not all that crazy about getting shit on, even when somebody's paying for it.'

'My God, who the fuck do you think you are? Who the fuck do you think you're dealing with? I need a fucking professional, and they send me a fucking extra from *Bonanza!*'

She's talking about the Tony Lamas, Spandau thought. Otherwise he was in Armani and impeccable. Spandau saluted her and turned toward the door.

'Hey, buster, don't you turn your back on *me!*'

'If you'd like, I can have the agency send someone over more to your liking.'

'Are you kidding?' she cried as he opened the door. 'Fuck you *and* your agency! Don't track horse shit on the carpet as you go out, Hopalong!'

Spandau opened the door and nearly ran into a slim, elegant middle-aged man in a pinstripe suit and a good haircut. 'Excuse me,' Spandau said, and started to pass him.

'Would you mind waiting just a few more moments?' he said to Spandau. His smile was a triumph of orthodontics. He graciously escorted Spandau back into the room and closed the door. 'Hello, Annie,' he said to her. 'I see you've been honing those social skills that made you so popular at Bennington.'

'This . . . *asshole* the detective agency sent me was just leaving.'

'I'm sorry,' he said. 'Mister Spandau?'

'David Spandau. Coren and associates, personal security and investigations.'

'I'm sorry, Mr Spandau. Annie is far too used to getting her way. Her idea of diplomacy is to scream loudly until people give in. It's not pretty but surprisingly effective. It works with most people. I apologize for her.'

'Robert,' she said. 'He's an idiot. He's all wrong for this. Just look at those shoes!'

'Sweetie,' he said, 'for somebody who can wear Versace and still look like a Hasidic Jew, I'm not sure I'd talk.'

'Robert, that's cruel!' she whined, but it made her laugh.

'Honey, you know it's true. You'd be wearing go-go boots with that dress if the shop hadn't given you instructions.' To Spandau he said, 'Chanel refuses to sell her anything.'

'That's an outright lie!'

21

'She's practically a legend. They're convinced she takes their clothes and has them altered by some little Chinese man in Reseda. Otherwise it doesn't make sense.'

By this time she'd collapsed into a fit of giggles. 'Robert, you are horrible!'

'I love you, that's why I can tell you these things. You do look good in that black thing, though. Is it DK?'

'God, no. Balenciaga, honey. You think it looks okay?'

'It looks great. Just the style for you. The lines suit you.'

'You think so?' she pleaded.

'Am I not the most honest man you know? Now be nice and quit picking on this poor guy.' He held out his hand and we shook. 'I'm Robert Aronson, by the way. I'm Bobby Dye's attorney.'

He motioned for Spandau to sit down again, then sat down himself, after adjusting the knees of his suit.

'Now let's see if we can get this sorted out. I've been on the phone all afternoon about you, Mr Spandau, and in spite of Annie's impression, it seems you are highly regarded in your profession.'

'I—' began Annie.

'Shut *up*, Annie. You remember the lunatic who was stalking Marcie du Pont last year? This is the gentleman responsible for putting him away. It seems Mr Spandau specializes in people like us. Tell me, Mr Spandau, are you really as good as all that?'

'Better,' Spandau said. 'I'm a genuine asset to any organ-ization.'

Aronson laughed. It would have been a pleasant laugh if Spandau thought he meant it.

'He's not going to work,' Annie insisted.

'The bottom line, dear, is that no one gives a shit what you *or* I think. I was just on the phone with Gil – Gil White,' he said to me, 'the head of Allied Talent – and Gil wants Bobby to see him. The rest is up to Bobby.'

Annie Michaels shrugged and gave a frustrated sigh. She sat down behind her desk, picked up the phone and pushed a button. Spandau heard a buzz on the assistant's desk outside. 'Millie, check and see when the *Wildfire* shoot is breaking for lunch.' She hung up the phone. 'And when this whole fucking thing blows up, it'll be my ass, as usual,' she said to no one in particular. Her phone buzzed. She picked it up, listened, then asked, 'Is he on the set or in the trailer?' then hung up again. She picked the phone up yet once again and quickly dialed a number. 'Hello, sweetie, it's me. The detective is here. Are you in the mood to see him? When? In about half an hour? Bye.' She replaced the phone with the tips of her fingers, as if it were a piece of bad fruit. 'Okay, let's try it.'

'That's all we can ask for,' said Aronson. 'That is, if Mr Spandau still wants the case, after being subjected to your charms.'

'I'd like to talk to him,' Spandau said.

'They're breaking in half an hour,' she said. 'They're shooting on 36 at Fox.'

She picked up her purse and marched out the door. Aronson looked at Spandau and rolled his eyes.

'We're going to the *Wildfire* set at Fox,' she told her assistant. 'Call and have passes for us at the gate. I'll be back after lunch. Transfer anything important to the cellphone. Everything else can wait until I get back. Are you clear on the difference between important and not important?'

'Uh-huh,' said the assistant, embarrassed and turning crimson.

'Are you listening to me?'

'Yes, Annie.'

'I don't want to be bombarded by calls from people who just want to chat.'

'Annie, how am I supposed to know if they want to chat or not?'

'Because, honey, it's part of your fucking job to know who's important and who's not, and important people don't have time to chat. Is this clear now?'

'Yes, Annie.'

'Why does everybody act as if they've just had a goddamned lobotomy? Robert, you come with me. Hopalong, you can follow us on your horse.'

'I'll just meet you there,' Spandau told her. 'I know where it is.'

She grunted and strode to the elevator and assaulted a button. Apparently the elevator was as frightened of her as everybody else, because it opened right up. 'Robert, are you coming?'

'Of course, Annie.'

Spandau followed him. Aronson purposely took his time about getting to the elevator. Annie had to jam her purse between the doors to keep them from closing. Walking away, Spandau distinctly heard the assistant mutter 'miserable bitch' under her breath. As the elevator doors closed and Annie Michaels began another stream of invective, Spandau made a mental note to send the assistant a bouquet of flowers and his deepest sympathy.

Spandau followed Annie Michaels' Mercedes out of the Allied Talent underground garage. She drove the way she talked, like a screaming banshee, nearly taking the ass off one of the attendants as she pulled onto Wilshire. She drove fast, but so reckless it was impossible to lose her. It was like following the path of a tornado; you simply traced the destruction in her wake. Through the rear window he could see her either talking on the phone or yelling and gesticulating at Aronson, who sat quietly and endured it. Every fifty feet or so, she looked at the road long enough to slam on her brakes and scream at another driver or pedestrian she'd nearly killed. It exhausted Spandau just to watch her. He eased back and let the Mercedes disappear in traffic. He'd been to the Fox lot a thousand times and could have driven to it blindfold. He turned the radio onto a country and western station and took his time.

Spandau's BMW was leased by the agency he worked for, so he couldn't smoke in it – and he badly wanted a cigarette.

Walter, his boss, had already reamed his ass a couple of times for lighting up in the car, so Spandau had to relinquish the a/c and open the windows. The moment he did Los Angeles came rushing in like the angry breath of Hell. It was late September but LA still hadn't managed to outrun a miserable summer. The air shimmered above the pavement, above the parked and waiting cars, and the western horizon turned a lovely but unnatural orange in the smog. A hot, fine mist, composed of equal parts road dust, motor oil and the exhalations of ten million anxious Angelinos, settled on any available skin and clung there to turn clothing into sandpaper. The eyes watered and the throat burned.

Spandau smoked, and thought the city gliding past was like an over-exposed film, too much light, all depth burnt away and sacrificed. All concrete and asphalt, a thousand square miles of man-made griddle on which to fry for our sins. Then you turn a corner and there's a burst of crimson bougainvillea redeeming an otherwise ugly chunk of concrete building. Or a line of tall palm trees, still majestic and still refusing to die, stubbornly sprouting green at the tops of thick dying stalks, guarding a side street of bungalows constructed at a time when LA was still the Land of Milk and Honey. If you squinted hard, you could imagine what brought them here, all those people. There was a beauty still there, sometimes, beneath all the corruption, like in the face of an actress long past her prime, when the outline of an old loveliness can still be glimpsed through the desperate layers of pancake and eyeliner. Spandau could never

figure out why he stayed, what kept bringing him back to
LA, until a drunken conversation he'd had in Nevada with
a cowboy who'd fallen in love with a middle-aged whore. It
was true, said the cowboy, that she was old and greedy and
had no morals to speak of. But sometimes when she slept
she had the face of a young girl, and it was this young girl
the cowboy kept falling in love with, over and over. And
also, added the cowboy, she had tricks that could make you
the happiest man alive when she was in the mood.

He was thinking again of leaving Los Angeles. He often
thought of it –hell, anybody sane thought of it a hundred
times a day –but like the cowboy's whore she inevitably
lured him back. This time it was hard. This time he nearly
didn't come back. Leaving his sister's place in Flagstaff
and rolling the truck back toward LA was like pushing into
cloud that only got darker, until crossing the California line
felt like having a curse lowered on you. He was too old for
this crap. He'd tell Walter he was quitting. Dee was gone,
and the detective work had begun to numb him to anything good and decent in the universe. He was already
drinking too much, and he could see himself ending up
like Walter, having spent the best years of his life chasing
things that, when caught, made no sense at all. With the
sale of the house and what he'd set aside, he could buy a
small ranch in Arizona. But no, shit, he was no goddamn
rancher, he didn't have the energy to start and build a
spread of his own. Not this late in the day. He'd started
collecting books on the American West, and he enjoyed

that world. Maybe he'd become a bookseller, fill up a little house somewhere with books, put out a catalogue. But no, he wouldn't do that either. He didn't know a damn thing about selling books. Beau McCaulay had always said that a man should do whatever he does best. All Spandau could do was fall off a horse. It wasn't much of a résumé.

The Fox lot was in Beverly Hills, across the street from the country club. What disappoints visitors to a movie set is that glitz is reserved for the paying public. From the outside, the place looked like a factory that produced canned goods or toilet seats. And as far as most of the executives were concerned, there was no difference. The only trace of Hollywood glamour was the three-story billboard advertising Bobby Dye's latest film, *Crusoe*, a hip remake of Defoe's classic, in which Friday was played by a pneumatic French actress in a loincloth. The film was about to open, and while serious critics were going to pan it, of course, there were only three of those left in the country, the rest worked for papers or magazines owned by the same people who owned the studios. The buzz was huge and the movie was expected to make back twice its budget in the opening weekend. So, for the time being anyway, Bobby Dye was as close as you get in Hollywood to being a god.

Willard Packard was on duty at the guard's shed when Spandau pulled in. Willard had worked for the studio for more than forty years, and said he knew all the great ones intimately from the chest up.

'Mr Spandau.'

'Mr Packard.'

'*Wildfire*, Stage 36, right?'

'Yep.'

'I don't have to tell you where it is, do I?'

'I think I can find it.'

'*Dead Letters*,' he said. '1976. *Horse's Mouth*, 1978. *Doublecross*, 1981. Am I right?'

'You forgot *The World and Mr Miller*,' Spandau said, naming one of the other films he'd worked on at Fox.

'No, sir, I was just too polite to remind you,' Willard said. 'I believe they handed out cranberry sauce with that one, didn't they?'

'I do believe they did,' Spandau agreed. 'Has Bobby Dye's agent got here yet?'

He made a serious face, then held up a hand with several fingers folded back, as if they'd been chewed off. Spandau nodded and drove onto the lot. He parked in the lot behind the executive building, locking the doors of the Beamer in case the VP in charge of distribution felt like stealing his Blaupunkt sound system. He dodged a flying golfcart, a Chinese man in a headless Panda costume, and two women in suits arguing if blackened catfish was allowed in a macrobiotic diet.

Spandau turned right and walked down a deserted city street past the New York Public Library and an Italian restaurant on the Lower East Side. He'd once fallen dead out of the second-floor library window, and been machine-gunned through the window of the restaurant.

Both had been routine stunts, nothing to be proud of, but he felt a twinge of nostalgia for the old work, until he remembered he'd cracked his wrist falling out the window. The airbag had interfered with the shot the director wanted and he'd moved it slightly while they were at lunch. As a result, it didn't deflate properly and Spandau bounced like a pingpong ball onto the sidewalk. The director had a track record of hits and was only mildly rebuked by the studio. Meanwhile Spandau spent a month in a plaster cast, unable to work and wiping his ass with the wrong hand.

Stage 36 was on the other side of the lot, surrounded by a maze of trailers, cables and equipment. A grip pointed out Bobby Dye's trailer, a small motorhome that would have looked at home in an Arizona retirement community. So much for Hollywood glamour, thought Spandau, though he knew that actors' trailers expand in direct proportion to egos and box office revenues. If *Crusoe* and *Wildfire* did as well as the buzz predicted, Bobby's next trailer might require its own area code. Spandau knocked on the door. Annie Michaels popped out like a ferret and shut the door behind her.

'Where the hell have you been?'

'Taking a stroll down memory lane,' he said.

'Can you make an effort here, please?' There was a slight panic in her voice. Spandau nearly felt sorry for her but stopped himself. 'Now listen. He's under a lot of pressure, he's tense, he's taking a lot of shit from the asshole producer and the asshole director. His co-star has the talent of a bran muffin. Just let me do the talking, just sit there until he talks to you first. If it's a bad time, you'll just go, nothing will get accomplished anyway. He's got good instincts. If he doesn't like you, you're history, understand?'

'Should I have brought a carrot or some sugar cubes?' Spandau asked mildly.

She sucked at her front teeth and gave him the Bronx death stare. 'Personally,' she said, 'I give you about thirty seconds.'

Inside the trailer, Bobby Dye sat wedged behind the small dining table across from Aronson.

'Bobby,' said Aronson, 'this is David Spandau from the detective agency.'

Bobby stood up and they shook hands. Annie hovered behind Spandau for a moment, then inserted herself between them, separating them as if protecting her client from contamination.

'Sweetie, you don't have to do this now if you're not ready,' she said to Bobby.

'I'm fine with it,' he said.

'Are you sure?'

'Dear God, Annie,' said Aronson, 'will you just get a grip?'

'Annie,' said Bobby.

'Yes?'

31

'You're driving me fucking batshit, okay?'

'Sweetie, I'm just looking out for you. That's what I get paid to do.'

'Well stop. Enough, okay?'

'Whatever you want, sweetie.'

'I want you to fucking stop calling me sweetie,' said Bobby. 'It gets on my nerves.'

'Well excuse me,' Annie said, and launched into the post-mortem of a call she'd had that morning from a Finnish director who was interested in working with Bobby. It could have waited, of course, but Annie was trying to save face and wanted the appearance of surrendering ground rather than having had it pulled from under her.

Spandau tuned out the family melodrama and sat down, taking the opportunity to glance around the trailer.

Fifteen-hour days are not uncommon on a movie set. For a starring actor, most of that time is spent sitting in a trailer, under a kind of house-arrest, since you never know when you'll be needed and you dare not leave the set. There's probably nothing in your contract to prevent it, of course, but there's something unsettling about popping round to McDonald's dressed as a cowboy or a flesh-eating zombie. And if you're a popular actor, there are the fans and the press to contend with. If you're filming on a lot, you could in theory go out for a stroll, though you would have to be pretty desperate, since film lots are marginally less exciting than a lumber yard. And like teachers who discover they're a child short at the end of a field trip, producers and directors –a nervous bunch anyway –display apoplectic seizures when they can't locate their actors, who, if left to their own devices, have been known to distract themselves in clever and interesting ways. Everyone is much happier if an actor simply stays nice and safe in his trailer.

Since motorhomes have never been known for their warmth, actors do what they can to make them 'homey'. Spandau had seen trailers decorated like Turkish brothels, opium dens, French boudoirs and gymnasiums. One star he knew traveled with a pot-bellied pig, and had a section of her trailer fenced off and covered with straw. The place smelled accordingly, and the star herself –an international sex symbol who'd ploughed through five husbands – was often redolent of *eau de cochon*. But if the star was happy so was everybody else, health codes be damned.

What made Bobby Dye's trailer special, in Spandau's mind, was its utter lack of distinction. There were no frills, no pillows or fancy curtains. No family photos – no photos at all, no memorabilia, nothing that provided any access to Bobby's personal life or past. The door to the bedroom was open, and Spandau could see a messy bed, some tossed clothing, and a set of weights. The rest of the trailer was as factory-issued, cool and impersonal, as if an effort was made to keep it that way. The only clues to the inner life of its inhabitant were the magazines and books laying about. Among the magazines were *Cahiers du Cinéma*, *Sight &*

Sound, the *New York Times*, *Esquire* and *People*. A diverse reading list, though Spandau unkindly suspected if you looked closely enough they'd each contain some reference to Bobby. On a small bookshelf Will Durant cuddled up with Charles Bukowski and Carl Jung. Had Bobby actually read them? Or were they a bit of theatre dressing?

'A real detective, huh,' said Bobby, calling Spandau's attention back.

'The genuine article.'

'You packing?'

'A gun, you mean?'

'Yeah,' said Bobby.

'No,' said Spandau.

Bobby was disappointed. 'I mean, what the hell is the point, then?'

'Sometimes I ask myself that very question,' Spandau replied.

Spandau liked the fact that Bobby had stood up when they shook hands – someone had given him some manners, at least. Bobby Dye was four inches shorter than Spandau's six-two. He'd gripped Spandau's hand and looked him in the eyes, though there was something exaggerated about it, as if he were playing a role and this was how his character behaved. Bobby was indeed still in costume – faded jeans, scuffed cowboy boots, a plaid shirt open to reveal a tanned but hairless chest. Sleeves rolled up on strong, wiry arms decorated by a collection of tattoos just visible beneath the makeup. A tangled mass of longish brown hair, made worse by hair extensions that were dramatically teased to look windswept for the camera but on close up looked more like a nest of garter snakes. The eyes were brown and a little sad – a fact much commented upon in the teen magazines. And there was the nose – the famous broken beak, slightly pushed in and crooked, the supposed result of a short boxing career, that gave Bobby's face most of its character and redeemed it from looking like a million others. Not for the first time, Spandau was amused at how mundane an actor could seem in person, then somehow blaze into magnificence on screen. There was some peculiar magic in those otherwise plain features that gave them a grandeur and romance through the lens of a camera. No one could explain why it happened with only a few chosen ones, though people had tried since the beginning of film.

'So how are you supposed to protect me?'

'Generally speaking, if it gets to a point where there's any shooting, I haven't done my job. And I always do my job.'

'What I think Mr Spandau means is—' started Annie.

'I know what he means,' Bobby said to her sharply. 'I got ears.'

She glared at Spandau. Spandau realized he must have been smiling. 'Mr Spandau, I don't think you are quite—'

'Oh, shut up, Annie,' Bobby said.

Spandau tried not to gloat. Spandau said to him, 'I thought we might talk.'

'Sure.'

'Alone would be a good idea,' Spandau said, 'unless we're having a tea party.'

Aronson looked over at Annie and nodded. She reluctantly followed him out of the trailer.

'You don't much want this gig, do you?' Bobby said to Spandau.

'I guess that depends on you. I can't do anything without your cooperation.'

He handed Spandau a sheet of paper with a message in cut-out letters glued onto it: YOU'RE GOING TO DIE, DYE!

Spandau handed it back to him. 'Cute.'

'I found it yesterday morning. Somebody'd slipped it under the door over there.'

'You get a lot of these?'

'It happens. Some chick falls for me in a movie and her boyfriend gets pissed and sends a letter.'

'How do you normally handle it?'

'There's a guy who does security. Mainly nobody does shit.'

'You show it to him?'

'Yeah.'

'And?'

'Nothing to worry about. We could tack on a couple of bodyguards. The production company will pay.'

'So why do you feel this one is any different?'

'Because they managed to slip it under the door of my fucking trailer.'

'Why call me? What can I do for you?'

'I want you to find out who it is.'

'You got any ideas who it might be?'

'No.'

'Then it's unlikely I'd be able to chase it down, brilliant shamus that I am. Like you said, it could be a pissed-off boyfriend. It could be anybody. Take the bodyguard and forget about it.'

'That's it? That all you've got to fucking say? Somebody threatened my life!'

'Some shithead sent you a note. I'm not blowing it off, but it happens all the time and I don't think it means much.'

'Fuck you.'

'Look,' Spandau said, 'if this sort of shit meant anything, half of Hollywood would be dead already. These things go around like supermarket flyers. I'm sorry to burst your bubble, but everybody gets them. You can chalk it up to the price of fame. If you think you're in serious danger, then there are people to protect you and you need to go to the police. But trying to narrow this thing down by a process of elimination isn't going to work. It could be anybody. Unless you know who it might be? Do you?'

'No.'

'Then there's nothing to say. Go to the cops and hire the bodyguards.'

'Then fuck you. I'll get somebody else.'

'You can always find people to take your money.'

'Fuck you.'

Spandau was getting tired of his mouth. He thought seriously about grabbing him by the lapels and lifting him up out of the seat and delivering a little lecture on the proper way to treat guests, especially ones who have nearly fifty-five pounds and four inches on you. And he might have, too, if Bobby Dye's hands hadn't been shaking as he lit a cigarette. He was trying to be tough and failing at it. Up until this point the whole thing had felt funny to Spandau but now he was sure something else was going on.

'Let me see the note again.'

He handed it to Spandau. Spandau held it at the corners, not that it would have done much good. Spandau held it up at an angle to the light. The letters were glossy and there were fingerprints all over them, but God knows whose they were.

'How many people have seen this?'

'I dunno,' he said. 'Annie. Robert. Maybe a couple of others.'

'What you mean is, it's been handed around like a plate of cocktail franks.'

He laughed a little. 'Yeah, I guess.'

'You mind if I take it with me. I'll bring it back tomorrow.'

'Yeah, I guess. Sure. You taking the case?'

'I need to think about it.'

'What are you doing? Playing fucking hard to get? Is this some kind of ego trip for you?'

38

'I won't take a case unless I'm sure I can do the job. That's just the way it works. You can hire anybody you want.'

'Robert says you're the best.'

'He's right. I am the best. Which means you can take my word for things.'

'Well don't fucking lose it.'

'I'll try not to. Anyway, I'll come back tomorrow.' Spandau stood up and shook his hand. 'And by the way, don't ever speak to me again the way you've been speaking to me. Maybe some people will put up with it but I won't. I'll see you tomorrow.'

Annie pounced on Spandau the moment he stepped out of the trailer.

'Well?'

'Well what?'

'How did it go?'

'Ask your client.'

'I'm asking you.'

'Yeah,' he said, 'but I don't work for you.'

Her first instinct was to unload on him, but she thought better of it. She smiled. 'You really are an asshole.'

'Maybe,' he said, 'but I'm an old-fashioned asshole, and you people keep calling me names and I don't like it. I'm sure it's only a sign of affection but I want it to stop.'

'Are you taking the job?'

'I honestly don't know. I have to check with my boss. I'll let you know tomorrow.'

Spandau turned and walked away. He half expected a rock to hit him in the back of the head. When it didn't come he kept on walking and tried to imagine the look on her face.

The office of Coren Investigations was on Sunset across from a Mercedes dealership and a French bistro. On clean air days you could open the window in the waiting room and smell the *daube au provençal* as you watched Iranians test drive the SLRs in circles around the block. The Coren office made an attempt at discretion – it was after all supposed to be a discreet profession – but allowed the vanity of a somewhat smug and successful brass name plaque next to the front door. The office itself was nothing more than the reception area, Coren's office and a small conference room, but the carpet was thick and the furniture was heavy. Trust us, it said, and people did. Coren rarely had more than five operatives employed at a time – he liked to refer to it as a 'boutique' agency, with its implication of class and selectivity, as opposed to a large and impersonal outfit like Pinkertons.

Walter Coren had inherited the business from his father, an alcoholic old-school gumshoe whose favorite reading was Sir Walter Scott but who was beaten down by thirty years of sordid divorces and skipped husbands. Walter got a business degree from UCLA though paid for it working nights for his old man. By the time he entered college he'd already spent three years aiming cameras through motel windows and picking incriminating condoms out of trash cans. The bleakness of a sound financial education only quickened the demise of whatever romantic notions Walter had about life in the City of Angels. Walter buried the old man and his calcified liver about the same time he got his degree, then set about recreating his father's legacy, turning down a shot for an MBA at Stanford. Everyone he knew thought he was nuts, since his father had never pulled in more than a subsistence wage his entire career. But Walter, unlike his father, didn't feel himself crippled by the moral failures of the world around him. Walter was gifted with an early understanding that human beings are flawed creatures who, as a result of these flaws, frequently got their asses in a sling and needed help. In much the same way that entrepreneurs can make fortunes hauling off human waste – Walter had done an enlightening college paper on the economics of waste management – Walter realized that lots of people in Los Angeles were willing to pay big bucks to dispose of other kinds of inconveniently accumulated shit. He reasoned that while all classes of people are capable of fouling their own nests, it was the rich ones who paid better and were the most entertaining.

Walter went into hock to lease an impressive car, purchase a good suit, and rent an upscale address in Beverly Hills, on the theory that the well-heeled only trust people who resemble them. He set about cultivating the rich and famous, who appreciated his country-club tan, his nice teeth, and the fact that he was discreet and didn't appear to make any moral judgments about them. The rich, too, wish to be liked. Within ten years, Walter Coren was a success and one of the best-kept secrets in LA society. He'd also accumulated three ex-wives, a peptic ulcer, a succession of young mistresses, and Spandau. Spandau was the only one he actually liked, and only Spandau knew that Walter Coren Jr. cared far less about making money than he did the vindication of a father he'd adored. In the end the old man had started a successful concern. A painting of Walter Coren Sr., the founder, hung in his office – Walter had it done from a photo – and every July 14 Walter got drunk in remembrance of his death. Sometimes Spandau went with him.

Spandau wedged the BMW into a rare space in front of the bistro and wondered if the *paupiettes de veau* was on today's menu. He checked that it was and made a note to complain to the chef, Andre, about using red wine instead of the Madeira. When he walked into the office, Pookie Forsythe – whose name had been Amanda until she went to a good school back East – looked up from her perusal of *Women's Wear Daily*. Pookie was a small and pretty brunette who believed in spiritual redemption through clothing. She also believed that one identity was never enough and changed hers daily. In this she was like most of Los Angeles. Today she'd decided to be Audrey Hepburn. She wore her hair up to show an exquisite pale neck, and if her pink suit wasn't Givenchy it was a fair copy. Pookie was in LA determined to make it on her own, though the monthly check from Daddums eased the strain a little.

'It's back!' Pookie announced. 'So how was the vacation?'

Spandau held up his thumb, which was looking more and more like an eggplant. Pookie wrinkled her face at it.

'What in God's name did you do to it?'

'I roped it.'

'It was my impression,' she said in her best Barnard voice, 'that you were supposed to rope the cow or something.'

'I missed. Is he in?'

Pookie nodded. Spandau went to Coren's door and knocked. Coren opened the door and looked surprised to see him. But he recovered quickly and said, 'Turn in your gas mileage.'

Walter Coren Jr. was tall and thin, and had the sort of good looks that age well but misleadingly suggest Old Money. His tan was still good though the fair hair was thinning and it was an effort to maintain the size 34 waist these days. He was just past fifty but looked near Spandau's age. Women found him attractive enough to keep him in trouble, and men liked him because he could stoke their vanity without coming over as a homo. Still, underneath all that he was in hock to all his wives and his liver was on its way to matching his father's.

'I just got back,' Spandau said.

'You never turn in your gas mileage, then you bitch that we don't pay you enough. We are here to help you.'

'You the Man,' Spandau said, dropping into the chair opposite Coren's desk. 'The Man is only capable of exploitation, never true understanding.'

'What is that?' Coren said admiringly. He'd been a radical at UCLA in his youth, one of the few with a stock portfolio. 'Is that Eldridge Cleaver?'

'Mr Rodgers.'

'How's the thumb?'

Spandau exhibited it. Coren flinched. 'Jesus, that's ugly. Why don't you put some makeup on it or something. It makes people uncomfortable . . . So what about this Bobby Dye thing?'

Spandau showed him the note. Coren looked at it and handed it back.

'Any idea who it's from?' Coren asked.

'He says not.'

'So what does he want us to do?'

'Investigate. Somebody told him we did that sort of thing.'

'And did you patiently explain the odds on tracing this.'

'Yes.'

'And?'

'He still wants us to investigate.'

'To which you replied?'

'I said I'd check with my Lord and Master.'

'You think there's any point?'

'I think the whole thing's bullshit. I think it's a fake.'

'You think he sent himself a death threat? Why would he do that?'

'I have no idea. My first thought was publicity of some sort, but he doesn't want it to get out, and he doesn't want to go to the cops. And he doesn't need this sort of notice anyway.'

'You think maybe he's trying to lead up to something, working up the nerve?'

'That seems likely. He's looking to trust somebody.'

'Like you and your St Bernard face.'

'That's right.'

'I agree. It sounds like bullshit and a great waste of time. There are a dozen other things you could be doing.'

'I'm still on vacation,' Spandau reminded him. 'I'm not even supposed to be here until Monday, remember? And by the way, I'm on the clock for this, right?'

'I've never understood the concept of vacation,' said Coren, skillfully gliding over Spandau's pathetic attempt to extract money from him. 'People ought to seek fulfillment in their work. That's what's made this country great. You think Thomas Jefferson sat around pissing and moaning about getting to Myrtle Beach for his mandatory two weeks every year? And anyway, you're utterly bored already and like an idiot you've bulldogged your own thumb. You're practically begging for something to do.'

'Thomas Jefferson had a hundred slaves and spent an inordinate amount of time trying to foist the tomato off on the American public,' replied Spandau. 'He farted around in his garden and never had to deal with agents, actors or the Ventura Freeway at six in the evening. I've got three more days.'

'Okay, what is it you want to do? You actually want to pursue this?'

'I'm going back over there tomorrow and talk to him.'

'Fine, but it's on your dollar. Like you say, you're still on vacation. I'll pay you for today but until you've got an official case you're on your own, sweetheart. I run a business.'

'And what a business it is.'

'There's no money in pretending to be a St Bernard. And turn in your goddamn mileage sheets, will you? I'm not putting up with any more of this crap where you guys hoard them like it's a goddamn savings account and expect me to come good on it.'

Spandau got up.

'Monday,' Coren told him. 'Bring me a case by Monday or I find you something else to do.'

Three

They buried the girl in the sand outside of Indio. When they finished it was nearly daylight and Potts was increasingly nervous about being spotted, though they were way the hell off the main highway and they'd dragged her up into the rocks. It was a full moon and they dug mainly without a flashlight. Potts thought several times he heard rattlesnakes but Squiers reminded him that snakes were cold-blooded and active in the day. Or maybe it was the other way around. Squiers was huge and strong but a lazy motherfucker. They were supposed to be taking turns but Squiers' turns kept getting shorter and shorter until Squiers was sitting there and it was Potts digging in the sand. They thought because it was sand the digging would be quick, but after a foot and a half the sand kept pouring back in. The hole was shallower than they'd hoped and the body made a huge lump. Potts reasoned that nobody would spot it in the rocks and even like this it couldn't be spotted from the air. There was the worry that coyotes would come along and dig it up but in the end they agreed it only made identification all that much harder. Soon enough there would be nothing but bone. Squiers wanted to strip the girl but Potts stood his ground about that.

Potts got back to his house in Redlands at mid-morning. He was tired and dirty and he wanted a shower and a cold beer. He'd sleep and have a late breakfast and then go out somewhere. He lived out of town at the edge of the desert. Underneath the yellowing stucco was crap cinderblock. It had been cracked innumerable times by earthquake and plastered over and every so often a bit would fall off to reveal a deep fissure where insects lived. Potts tried not to think of what went on under the floor beneath him. Off to the side there was a wooden garage that leaned slightly and let sand and wind in through the chinks. Potts had wanted a better place, maybe even an apartment, but the bastards all did credit checks these days and Potts' credit was shit. There was one small bedroom and a tiny kitchen and living room. A fucking crackerbox. But it had a yard.

Potts parked his truck in front of the garage and went inside the house. He'd forgotten to leave the a/c running and the place was hot. He turned it on and went into the kitchen for a cold beer. He opened the beer and took a sip and then downed the whole thing. He opened another. It would help him sleep.

Potts went into the living room. He sat in his easy chair and looked around. It wasn't much but it was something, and Potts was happy to be back. The place was furnished mainly from Goodwill with accents from Target. Maybe it was cheap but nothing like the shithole he'd been brought up in, or the shitholes he'd lived in often enough. There was a big painting hanging on the wall of somebody called Blue Boy by somebody called Gainsborough. All in all it was a pretty faggoty painting, but Potts liked it. He liked the soft colors and the way there were no hard lines in it anywhere, everything kind of blended together. It relaxed him, and, anyway, he never brought people here. In the year he'd lived here nobody else had been in the place except the landlord and a guy to fix the toilet. There was a word for what the place was. Sacro-something or other.

The telephone answering machine was blinking. Potts played it back.

'Mr Potts, this is Gina Rivera from Consolidated Credit. We've been trying to reach you concerning your account, which is seriously past due . . .'

(beep)

'Mr Potts, this is Kevin Pynchon again. I've come by about three times now for my rent . . .'

(beep)

'Mr Potts, this is Leslie Stout from McCann, Pool and Foxle. In regards to the appeal we filed for you about visitations to your daughter, it's been denied. If you'd like to call me I can give you the details. We can try again of course, but it would require additional fees . . .'

Potts went over to the sliding patio door. As usual he

had to wrench it open. Potts would have preferred a real door with hinges and all, since he knew how easy these were to break into. All it took was a jimmy. God knows he'd done it often enough himself back in Texas. The door led out to the backyard and sometimes you could sit in the living room and look out and watch the sky change colors.

In the backyard, mainly sand with clumps of crabgrass, was a barbecue grill and a plastic table and chairs. Potts had strung up Christmas lights and sometimes he turned them on when he got drunk. There was a birdfeeder birds ignored and a jerry-rigged horseshoe court. He went over and picked up a rusty horseshoe and threw it. He missed. He sat down in one of the plastic chairs and for a while looked out at the desert. He finished the beer and dragged himself out of the chair and went inside. He got another beer and then he went into the bedroom and emptied his pockets onto the dresser, tossing the thick wad of bills Stella had given him into his sock drawer. He undressed and got sand all over the floor and cursed but he didn't have the energy to clean it up. He went into the bathroom and took a long hot shower and tried to think about a woman but he couldn't do that either. He felt like breaking something so he got out of the shower and put on his kimono and drank two more beers.

He woke late that afternoon on top of the bed in his dressing gown. His mouth was thick and his head throbbed. It might have been the beer but more likely it was because he'd forgotten to eat. He shuffled into the kitchen and made some instant coffee and took it with him into the bathroom while he had a watery shit. His guts were churning and he felt weak. He'd dreamed, in flashes, of the dead girl's face.

Potts dressed in jeans, boots and his ragged leather bike jacket. He went out to the garage and unlocked it and lifted the door. The large classic Harley-Davidson sat in the middle of the garage, surrounded by spare parts and boxes of tools. Potts went over and ran his hand along the bike. He straddled it and rolled it outside, then got off and closed the garage door. He put on his skid-lid – the minimum the law allowed – and kicked the bike to life. When Potts rode he forgot about everything, which was the reason anybody rode. The fucking world was everywhere but when you rode you broke free and skimmed over the top of it.

Potts rode to Kepki's Roadhouse. There were a dozen or so bikes outside and a few trucks from guys just getting off work. Potts knew some of the people and when he went inside only a few said hello or waved even though he'd been coming here regular for a year. Potts went up to the bar and sat on a stool. Kepki was behind the bar.

'Beer?' said Kepki.

Potts nodded. 'And some of that chili, if you got any. And a bunch of crackers.'

Kepki brought him a beer and Potts drank it quickly. He held up the bottle for Kepki to bring him another.

51

'You starting early or just keeping one going?' Kepki asked him.

Potts ignored the question but attacked this beer a little slower. He turned around and checked out the room. A couple of bikers were shooting pool at the table in back and a few people were standing around watching. One of them was a woman in her thirties wearing a tight blue dress and drinking a beer. She looked up and saw Potts watching her. Potts turned back around.

Potts had started in on the chili when the woman turned up at his side.

'You want to give me a Miller?' she said to Kepki.

Kepki brought her one and she drank it standing next to Potts. Potts opened several packs of saltines and broke them up into his chili and stirred it around. He was hungry and when he took a bite it was too hot and he had to spit it out into his hand. 'Shit!' He took a swig of beer to cool down.

The woman laughed. 'Didn't your mother never teach you to blow on it first?'

'Damn, I burnt the hell out of my mouth! God damn, Kepki, you coulda warned me.'

'Just cause it says chili don't mean it ain't hot,' said Kepki, winking at the woman.

Potts took another swig of cool beer.

'You always eat like that?' the woman asked him. 'Big gulps of everything? I reckon that's a good sign, though. A man just taking big bites out of everything, like taking big bites out of life. That the way you are?'

'I never thought about it.'

'I bet you are,' she said. 'I bet you that's the way you do things. My name's Darlene.'

'Potts.'

'Just Potts?'

'Just Potts,' he said.

They drank up the rest of the evening. Potts had some of Stella's money in his pocket and the beer bottles and whiskey glasses accumulated on the bar in front of them. They laughed and talked, Darlene resting against Potts with her arm around him. Somewhere early on Darlene leaned over and kissed Potts and slid her tongue deep into his mouth and rubbed his crotch through the blue jeans. Potts got up to have a piss and was standing at the urinal when Darlene came in. Potts started to zip up but Darlene said, 'Don't bother,' and she grabbed Potts by the dick and led him over and pushed him up against the wall. She raised her blue dress and jammed Potts' hand down into her panties. Potts was a little overwhelmed. A biker came in and said, 'Hot damn! Well don't let me interrupt nothing,' and took a leak watching Potts and Darlene administer to each other. The biker whistled appreciatively before he left and winked at Potts.

'Why don't we go to your place?' Darlene said to him.

'No,' said Potts.

'You married?'

'No,' he said.

'Then how come? I don't give a shit how clean it is, long as the bed is okay.'

'I never take anybody there, that's all.'

'How come?'

'Why you asking all these questions? I just don't, that's all. Now you want to get it on somewhere or not. Let's go to your place.'

'Can't. I got a kid. I bring anybody home and the kid'll blab to the goddamn social worker.'

They drove in her car to a motel. Potts was drunk so he handed her a wad of cash. She was perhaps slightly less drunk than Potts and she went in to book the room. She came back out a few minutes later with some cash still in her hand. She looked at the money, looked at Potts, then jammed the money into her bra.

'You want it,' she said to Potts, 'you got to come and get it.'

In the motel room Darlene sat on the bed and took a pint of vodka from her purse. She took a hit and offered it to Potts.

'You look nervous. You always like this or is it just me?'

'I ain't nervous,' said Potts.

'Fun to be a little nervous,' she said. 'I like being a little scared.'

She sat back on the bed and motioned for Potts to sit next to her.

'Come on, honey,' she said. 'Come and talk to Mama Darlene a little while.'

Potts climbed onto the bed. Darlene pulled his head to her chest and gently stroked his hair, his face. Potts closed his eyes.

'You had a hard life, ain't you? I can tell. You can always tell a hard life. What you need is a little love, ain't it, sugar? What you need is someone to be gentle with you, someone to be soft. Life's too hard. Life ain't got to be this hard all the time, is it?'

She tilted his chin up and brought her lips down to his, tenderly kissing him. She looked into his eyes.

'You got beautiful eyes, you know that? I noticed that right off. Them big sad eyes of yours. That's why I liked you. I thought: anybody with them eyes got to need some love.'

Potts watched her undress. She was beautiful, in her way. Her pale body was lush and soft but there was an ugly deep scar across her abdomen. She caught Potts looking at it.

'That upset you?'

'No,' said Potts.

'Ugly, ain't it? A doctor did that to me, when I had my kid. An infection. I like to have died. Maybe you don't want me now. Some men don't.'

'No, I still want you.'

She let him touch the scar softly. He ran his fingers the length of it.

'You're a good man, ain't you? Are you?'

'Yeah. I am. I'm a good man.'

'Come on. Get undressed. I'm going to hold you for a while, then I'm going to love you.'

Potts undressed and climbed into bed with her. She seemed shy now. Potts touched her all over and she giggled. It was like high school. She pulled Potts close to her and it was as if she enfolded him. She pushed Potts onto his back and she slid him inside her. She smiled down at Potts and in that moment Potts thought she was the most beautiful thing he'd ever seen. The ceiling light was behind her and she looked like an angel; there was a halo round her head. Potts was in heaven. Like an angel.

She rolled over onto her back and pulled Potts on top of her. He kissed her as he made love to her but as she became more and more aroused she turned her face away. Her fingernails bit into Potts' back and her legs wrapped round him as she arched beneath him, urging him harder, faster, harder. Potts thought she was going to come but she stopped and grabbed Potts' hands and placed them on her neck. Potts wasn't sure what to do. Darlene glared at him. 'Do it, for God's sake, do it!'

Potts tightened his grip on her neck and she relaxed and he could feel her begin to move beneath him again. Potts was worried about her but whenever he loosened his grip she became angry. Finally she grabbed his hands and squeezed them herself into her neck to show him what she wanted. She turned red and then began turning purple and made gurgling noises in her throat. Potts wanted to stop moving but she hit him on the arms and he kept on. She began to twitch and her eyes began to roll and Potts was afraid he was killing her, he didn't want to hurt her. She started slapping the bed with her palms and Potts stopped and took his hands away. He looked down at her as she fought for air and seemed to come round to consciousness again. Her eyes focussed and she stared at Potts curiously and then she screamed at him:

'Why the fuck did you stop? I was coming! I was almost there, you stupid son of a bitch! I was nearly there!'

Potts backed off the bed and Darlene became hysterical. She sat up in the middle of the bed crying, cursing, tearing at the sheets that tangled her. Potts pulled on his pants and ran from the room carrying his boots. He stumbled out into the parking lot and the cool night desert air hit him and made things worse. It only increased his confusion. He looked around for his bike and remembered they'd taken her car. He sat down with his boots and tried to pull them on when Darlene appeared in the doorway, naked, shouting at him.

'What is wrong with you? Am I too much woman for you, you fucking faggot? Is that it? You fucking loser, you fucking goddamn little faggot!'

She kept shouting at him, shouted as the doors around the motel opened, shouted as Potts hobbled carrying his shirt and boots out into the street and away.

57

Four

After Spandau left Coren's office it was nearly 3 p.m. when he got back to his home in Woodland Hills. He lived in an older two-bedroom house, small, but it had a nice backyard. Spandau had put in a pond with some fish and a turtle. The turtle seemed to be doing well but the fish were being eaten by the raccoons. Every few days Spandau would look into the pond and notice a fish was gone, and sometimes he'd find the tail and a fin or two under the hedge. Then he'd go buy another fish. He thought about sitting up some night in the dark lurking behind the open window with a pellet rifle and catching the damned raccoons in the act, and the fact that he did think seriously about doing this worried him a little. They were just animals, after all. Thinking about them in human terms like revenge was already halfway to being crazy and best not explored. But he wished he'd never put in the goddamned pond. It was supposed to relax him but now whenever he looked at it he got angry.

He pulled the BMW into the drive, got out and opened the rickety two-car garage, then parked next to his pickup truck. It was a refurbished 1958 Chevy Apache shortbed, which he would have far preferred to drive than the BMW, a car that struck him as pretentious but was what Coren leased for his agents. Coren's reasoning was that a BMW was familiar enough not to be much noticed in LA but hip enough to allow his people to fit in. As far as Spandau was concerned it was a goddamn large and hot kraut car that he wasn't allowed to smoke in.

Spandau himself was of German extraction, his father a butcher coming from Düsseldorf just after the war, and he thought perhaps the car reminded him of his father. Dark, cold and aloof. The old man used to beat him with a wide strip of military webbing, and Spandau always suspected it was some romantic vestige of his military service defending the Reich. Spandau once asked him if he'd been a Nazi and old Horst knocked him across the room. In the shop the old man hacked angrily all day at carcasses of meat, as if they were Jews, homos or gypsies, and came home to drink schnapps and terrorize his wife and children. Katrina, his daughter, two years younger than David, he never beat, but merely slashed with invective. Something in his German genes that wouldn't let him hit a woman made it alright to reduce them to emotional rubble, dismember them as surely and deeply as the flesh he worked with. Whenever someone praised the BMW as a 'fine piece of German engineering' Spandau recalled his father's own ruthless efficiency at carving meat and human beings. But in the end that too was the road to madness. In the end, it was just a car.

Spandau had stopped at the market, and now he balanced the bag of groceries in the crook of his arm as he pulled shut the garage door. No fancy electronic openers for him. It was a hot day and the back of his white dress shirt was soaked underneath the thin Armani jacket. Inside the house it was cool and dark; he'd pulled the shades and left the air-conditioner on. It was a relief to be inside, safe, quiet, private. He missed Dee but in truth it felt good to come home like this, to shut the world out, not to hear anyone talking.

Delia had left him the year before. It had been an amicable divorce – if a divorce could ever be called such – and he did not contest it. He had long seen it coming, they both had. The marriage had been fine during the stunt work, because she understood that, it was what her father did too. Then Spandau had that run of bad luck where too many bones got broken in a single year, and Spandau had hit that producer.

A broken hip and arm and collarbone in the span of ten months were bad enough, but Spandau had lost his temper on the set one day and clocked a Suit with a nice, crisp short one to the chin. The Suit cracked several expensive dental crowns and summoned his attorney. The attorney threatened to sue the stunt coordinator, Beau, who owned the company and was also Dee's father. Beau chewed

Spandau out but would have fought for him and lost his ass in the process. Beau refused to fire him. Rather than jeopardize Beau, Spandau appeased the Suit by quitting. He sat home for three months, drinking through most afternoons toward the last. Then Coren had come through with the detective job, and Spandau found out he was good at it, and it required the injury of hardly any body parts.

It was the detective work that had ruined the marriage. Dee didn't care how much he drank and caroused, what he damaged, who he punched out. Hell, she was Beau McCauley's daughter and she was used to all that. What she wasn't used to was the change that came over Spandau, and how readily he took to a job that she found morally offensive. On one early job, Spandau had been required to befriend a man, a personal manager suspected of 'misappropriating' some of his client's money.

The client was a bitch-goddess of a TV star, a pneumatic peroxide blonde with a body like Barbie and a mind like J. Paul Getty. She worked the manager like a dog, paid him a minimal amount of kibble, and thoroughly enjoyed humiliating him in front of whoever happened to be around. The manager put up with it but took his revenge by siphoning small amounts of her money into an account in Nevada. It wasn't much, the man just wanted to pay off a little cabin at Tahoe, where he went to fish and relax whenever he could escape the clutches of his boss, which wasn't often. Spandau arranged to meet him in Tahoe, they went fishing together, became pals.

One drunken dusk while sitting in his johnboat and fishing for bass, the man confessed the whole thing to Spandau. He explained how he'd been draining the money little by little for over a year, hardly enough to notice, so that he could finish paying off this place and have somewhere to live when he quit working for Queen Titzilla, which he planned to do within the next few months. The way he told the story to Spandau, you could see he felt there was nothing wrong in what he was doing. To him the actions were justified and he felt no guilt about it. Titzilla overworked and humiliated him, so he extracted an amount from her he felt was fair, and that was that. It wasn't like she'd miss it. She was loaded and owned real estate up the wazoo. But of course she did miss it. She said she began to suspect him when he quit looking hurt whenever she insulted him. She said it was cheaper to hire a detective than to audit her books, which she wasn't keen to draw attention to anyway. Spandau helped the poor drunken fool off the lake and back to his small cabin, put him to bed, called Titzilla and told her the whole story.

Dee found this appalling, and was surprised that Spandau didn't. How could he betray a friend, someone who liked and trusted him? Spandau didn't see it that way. He felt no qualms at all, not a trace of guilt. He tried to make his position clear to her, but it was useless. The man was a crook, Spandau explained. Spandau had been hired to catch him. He did. End of story. But for Dee, friendship and family were sacred. You didn't betray a friend, no matter what, especially if there was even a remote justification for his act. You just didn't.

'But he's not my friend,' pleaded Spandau. 'He's a thief.'

'But you told him you were his friend!' she accused. 'You made him feel safe, you let him think he could trust you. And then you used it against him.'

There was nothing Spandau could say. Her whole argument seemed irrational to him. But the case had opened up a rift between them, an unbridgeable chasm. He suspected there was something more at stake, that something else was going on, but he couldn't grasp what it was. The incident struck some hidden weakness in their relationship.

It wasn't until Dee had been gone for a few weeks, when Spandau had time to sit and obsessively go over each and every marital fuck-up, that he suspected he had an answer.

Dee herself had pointed it out once, early on. Spandau had told her about his father. About the beatings, the verbal abuse, the coldness and cruelty. How he and his sister and his mother became close because of it. How that closeness excluded everyone else, how it isolated them from friends and confidences, but made bearable the daily mortification that old Horst inflicted.

It was possible, David understood, to watch someone you love be abused and to say nothing to defend them, because that was simply the way of things. You accepted, you let the pain and humiliation ride through you like cold wind through a hole, and you made up for it later by doling out the tenderness you'd kept hidden.

This had meant nothing to Spandau when he told it to her, except for the embarrassment of coming from such a home, such a father. Dee had tears in her eyes. Spandau made fun of her, but truthfully could think of nothing he'd said that should move anyone to tears.

And this, said Dee, was exactly why she was crying. That he had no idea how tragic it was.

That was the word she'd used: tragic. Dee's upbringing had been boisterous but loving. Beau might get shitfaced after a night out with the boys, but otherwise he was a model husband and father. Two sons and a daughter adored him, as he adored them. He'd raised his voice often enough but had never been malicious and never, never struck any of them. Dee had grown up so loved that she was in college before she realized what a privilege that was.

She thanked David for telling her, and said it explained some things.

Like what? Spandau asked.

Like your ability to distance yourself when you feel threatened, Dee told him. Your ability to turn inside yourself, like a hedgehog.

David said he had no idea what she was talking about, and she wouldn't discuss it anymore.

The fault lay in their concept of family and loyalty. Dee had grown up expansive in her love, in her trust, in her loyalties. For Spandau, life was like rowing in a very small boat, and you were either in the boat or out of the boat.

If you were out of the boat, how long you could tread

water was up to you. He loved his mother, his sister, he loved Dee and Beau. A tiny crew for a tiny yacht. The rest of the world wasn't his problem. You protected like a tiger those closest to you and to hell with everyone else; there wasn't even time to be sorry.

Had this been what ruined his marriage? He thought it might be.

The destruction was as simple, perhaps, as the difference between happy families and miserable ones. They approached the world differently, and perhaps even loved differently. For Spandau, the world was something to be mistrusted except for those proven and close to you. For Dee, the world was to be loved and embraced.

The tragedy was, that was why Spandau loved her. Because she was so much unlike him.

Spandau understood that he had wanted Dee to make him a better person. He hoped that he would become more like her. Instead, he had remained the same. As much as they had loved each other, as much as they still loved each other, she had not changed him. He was incapable of change and that was why she was gone, and why he was so good at the profession of betrayal.

They were married for five years. She was a teacher. She taught second grade at a school in the Valley. There were moments, days even, of enormous happiness. Happiness that for Spandau brought a guilt with it, a sense that it was too good to be true, that it was (at least for him) unearned.

The marriage was never bad, though sometimes hard.

At the beginning of the fourth year Beau had died. A heart attack at seventy. Beau McCauley was as healthy as one of the horses he'd wrangled all his life. He was the sort of man who was supposed to live forever. A character bigger than life, for whom the normal rules of mortality could not apply. His death opened a great hole in all their lives.

It was hardest on Dee, Beau's little girl. Her brothers came for the funeral but could not remain. They were far-flung, one living in France and the other in New York, both with families of their own. Beau's wife Mary, a tough old bird, was left to honcho the ranch in Ojai with the help of a Mexican family who'd been with them for years. Dee had practically lived out there the last couple of summers, helping with the stock, the intricacies of ranch bookkeeping, and just keeping Mary company. Spandau came out when he could.

It was no surprise when she told him she wanted to move back to the ranch full time. They lived apart for a year without divorcing, then she said she thought it best to make it official. Spandau wondered about another man but no one appeared, at least not until now.

Maybe Dee wanted to release Spandau to chase other women. It was only after the divorce papers were signed, within the last year in fact, that Spandau could look at anyone else. Even now it was awkward. He didn't expect to find another Dee.

He didn't, in fact, expect to find anyone at all and he preferred it that way. The divorce papers were signed and when it was clear she wasn't coming back, Spandau bought her half of the house. There was nothing else they owned. She took the Toyota 4-Runner. Spandau kept the Apache and most of the furniture.

Spandau took the groceries into the kitchen and sat the bag on the table and put them away. It wasn't quite two o'clock. He made a sandwich and ate it quickly, bachelor-style, over the sink. He went into his office to check his messages.

The second bedroom was to have been a baby's nursery. Now it was what Dee called 'the Gene Autry Room'. It started out simply as an office where Spandau did his accounts and wrote his reports for Coren. Gradually it became a depository for memorabilia, mementos and photos of movies he'd worked on and rodeos he'd competed in. The occasional trophy from some dinky local rodeo – usually for roping, since Spandau stayed on a horse, as Beau told him once, like his ass was coated with Teflon.

When Dee moved out, the never so latent cowboy in him took over completely. Navaho rugs, Native American totems, Mexican blankets draped over an old sofa and a saddle-leather chair, his favorite spot. His collection of books on Western Americana in a glass bookcase. Some antique guns hanging on pegs on one wall. A large poster of Sitting Bull on the wall behind his wooden desk chair, the desk itself an old roll-top that needed three men to wedge it into the room.

It was a museum to a time long gone, as the few friends invited quickly pointed out. The only concessions to the twentieth century – which, like Evelyn Waugh, Spandau believed to be a huge mistake – were the answering machine and the laptop computer, tucked away in a corner out of eyeshot. Spandau was more at home here than anywhere in the world. He whiled away many a long and lonely night in his easy chair, smoking a pipe, sipping Wild Turkey and reading books on the American West.

There were no surprises on the answering machine. Pookie reminded him, in that Marilyn Monroe voice she affected over the phone, that Coren wanted his mileage sheets. A friend from Utah, a genuine cowboy, drunk and bored, called to say he was coming to LA soon and wanted to know if Spandau knew any available starlets.

Dee had called. She wanted to know if Spandau was still coming out to the ranch that afternoon. Spandau replayed her voice several times, coasting the familiar drop and rise of his heart.

He pulled off the Armani and dressed quickly in jeans, a work shirt and an old pair of boots. It was like shedding a false skin in exchange for his true one. He felt his life become lighter. He opened the garage and after a few attempts cranked up the Apache. It hadn't been driven in weeks. He backed it out and shut the garage. He sat in the truck in the driveway, relishing the feel of it. He'd restored the truck to its original state, right down to the baby-blue and white paint job and the functioning AM radio. With

three speeds and six cylinders, it wasn't a hellcat on the
road, and drove like what it was, a work truck. On the
bench seat next to him were a banged-up straw Stetson and
a baseball cap advertising the Red Pecker Bar & Grill. He
put on the baseball cap.

He was home.

The McCauley ranch was seven miles outside of Ojai,
reached by a twisty and dusty road that dodged between the
hills. Beau McCauley had purchased the fifty acres of mostly
hilly land forty years before, not long after his marriage to
Mary and his start as one of the best stuntmen in the business. Beau never trusted movie money and felt that raising
quarter horses was a safer bet. Horses were the stupidest animals God ever put on this planet, but he still preferred them
to most people. Beau and Mary both had good heads for
business, and soon they owned the land outright. Beau continued to be in demand as a stunt coordinator, forming his
own company, and the ranch did well for itself. When Beau
died, Mary decided to continue running the ranch. She
didn't have to. She could easily have sold off most of the land
and lived well without working. But that wasn't Mary. She
still raised horses but was pushing seventy herself and had
slowed down a little. She ran the ranch with a Mexican
named Carlos and his wife and son. The son was twenty and
drank on weekends but was still a good hand.

Spandau loved the ranch, and if he had a home this was
it. He approached the ranch driving up a hill, and over the

crest the ranch lay spread out on a piece of flat land below. A gravel road hugged the side of the hills weaving its way down. There was a creek that ran through the property and the white two-story frame house sat in a green oasis in the middle of the usually brown landscape. There were the outbuildings and the barn and the stables and the corrals and the small house where Carlos lived. A few horses wandered in the pasture. There were not many. Just enough, as Mary said, to still call it a working ranch. The sale of the horses in fact barely covered Carlos' salary. But a ranch without horses was a dead thing, just a pointless hunk of land, as Mary pointed out, and as long as the ranch was alive there was some large part of Beau still alive with it.

Spandau wondered what would happen to the ranch when Mary died. Dee loved the place but loved teaching more and had no inclination to run a ranch. The brothers had been happy to get off the place and were now citified with no desire to return. The land was worth about ten times what Beau had paid for it, and there was pressure to sell. A decade after Mary was gone the place would be a suburb, full of tacky-box houses, cable television towers and other remnants of the American Dream. One more part of Spandau would be gone as well. It didn't pay to love something you didn't own, that wasn't yours. He ended up loving this place in spite of his common sense.

Carlos was giving his son hell about something as Spandau pulled up in back of the house. The son stood with his head hanging down as Carlos wagged his finger at him. Carlos looked up long enough to smile at Spandau and raise his hand in greeting, then went back to his son. The son glanced up at Spandau, looked sullen but said nothing. Now Spandau could see that the boy had a black eye. The boy hung his head again, letting it all pass over him, not really listening to a word. The boy had always seemed to dislike just about everything and Spandau had always disliked the boy.

Spandau rapped on the screen door to the kitchen and Mary emerged from inside the house. Mary McCauley was a small, wiry little woman who still looked like Myrna Loy, the actress in the *Thin Man* movies. Beau said this was one of the reasons he had married her. Mainly though, he said, it was because he needed a woman even meaner than he was to keep him in line.

This wasn't far from the truth. The previous year, she had picked up a shovel and threatened to stove in the head of a real estate developer who'd been hounding her about selling the ranch. The man had known better when Beau was alive and thought to take advantage of Mary's bereavement. It would have been fine if the man had left off at paying his respects, but he brought up the sale of the ranch and Mary felt this was a violation of decorum. She chased the man to his car and put out one of the rear lights of his Mercedes before he could get away. It was impossible that Spandau should not adore her.

Mary opened the screen door and gave Spandau a dry

peck on the cheek. 'We didn't know if you were coming,' she said. Mary wasn't much on demonstrations of affection – Beau had been the great hugger and kisser in the family – but she went directly to the refrigerator and set out on the table a bowl of potato salad, sliced ham, salad and a pitcher of iced tea, all things she knew Spandau liked, all made earlier in the day just for him.

'I like to cultivate an air of mystery,' he said.

'Mystery, hell,' Mary said. 'You're the most un-mysterious person I ever met. You're like Beau. You're an open book, honey, I hate to tell you.'

'What's all that about?' he asked, nodding out the window toward Carlos and his son.

'Miguel's knocked up some girl down in Camarillo,' she said.

'No wonder he looks like hell. Carlos give him the shiner?'

'Nah, it was the girl's old man. A good Catholic, too, so he wants wedding bells.'

'Poor bastard.'

'He's turned into a nasty little shit,' Mary said. 'Do him good to get saddled with a fat little wife and about fifteen kids, before somebody knifes him.'

'You're in a rare mood today.'

'We buried Beau two years ago this week. I always go through an angry spell.'

Spandau sat down at the table. Mary put a plate, cutlery and a glass in front of him. She filled the glass with tea and

72

removed the plastic wrap from the food. Spandau helped himself and began eating.

'You're not going to ask where Dee is?'

'It's all part of my program of being mysterious,' he said. 'Besides, I'm hungry.' The truth was he couldn't wait to see Dee, he ached to see her, and they both knew it.

'She's out in the stable. She's got Hoagy all ready for you.'

'Good,' he said.

'You're so full of shit,' she said, smiling. 'She's been nervous all morning, waiting for you.'

'Are you supposed to be telling me this?'

'I don't know what in hell is wrong with you two. You act like all this is some sort of game. I never could understand why you got divorced in the first place. You still love each other. Neither one of you is ever going to get over it, or wants to, for that matter.'

'It's a complicated world.'

'No, it's not,' she declared flatly. 'It ain't now, and it never has been. It's the goddamned intellectuals like you two who screw things up by pretending it is. The world goes around just fine. All you got to do is learn how to hang on,' she said. 'Just like horses.'

'Is this some kind of comment on my recent showing up at Salinas?'

'No,' she said, 'but I heard it was less than brilliant. Let me see that thumb.'

Spandau showed it to her. She laughed. 'You always did

73

have a tendency to get that thing in the way. Beau said you were going to snatch it off one day. Looks like you damn near did the job this time.'

She sat down across from Spandau and looked at him.

'Hasn't it occurred to you,' she said, 'that I'm going to die one of these days?'

'You got mortality on the mind, do you?'

'They're going to chop this ranch up into little gibbety-bites and sell it to people who watch Oprah Winfrey,' she said.

'I wouldn't die, then, if I were you.'

'The boys don't care anything for it, and Dee won't run it by herself. She could, I guess, but she won't.'

'This doesn't have a thing to do with me, Mary,' he said. 'Lord, you wouldn't be picking on me this way if Dee was in the room.'

'She's bullheaded. Maybe you've got some sense left.'

'Dee's the one who left me,' he said.

'You let her go.'

'Since when could anybody ever stop Dee from doing what she wanted.'

'Hell,' she said. 'Let her teach. You could be running this ranch.'

'Don't you think your sons might have something to say about that?'

'All this is to them is a patch of dry land in the middle of nowhere. It don't mean a thing to them. I got money and I can make them a good settlement. Not that they need it.

74

The ranch can pass on to Dee, if she wants it. They won't squeak about it.'

'You'd better talk to Dee.'

'I'm talking to you, mister. You better get your head on straight about what you want. There might not be much time.'

'You're as fit as a fiddle, unless there's something you're not saying.'

'That's not what I'm talking about.'

She got up and started to wash dishes in the sink that had already been washed.

'What are you saying?'

'I'm not saying a word,' she said. 'It's not any of my business what you two do with your private lives.'

'Are you trying to tell me she's seeing somebody?'

'It's not my place to say. You ought to talk to her.'

'Goddamn it, Mary,' Spandau said.

'All I can say is you two better work it out. I won't be around forever.'

'Work out what?' asked Dee from the screen door.

'Work out what it is you two want for dinner,' Mary said. 'I don't mind cooking but I can't be bothered with menus. People have to tell me what they want.'

Delia McCauley was tall like her father. She'd inherited his family's auburn hair, which she wore long and was now twisted and curled, pinned up on the back of her head. Spandau had seen her many nights standing above him at the side of the bed, pulling the pins loose and letting the hair cascade down in a breathtaking autumn flow. From her mother she had a fineness of bone and features, an almost regal elegance. She was long and slim and beautiful and Spandau desired her as much now as he ever had.

She came in the screen door and let it close with a sharp thwack, done mainly to irritate her mother. She crossed to Spandau and kissed him lightly on the cheek, laying her hand on his upper arm. Spandau smelled the faint odor of horse and leather tack, which was not unpleasant to him. It rooted her into this world, this place he loved as well.

'I didn't think you were coming,' she said.

'I got held up in town. I should have called, but I got home and just came straight out here.'

'I got Hoagy all ready for you,' she said. 'If you still want to go for a ride. We can be back in time to cook dinner.'

'You all just go on,' said Mary. 'I've learned how to cook all on my own. Just enjoy yourselves,' she added sweetly.

Dee gave her a warning look. Mary ignored her. Dee disappeared back into the house.

'I guarantee,' said Mary, 'that you'll hear water running in a minute. She'll want to wash the horse off of her. And don't be surprised if there's a hint of perfume.' Mary sighed. 'I've never seen two dumber people.'

Spandau finished his food, and when Dee returned Spandau could detect the faintest hint of Chanel. Mary looked at him and shook her head. 'Hmpf,' she grunted.

'You all set?' asked Dee.

He followed her out to the stables, watched her walk

across the yard, the sway of her hips in the clinging blue jeans. Seeing her here, so natural in this place, it was hard to imagine her in the classroom, standing in front of a bunch of second-graders or a meeting full of teachers. But he'd seen both, seen her dressed in the severe blouse and skirt, crisp and formal, the auburn hair done up in a tight spinster's bun, the reading glasses perched on the end of her nose, standing there tall, uncompromising and unapproachable. He suspected some of the teachers were afraid of her. She stood her ground. But she was a fine teacher and loved the work, loved the children year after year. Still it was like watching some stranger. It wasn't the same woman who had done a striptease for him in the bathroom doorway, then, damp and soft and smelling of scented soap, climbed into the bed like a cat and lowered herself onto him, holding his hands on her hips, whispering to him, beads of moisture running from her still wet hair down her neck to trickle between her breasts and down her stomach, dampness too falling on Spandau, like a fine rain, as she put her hands on his shoulders and leaned forward above his face and cried out in a small voice that she loved him, that she would always love him.

They called the horse Hoagy because he always looked so damned sad. He was the first birthday present Dee had ever given him, a skinny little yearling then that nobody but Dee thought was going to amount to anything. He was too thin, too long, and showed none of the signs that made for a top-dollar quarter horse. Dee said anyway he had soul. Beau said he was built more like a goddamn llama than a horse. Mary said that he looked in the face like Hoagy Carmichael, always a little blue. The name stuck. When the time came, it was Spandau who broke and trained him. Even now he was too tall, too long in the leg, with a center of gravity too high to be a good roping horse. But he was. They'd meant for him to be just something for Spandau to ride when he came out to the ranch, but Spandau set him to work with cattle on a neighboring spread. He wasn't quick to turn and you were sitting up so high he'd damn near shift you off, but he was smart and he had an instinct for what the cow was going to do before it did and that more than made up for it. And he was fast. First time he put Hoagy in a rodeo chute the cowboys laughed their asses off about whether or not camels qualified for roping events. When the chute opened that was the last Spandau heard of it. Hoagy shot out so fast he was nearly on top of the calf and all Spandau had to do was practically lower the rope onto it. Then Hoagy stood firm with a slight backward tug that Spandau had never taught him and the calf flipped onto its back and Spandau had only to tie it. When Spandau left the arena the same cowboys were now asking why the hell the horse even bothered with Spandau, since all Spandau had done was carry the damned string.

As Spandau came into the stable the horse caught his smell and in recognition snorted and shuffled in his stall.

'He's missed you,' said Dee.

78

Spandau stroked the horse's forehead and patted him roughly on the neck.

'I should have brought something.'

'He'll be happy enough to be ridden,' Dee said. 'Nobody's been on him since you left.'

They saddled the horses and led them out of the stables, through the gate and into the pasture. Spandau closed the gate and they mounted up and rode slowly, without speaking, across the pasture, through another gate, and uphill into the trees. The trail wound upward through the forest and soon became steep enough that the horses were lazy and inclined to stop unless you kept nudging them. After a time they came out of the trees and into a high clearing, where you could see the ocean far below and away. The cliff itself dropped swiftly down into the valley. You could see the ranches and part of Ventura and the ocean glimmering in the distance. A rough wooden bench had been constructed near the edge, facing out to sea. Spandau and Dee dismounted and tied the horses. They went over to the bench and Dee sat down, stared out at the sea, and took a long breath.

'Mom tell you it was two years ago today?'

'Yeah.'

'He used to love this spot,' said Dee, speaking of her father. 'This was our secret spot, you know. I dragged this wood up here myself to build this thing. We worked on it together all one Saturday afternoon.'

Spandau picked at the coarse wood of the bench with his fingernail.

'Are you nervous about something?' she asked him.

'Just the end of vacation,' he lied. 'I don't want to go back to work. You know.'

'I thought you loved your job.'

'I never said I loved it. I'm just good at it, is all. I don't expect much of a future as a cowboy.'

'Not if you keep trying to snatch off digits.'

'I'm getting old,' he said.

'You always say that. You've been saying that as long as I've known you. What are you now? Thirty-eight?'

'Thirty-eight,' he repeated. 'Jesus, I feel ninety.'

'Well, that's the problem right there. Stop feeling so damned old. I don't feel old.'

'You don't?'

'Hell no,' she said. 'I'm still feeling frisky.'

'Frisky enough, I guess,' meaning the other man, though he didn't mean to say it.

He was jealous, and she could hear it in his voice. She hadn't wanted to talk about this, at least not now, not here. She'd hoped they could have a quiet ride, perhaps not talk at all, just spend some rare time together.

'What did Mama say?'

'Nothing,' Spandau said. 'I just sort of figured it out.'

'I was going to tell you.'

'You don't owe me any explanations,' he said. 'We're not married anymore. You can do what you want. There's nothing wrong with it.'

'Well,' she said, 'it feels wrong.'

'It shouldn't. It makes sense. Or maybe it just feels wrong for some other reason.'

'No,' she said, 'it feels wrong because I still feel married to you.'

She hadn't wanted to say that, either, though that was how she felt. Spandau didn't say anything.

'Shit,' said Dee.

'What do you want me to say? You want me to be jealous? Okay, you're goddamned right I'm jealous. But you knew that, so why make me say it?'

'We're not married anymore.'

'Look,' he said, 'I'm not arguing with you. You want me to stop coming out here?'

'Maybe that's the right thing to do,' she said, although this was something she didn't feel, and she said it because she was angry and she wanted him to fight it.

'Okay,' he said.

'It just doesn't seem right, though,' she said quickly, backtracking. 'I mean, I know this place is like—'

'It's okay,' he said. 'It's probably the best thing. We should have made a clean break of it anyway. The way things are, neither one of us can get on with our life.'

'What about Hoagy?' she said. 'What are you going to do about—'

'It'll be fine,' he said. 'I can put him up at my sister's place in Flagstaff. He'll be fine.'

'I'm sorry,' she said.

Spandau dug harder at the back of the bench. Small

splinters had wedged themselves under his nail and now it was beginning to bleed a little.

'Is he a good man?' Spandau asked her, finally.

'He seems to be. We don't know each other all that well yet. But he seems like a good man.'

'What's his name?'

'Charlie,' she said. 'For some reason it always reminds me of a damned parakeet. He's a guidance counselor.'

'No more cowboys, then.'

'No more cowboys.'

There was another long silence. Dee slapped her thighs and stood up. 'Well, everything changes.'

'Yeah,' said Spandau, 'and I hate it.'

She went over and put her arms around him. He held her and they remained this way for a little too long, outlasting the pretense of being innocent. She pulled away and wiped her eyes. They mounted the horses and began the ride back down.

They combed and curried the horses without speaking. When Dee finished she simply put the brushes away, closed the stall and walked back toward the house. Spandau followed a few minutes later. Mary was in the kitchen.

'What the hell happened?'

'We had a talk,' said Spandau.

'God damn it,' said Mary, 'I told you the secret of any relationship is not talking. That's your problem. Beau and me worked that out a long time ago. In thirty-five years we hardly said a word to each other. But when we did, by God, it was choice.'

'It's probably better if I stop hanging around here so much. I'll move Hoagy some time this week.'

'You're a fool,' Mary said to him. 'The thing with this fella, it won't last two weeks. It's not what she wants.'

'It's up to her to decide that.'

'You know,' she said, 'I hate it when people go around pretending that human beings actually know what they want. Just what goddamned evidence you ever seen of that?'

'It's not my place.'

'What is your place, then? If it's not here, if it's not with her? You got some sort of little goddamned island paradise I don't know about? Because you look pretty goddamned miserable to me, buster. You both do.'

'Mary, I can't argue about this.'

'Hell no, of course not. You're all set to let nature take its course. You're going to sit back and let whatever will be will be. Ain't that right? You go find a mountaintop, buster, and chant hari krishna while you both screw up your lives. Why don't you do that.'

'Well,' said Spandau, 'thank you for the grub. I won't be staying to dinner.'

He kissed Mary on the cheek. She was stiff but she let him.

'Tell her I said . . .' But there wasn't anything he could say. He walked out the screen door without bothering to finish the sentence.

Five

The next morning Spandau picked his way across the *Wildfire* set toward Bobby's trailer. When he got there a large, heavy-set guy was standing outside the door. He looked like a bouncer, and Spandau supposed Bobby had finally agreed to a bodyguard. This one was big but looked as intelligent as a bowl of wax fruit. People liked to hire the big ones, it made them feel safe, though in Spandau's experience the big ones were too slow and drew too much attention. They were okay as deterrents for over-aggressive fans, but ninety-five percent of the real job was spotting trouble before it happened and size never managed to impress a bullet. Spandau nodded to him and started to knock but the guy put his hand on Spandau's chest and pushed him away.

'You working for Bobby?' Spandau asked him.

'He's busy,' said the bouncer.

'You mind if I wait?'

The bouncer shrugged. Whoever he was he wasn't a pro, since it was drummed into every security worker that you never touched anybody first, since it could be taken as 'initiating a hostile act' that could start trouble and would bite you in the ass if things got legal.

There was the sound of a scuffle inside the trailer and Bobby's voice, shouting: 'Look, man, I don't give a fuck! Who the fuck you think you are, you can't—'

Bobby's voice was cut off by a sharp grunt. Spandau moved toward the door but the bouncer stepped in his way to push him off again. When the man's hand touched his chest, Spandau grabbed the hand and bent it backwards and down. When the guy was off balance Spandau rolled him onto the asphalt a few feet away and went in the door.

Bobby was leaning against the table, bent over and holding his stomach, struggling to get his breath. A thin, rat-faced man in a three-piece suit stood in front of him.

'Step away,' Spandau said to him.

'Who the fuck are you?'

'Step back and put your hands where I can see them.'

'What is this? *Gunsmoke*? You don't even have a gun.'

The trailer door opened and the bouncer started to come through. As he was heaving himself up the steps, Spandau shoved him with his foot backwards through the door and locked it. He turned to the rat-faced man and gave him a short but hard jab to the solar plexus. The man doubled over.

'Feels good, doesn't it?' Spandau said to him. 'You okay?' he said to Bobby.

'Yeah . . . I just . . .'

Bobby turned and puked on the floor. Spandau looked around and found a towel. He wet it in the sink and gave it to Bobby, who wiped his mouth with it.

'Just sit down,' he said to Bobby. 'You'll be okay in a few minutes. And you,' he said to Rat Face, 'you stay right there. You move and I'm going to break something valuable.'

Spandau got out his cellphone and started to dial.

'Who you calling?' demanded Bobby.

'I'm calling security.'

'No.'

'I need somebody to get over here to—'

'I said no!'

Spandau stared at him. He was serious. Spandau put away the phone.

'Who is this guy?' he asked Bobby.

'I'm a friend of his, asshole,' said Rat Face.

'Some friend.'

Meanwhile the bouncer had been rattling the door.

'Richie?' called the bouncer. 'You okay, Richie? Richie?'

'I think your girlfriend is worried about you,' Spandau said to Rat Face.

Rat Face stood up to his full height and pretended his stomach didn't hurt. 'I'm fine, you fucking idiot, no thanks to you,' he called through the door.

'You want me to break down the door?' the bouncer asked him.

'It's a little fucking late, don't you think?' Rat Face replied to him. 'Just wait there, I'll be out in a minute.' He turned to Spandau. 'You'll be lucky if I don't sue your ass for assault.' To Bobby he said, 'Who is this guy?'

'Nobody,' Bobby said. 'Just a bodyguard Annie wanted to hire.'

'You don't need a bodyguard,' Rat Face said. 'You got me.'

'And what a class act you are,' Spandau said to him.

Rat Face said to Bobby, 'I'm going to go. You call me, right? About what we talked about?' As he passed by Spandau he said, 'You ever fucking touch me again and I'll make you wish you were dead.'

Rat Face unlocked the trailer door and went out.

'Jesus, Richie,' said the bouncer, 'I'm sorry, he got the drop on me.'

Rat Face slapped him. 'Don't you ever embarrass me like that again.'

'Sure, Richie, Jesus, never again . . .'

'You okay?' Spandau asked Bobby.

'Yeah.'

'I thought you said you used to box?'

'I'm out of shape, okay?' he said angrily.

'Who was that?'

'Just somebody I know.'

'You let all your acquaintances slap you around?'

'What the fuck do you want? You filling out a form or something?'

'I came by to tell you I'll take the job.'

'Swell. I don't want you. Thanks for nothing.'

'From the look of things, I'd say you need me even worse than yesterday.'

'Well I don't. I got everything under control.'

'I can see that.'

'Just go away,' Bobby said tiredly. 'Annie'll write you a check for your time.'

Spandau sat down in a chair and crossed his legs. He looked at Bobby and sighed and shook his head and thought about walking out. Then he said, 'What kind of trouble are you in?'

'I'm fine. Just leave me alone.'

'Why'd you fake the letter?'

'Who says the letter is a fake?'

Spandau picked up one of Bobby's popular magazines and tossed it at Bobby's feet. 'Nice glossy letters, cut out of *People* magazine or something. It's probably still laying around here somewhere. Fingerprints stand out on it like 3D.'

'Look, I don't need your goddamn help, okay? You want me to have you thrown out of here on your ass?'

Spandau looked at him for a few moments longer. He stood up, took out a business card and wrote down a number. He held the card out to Bobby, who wouldn't take it.

'This is my service. You change your mind about this, you call me. Maybe you are a tough guy, kiddo, but you're hanging around with the wrong bunch of people.'

Spandau tossed the card onto the table and left. Walking back to the car, he decided not to call Walter. Walter would either try to get him started on another job or coax him into getting the jump on a weekend bender. Walter could wait. It was a nice day, the sun was shining, and though Elvis was dead Spandau was still alive and kicking. He'd go to Santa Monica, have lunch on the beach and wait for the girl of his dreams to come roller-skating into his life. He thought about Sarah Jessica Parker in *L.A. Story*, doing cartwheels in the sand for Steve Martin. There was a lot to be said for a girlfriend who could do cartwheels, and potentially dozens of them waited in Santa Monica to be fulfilled by an older man sporting cowboy boots and a gigantic purple thumb. It was an amusing fantasy and lasted Spandau well onto Highway 405 and most of the way home.

That night Spandau sat in the Gene Autry room drinking Wild Turkey and smoking a pipe. From a bookstore in Flagstaff he'd managed to score a first edition of Mari Sandoz's *Cheyenne Autumn* and had been waiting all week for some quiet time to read it. He propped his feet up on a hassock made of saddle leather and took a sip of his whiskey, then picked up the book and turned it around in his hands, admiring the simple brown dust jacket still in good shape under the protective cover. He'd started collecting books on the American West just after Dee left him. Until then he'd felt guilty about spending the money – it was an expensive pastime – but now he was hooked and had accumulated a few dozen valuable copies. He justified it by telling himself they'd accompany him through a lonely and wifeless old age, and it was true the volumes had a way of lifting him out of himself, lifting him out of the quarrelsome world he inhabited. As he sat in this ridiculous room, surrounded by a dead age and smelling of smoke and leather and whiskey, full of anachronisms, readily admitting to being an anachronism himself, he could feel the perpetual knot in his shoulders unwind and his soul begin to seek its balance again. It was absurd, Spandau knew, this business of a grown-up playing at cowboys. Of pretending that time could be reset, however briefly, to a period of innocence, or that America had ever had a period of innocence at all. Wasn't that in itself the most American of sentiments? If we had a national identity at all, wasn't that the key to it, the belief that there was ever any sort of purity to be restored? That somehow, once, we had gotten things right, which opened the possibility of setting them right yet again. No matter where you looked there were illusions, and Spandau was tired of squinting and straining to see through the fog of it all. Perhaps in the end everything *was* bullshit, as Walter was the first to tell him. America. Cowboys. Love. All of it crap, all of it myths created to peddle something. Welcome to Hollywood, welcome to LA. He'd once heard a sociologist proclaim that, if you wanted to see into the future, take a look at Los Angeles today. Spandau tried hard not to believe this, and he could feel his mind resisting it even now. No, some faint but redeeming voice told him, not everything is shit. Remember how it feels to ride a horse. Remember coming out of the chute and the thrill of the rope when it comes taut on the saddle horn and the sharp sudden tug and release. Remember the smell of tall grass and the brush of it against your legs as you ride through it. Remember Dee. The whole of existence might well prove to be no more than an infinite, maggoty, festering dungheap. But as far as Spandau was concerned the memories of holding Dee in his arms made it worthy to continue.

The phone rang on the desk behind him, prodding him like an electric shock. He should have turned off the damned phone. There was nothing on his plate right now, nothing he had to answer to. He looked at the caller ID – it was blocked. The answering machine picked it up before he could turn it off. It was Gail from his answering service. He lifted the receiver.

'Spandau.'

'You've got a message from someone named Ginger Constantine. He says it's urgent.'

'Yeah, okay, give me the number.'

Spandau scribbled it on his hand. He rang off and dialed the number. A man with a light English accent answered.

'Yes?'

'This is David Spandau. You said it was urgent.'

'Oh my lord, yes! I'm Bobby Dye's assistant, I saw your

card and I knew he'd talked to you . . . Look, it's Bobby, he's in trouble. He's gone to see Richie Stella. He took a gun with him. I didn't know who else to call.'

'Thin guy with a rat face?'

'That's Richie.'

'How can I find him?'

'He went to Richie's club. You know the Voodoo Room on Sunset?'

'Yeah, I know it. How long ago did he leave?'

'Maybe ten minutes.'

'I'm leaving now.'

The Voodoo Room was the most popular club on the Strip, wedged between a liquor store and sushi bar. From the outside it looked like the sort of hopeless dive where alcoholic grannies could be found resting their cheeks in a puddle of bar sweat. Prior to this it had been a yuppie hangout done up in Philippe Starck, all shiny metal and mellow glass, and it cost the new owner a cool quarter of a million to rebuild the façade, carefully removing any taints of success or beauty and replacing it with a texture and design that resembled a matte-black cardboard box. This was designed to attract the truly hip, who were already smothered in the higher aesthetics and required a place where they could pretend to slum in comfort and safety, like Marie Antoinette's goat farm in the backyard at Versailles. When Spandau arrived there was the inevitable Friday night crowd of the terminally stylish waiting to be allowed past the gatekeepers. Spandau managed to park in a lot nearby and wondered how he was going to get in. He looked in his wallet to see if the fifties were still there.

A girl sitting on a stool at the door, flanked up by a couple of professional-looking bouncers, was culling humans like dried legumes. Bad this way, good over here. Only the beautiful or the well known got inside. Spandau was aware he was neither. The line kept growing. Spandau went up to two lovely young things toward the end.

'Look, I'm an actor, and there's a producer in there I've really got to meet. It's worth fifty bucks each. You don't have to stick around, all you've got to do is get me past the door.'

They sized him up and for a moment Spandau was sure they were going to start laughing. Then one of them said, 'Sure, for fifty bucks.'

'Anyway, you don't look so bad for an old guy,' the other one said.

As they reached the door the girls looped their arms through his. The girl on the stool looked at the girls, then at Spandau. She shook her head. Spandau thought it meant no, but she was merely expressing disbelief. She waved them past.

It was early yet but the club was packed, the floor filled with couples writhing to a near-deafening beat that filled the room. It was like being on the inside of a drum. Spandau had been to enough clubs like this before, though never by his own choice, always on some case. He hated them, of course, but he could see their attraction. It was a kind of licensed orgy where beauty and fame bought you permission to behave as you wanted. Places like this existed everywhere and always had. Like Steve Rubell's legendary Studio 54 in New York in the seventies, nobody would tell on you, provided you could get through the door. You could snort, fuck, grope and exhibit as much as you pleased – and share it all with the glitterati. There was a weird sort of democracy at work here. Where else would Lulu Snekert, homecoming queen from Grand Rapids, get a chance to do lines of coke with her favorite stars?

After buying them drinks, Spandau left the girls at the bar and looked around. He made a couple of rounds of the packed floor and didn't see Bobby. He wasn't worried about Stella spotting him – Bobby would be wherever Stella was.

The room was dark and smoky. Smoking was only one of the many municipal laws the place ignored, for which the management paid handsomely at the end of each month. The general idea was to recreate a 1940s Harlem nightclub, the sort of exotic place where white people went to watch negroes smoke reefers and look sensually menacing. You still occasionally found jazz in the Voodoo Room, but mainly it was rock and the bands were as ofay as the clientele. That special frisson of menace – de rigueur for all successful slumming – was provided by the flashy gangbangers modeling bling and girlfriends, and upscale drug dealers, who on some nights turned the place into a dope-addled souk that extended from the restrooms out onto the street.

There was a large mirror covering most of one wall. Behind that, Spandau reasoned, would be the infamous VIP room, where celebs hung out to avoid the hoi polloi. Spandau looked for an entry to the place. There were two closed doors at the end of a hallway. Spandau opened one. It was an office, and a pretty blonde in her late twenties sat at a desk hunched over a pile of receipts.

'Oops, sorry,' Spandau said in a fuzzy voice. Pardon me, just another lost drunk. 'Looking for the bathroom.'

'Other side of the club,' said the blonde and went back to her calculations.

Spandau tried the other door. Unlocked. It opened into a short, narrow corridor and another door. Spandau heard voices on the other side. One of them was Bobby's. He pushed open the door.

The room itself was in half-light, as if lit by candles. Through the glass plate on the opposite wall you could see the entire club floor and the stage. It was like watching some high-definition television program of *Hollywood Gone Wild*, broadcast on a giant screen. The room was soundproofed and music piped in through speakers, which made it even more unreal.

Richie Stella sat on a sofa. Bobby stood in the center of the room, backlit by the panorama of the club floor. There was a pistol in Bobby's hand aimed at Richie. The hand shook and the barrel of the .38 made small circles in the air. Bobby was soaked with sweat and though Spandau couldn't see his eyes he knew he was high on drugs or booze, probably both. Richie sat quietly with his legs crossed. He didn't seem particularly worried, though there was a good chance of Bobby shooting him by accident if nothing else.

When Spandau came in, Bobby turned quickly and brought the gun around.

'Whoa,' said Spandau, 'it's just me.'

'What the fuck do you want,' said Bobby in a plaintive voice. 'Leave me alone.'

'Ginger sent me to find you,' Spandau said. 'He was worried you were going to do something stupid.'

'I'm not going to do anything stupid,' Bobby said, his voice quivering. 'I'm just going to kill this miserable fuck.'

'I was just trying to explain to the kid—' attempted Richie.

'Shut up!' said Bobby. 'Don't talk, don't move!'

Stella continued anyway. 'I was just trying to tell him how dumb all this is. I'm a friend of his.'

'You're a fucking maggot and you deserve a bullet between your eyes,' Bobby said.

'Why don't you tell him how wrong this is?' Richie said to Spandau.

'I'm the wrong guy to ask,' said Spandau. 'I don't like you either.'

'Why don't you tell him about life in prison,' Richie said. 'He shoots me, that's what he's going to get.'

'He's got a point,' Spandau said to Bobby. 'You think it's worth it?'

'Oh yeah,' said Bobby. 'It's worth it.'

'Hell, then,' said Spandau. 'Just shoot him and we can all go home.'

Stella gave Spandau a long, withering look. They waited and when no gunshot came, Spandau said:

'Give me the gun, Bobby. That's a lousy .38, and unless you hit something major you're not going to kill the son of a bitch anyway. You'll just wind up going to jail and ruining your career.'

'I'm going to kill him.'

'Then do it,' said Spandau, 'and quit fucking around.'

Bobby stared at Stella. He raised the gun and aimed it at Stella's chest. His damp hand tightened on the gun, relaxed, tightened again. He waited.

Spandau went over to him and took the gun away. Bobby slumped and dropped down onto the sofa next to Stella. He sat with his face in his hands.

'Well that was just fucking lovely,' announced Stella. He looked at Spandau and shook his head, then turned to Bobby.

'How are you? You okay?' Stella said to Bobby.

Bobby didn't reply, just sat with his face covered.

'Jesus, kid,' said Stella, putting his arm around Bobby's shoulders, 'I thought I was fucking done for there for a minute. Look at you, all upset. You want a Xanax? I'll get somebody to find you a Xanax.'

'Leave him alone,' said Spandau. 'I'll take him home.'

'You,' Stella said to him, 'I have had enough of. You're lucky I don't off you. You nearly got me shot.'

'He wasn't going to shoot anybody.'

'No thanks to you and your cheerleading. Go ahead and shoot him, he says, so we can all go home. Where the fuck is Martin?' To Bobby he said, 'I'll have Martin drive you home.'

Stella picked up a phone and demanded Martin. In a few moments the bruiser who'd been with Stella at Bobby's trailer came in the door.

'I want you to take Bobby home,' Stella said to him. 'Get him anything he wants. Get him some Xanax or something. He's upset.' To Bobby he said, 'We'll get you something, you'll sleep like a fucking baby.'

'Leave him alone,' Spandau said again.

'Martin will take him home,' Stella said to him. 'You, you're not going anywhere.'

Martin lifted Bobby to his feet. Bobby was like a zombie. Martin led him out. Bobby passed Spandau without looking at him, just stared at the floor.

'What a fucking night,' said Stella. 'You want a drink?'

'Sure. Bourbon.'

'Have a seat,' Stella said to him.

Spandau sat down and looked through the two-way mirror at the dancing bodies. Stella turned off the sound as if to gain his attention. He picked up the phone. 'Send a bottle of Makers Mark in here, some ice and a couple of glasses.' He put down the phone and turned to Spandau. 'This is all your fault.'

'How do you figure that?'

'You hadn't stuck your beak into things, this would never have happened.'

'I hadn't stuck my beak into things,' said Spandau, 'you might be pushing up daisies about now. We could look at it that way.'

'I like my way better,' Stella said to him. 'This way you owe me.'

There was a knock at the door and the blonde from the office came in with the tray of the drinks. She gave Spandau a curious glance then looked away. Stella smiled at her and put his hand on her hip as she put the tray on the low table in front of him. She didn't shrug off the hand but she didn't seem pleased it was there either. She left the room without saying a word. Stella dropped ice into the two glasses and covered them with whiskey. He handed one to Spandau.

'You,' he said to Spandau, 'are a pimple that is uncomfortably close to my asshole.'

'Is that a metaphor for something?' Spandau said.

'I'll give you a metaphor in a minute. Who the fuck do you think you are, messing around in my business?'

'I was thinking along the lines of keeping Bobby from ruining his life. You I'm not much concerned with.'

'You think he'll be okay?' Stella said with genuine concern.

'He'll go home and sober up. Hopefully he won't get the same idea tomorrow night.'

Stella sat down on the couch and crossed his legs. 'You want to work for me?'

'No.'

'Why not?'

'I need an HMO and a dental plan. Besides,' said Spandau, 'I don't like you.'

'In the great scheme of things, likes and dislikes are of no importance. For the superior man, the key to success is the conquest of the ego.'

'Sun-Tzu?'

'Mike Ovitz reads Sun-Tzu,' said Stella. 'Business is warfare. You can learn a lot from the chinks. And they've got a lot of fucking money now.'

'You doing a movie with Bobby?'

'You bet,' said Stella. 'He's my star.'

'Does his agent know this?'

'Fuck her. They work for him, he doesn't work for them.'

'Well that's certainly a novel way of looking at it. Maybe it will catch on.'

'It doesn't make any difference,' said Stella. 'I got a script and I got financing. All I need is a start date.'

'And let's not forget a star who's willing to work for you.'

Stella laughed. 'That crazy little fucker, he's killing me. He doesn't know what's good for him. He fucking runs hot and cold. He says he'll do it then he cold-shoulders me. Then he fucking hires you, for chrissake.'

'He didn't hire me.'

'Well you're fucking here, aren't you, and in my fucking way.'

'This has nothing to do with me.'

'He likes you. I can tell. He respects you,' said Stella.

'You got a contract?' Spandau asked him.

Stella looked hurt. 'A man gives me his word, I don't need a contract.'

'Look – and I mean this in the nicest possible way – this isn't *The Godfather* and there is no romantic code among crooks. This is Hollywood and everybody is a liar until the check clears. I hate to be the one to shatter your innocence.'

'You don't work for him, why are you here?'

'His assistant called me and said he was coming down here to shoot you. Ordinarily that would have seemed like a pretty good idea to me, but it would have fucked up his life. He seems like a nice enough kid, at least until you and the fucking studios get through with him. Leave him alone. His life is going to be ugly enough without one more vulture sucking at him.'

Stella pretended he didn't hear the last sentence. He picked up the phone, dialed a number. 'How is he?' he said into the receiver. After a pause, he hung up and said to Spandau: 'He fell asleep in the back seat.' He sighed. 'A filmmaker has got no end of worries.'

Spandau drained his whiskey and stood up. 'I think you are all fucking deranged,' he said, 'and I'm going home.'

'You sure you don't want to work for me?'

'I think my being an employee would jeopardize our friendship.'

'Fucking smart-ass. Stay out of my way. Opposition should be destroyed in its infancy.'

'Sun-Tzu?'

'Nah, my old boss, Vinnie the Gag. Best garrotte artist in the business. I still got his number.'

Stella gave him a wolf-like smile. Spandau put down his empty glass and went home.

The following afternoon, a thankfully quiet Saturday, Spandau was working in the garden. The raccoons appeared to have forgotten about the goldfish for a while. It was nice and quiet and he was relaxed for the first time since his vacation had ended. The phone rang inside the house. He didn't answer it, let it go through the machine. He tried not to listen to it. He cleaned the pump in the bottom of the pond and fed the fish. They were like dogs now, they gathered in a clump whenever they saw him. He dropped in the pellets and they ate and wriggled around happily. He tried again to think of some way to protect the goldfish from the raccoons. Short of putting a top over the pond there was nothing he could do. He thought about killing the raccoons again. But there was the problem of what to do with a dead raccoon and, anyway, there were always more raccoons. His golden moment was spoiled and he went into the house and listened to his message.

'Hi, this is Gail. You've got a message from Bobby Dye. He wants you to call him. His number is . . .'

Spandau scribbled down the number. He thought about not calling. It was a mistake to get involved any deeper in this, a clear lose–lose situation, as Coren would have been the first to point out. The job was hard enough without working for a client who didn't know what the hell he wanted. Spandau crumpled the bit of paper and tossed it into the trash. He went into the kitchen and opened a beer, then went back into his office, dug the paper out of the trash and made the call. A machine picked it up. Bird noises and gorilla sounds, then the beep.

'This is David Spandau . . .'

Bobby picked up quickly. He sounded sober and crisp. 'Hey, man, thanks for calling me back. Can you come over here, to my place? I need to talk to you. I live up at the top of Wonderland . . .'

Head east on Sunset Boulevard, starting at the Beverly Hills sign, the most famous residential locator in the world.

You're well in from the sea now, and the funkiness of Santa Monica is but a memory. You've endured the twisty, disappointing paved section past UCLA (with all this dough you'd think they'd fix the potholes) and by now you're coming to terms with the fact that the houses in Beverly Hills don't look a thing like Jed Clampett's, since the yards are diminutive and there's nary a Southern Revival mansion to be found. Did we fly all the way out

103

here for this? you ask. You've passed Brentwood where O.J. Simpson did (or did not) off his wife and her lover, and where Ray Bradbury was once arrested for just walking. (You just kept driving, since they would not let you in. Standards have to be maintained. The snotty bastards.)

Finally you reach the sign, which, for some reason, doesn't look quite the way it does in the pictures. (This is because the sign you're thinking of, the big one, the really famous one, is actually a few blocks away on Wilshire. This is a second-string sign, and it's just as well you don't know this, because then you'd really feel like a putz, wouldn't you?) Your teenage daughter in the back seat wants to stop, to get her photo taken beneath the sign. But half a dozen people are doing that already, and there's no place to park without getting run over or another ticket like the one you got for trying to park in Westwood. And your old lady is tired and her sinuses are killing her. Maybe it's the flowers. You tell your daughter no and keep on driving and now she hates you, just the way she's hated you ever since you left home. She hates you. Your wife hates you. You suspect you may be about to get lost. You have a map but nobody except you is willing to read it, and you can't read it without getting everybody killed or pulling over, and there is nowhere to pull over. There are too many cars driving too fast, and the people in these cars apparently hate you too.

Keep driving.

You're approaching the Sunset Strip. The Lamborghini

104

dealership hints that there might be some glamour ahead. But no, this too is disappointing. It could be anywhere, and looks a little white-trashy, if anybody were to ask you. You wouldn't be caught dead in a neighborhood like this back home. Just look at those giant billboards, covering the entire sides of respectable buildings with bulging tits and crotches! Good lord! Restaurants, hotels and nightclubs whose names you vaguely recall sail past, but they don't look anything like the way you'd imagined. Look! There's the Whiskey A Go Go, where Jim Morrison and The Doors used to play, though nobody in the car but you knows or gives a shit who The Doors were. Your wife tells you she thinks you've passed Rodeo Drive, but you're damned if you'll turn back, not in this traffic, and anyway that's what she gets if she won't read the goddamned map. Your daughter thinks she's spotted that club where the famous young actor overdosed and died in the street. She wants to stop again and get her picture taken on the very spot. Screw her too, and keep driving.

Drive past the clubs and the bistros. Past the Chateau Marmont, that Gothic elephants' graveyard where stars go to kill themselves. Keep driving until it seems as if the dubious history and the chintzy glamour of the Strip have all been exhausted, and the world starts to give way again to strip malls and taco stands, the domain of us regular people. This would be Laurel Canyon Drive. Do not give up hope. You have not yet left history and glamour after all. Turn left into Laurel Canyon and you are entering the

Hollywood Hills, where life in LA *really* begins to get interesting.

On the other hand, none of this has any meaning for you at all.

Because you, being one of us regular people, one of the unprivileged, one of the hoi polloi, will never get to see it.

Because the whole point of this world, in case you haven't noticed yet, is to keep you out.

Wonderland Avenue crawls up the eastern side of the Santa Monica Mountains, pushing itself off from Laurel Canyon like a tired and indecisive burro. You do not drive up Wonderland so much as slog up it, since it is steep and twisty and even the few street signs appear to have abandoned hope. There are so many abrupt changes that it's useless to give directions, and most popular guidebooks don't even bother, instead recommending that tourists arm themselves with a Thomas Guide and hope for the best. Of course it is precisely this sort of confusion that makes the place so desirable for the people who live there. It's like living at the end of a gigantic garden maze and only a few people know the key. Who needs to live in a gated community when nobody can find you anyway? The result is a closed community, a community of secrets, while giving the appearance of being just another laid-back neighborhood. Musicians and actors have always liked the place because of the unspoken rule of keeping your mouth shut and minding your own business. This code of *omerta* has interesting consequences. Its seclusion made it attractive to the creative rock revolutionaries of the sixties, a place where they could hide away, drop acid, fall in love with each other's mates, and change the course of popular music. On the other hand, in 1981 porn star John Holmes was involved in a dope-infused, deal-gone-wrong blood-bath at 8763 Wonderland, in which police found an entire house redecorated in blood and guts. Privacy can have its drawbacks.

Spandau was thinking of the Wonderland murders as he drove upward through the exclusive neighborhood. He thought about growing up in Arizona, a place where the dream was to work hard and make enough money to buy into a neighborhood where everything was guaranteed to be clean and safe. It was a world where income alone weeded out the riff-raff. A world where your neighbor in the big shiny house was going to be a doctor or a lawyer, not a successful drug dealer or porn star or a bunch of strung-out and psychotic thieves. In LA, you couldn't be sure. That little house with the white picket fence might belong to the next Charlie Manson, just waiting to write your name in blood. You never knew where you were in this place. Spandau thought of five people getting hacked to death – a noisy enough enterprise, one would think – while ten yards away someone went on eating their corn-flakes. In what sort of world does a blood-curdling scream seem commonplace?

Spandau had often driven up Wonderland. The trick

was to always hang to the right. Soon he came to the top where it leveled a bit, and there was a small selection of large but tightly closed gates to choose from. Spandau drove up to the security post outside Bobby's gate. He pressed a button and let the camera have a good look at him. Waited, while they decided that a guy in an Armani suit and driving a new BMW probably wasn't the new John Wayne Gacy. You couldn't be sure though. The gate buzzed and opened. Spandau drove up and parked on the landing outside the garage. He glanced at the Porsche and the Harley, neither of which looked used. You had to feel a little sad for a guy who had those kind of toys and never got a chance to play with them. He walked up the hill to the house.

Bobby Dye's house – which, on the advice of his accountant, he did not yet own but merely rented for an exorbitant sum – sat on an outcropping that stuck out over a precipice like the hood mascot of a 1950s Pontiac, jutting its chin at the dried plains of Los Angeles. The house was all natural wood, glass, and high ceilings, built by a rock star in the sixties who liked the idea of living in a cabin somewhere but knew better than to let his manager or his record label out of his sight. The result was what one guest had called a 'hippie Valhalla' and Spandau thought it lived up to the name. A patio hugged the perimeter of the house, not the most burglar-proof arrangement but it led to some spectacular views. Spandau wondered how many drunks had toppled down into the hillside bushes. It wasn't high enough to kill you unless you landed badly or kept rolling. He walked over to the edge and looked toward the back. A long flight of wooden steps led down to a pool and a cabana. Another shorter flight led to what was probably a guest house. Spandau turned and through the plate glass saw Bobby watching him. Bobby came over and slid open the patio door.

'I really appreciate your coming over here,' said Bobby, extending his hand. Spandau shook it. It was a different Bobby from last night. He was cool and confident. The eyes were bright and alert, and his grip was firm. His skin had regained its color. It was as if the previous night had never happened.

'You ever think I wouldn't?' Spandau asked.

'Nah,' said Bobby. 'Not really.'

Bobby led him into the living room. A tall cathedral ceiling and acres of glass that looked down on most of Los Angeles. So this is what it's like on Mt Olympus, thought Spandau. At first glance the furniture was a collection of odds and ends, but the dining table was genuine Spanish mission and the childlike scrawl above the couch was a Basquiat. The couch itself was art deco, rescued from a 1920s ocean liner, and the lamp beside it was Lalique. The room had a southern exposure so the sun never managed to penetrate the window directly. The house was light and cool inside though all the wood still gave it the feeling of being in a forest somewhere. A good architect can do wonders. There was no consistency but the kid had taste and a good eye, Spandau had to admit. He'd been working class, Spandau had read. Maybe not poor but enough that the money would have been a shock. There were a few auction house catalogs around, and Spandau imagined him feverishly picking through them, researching the names, desperately trying to make up for all that time without. The trailer had been a blank screen, but this was different. Spandau felt he was beginning to get a handle now. Again there were no personal photos about, nothing to display his past, but that itself was telling. It was the place of a young man trying to recreate himself.

'Thanks for last night,' said Bobby. 'I might've shot him.'

'No, you wouldn't have.'

'What makes you so goddamn sure?'

'You may be dumb, but you're not a complete idiot.'

'What the hell is that supposed to mean?'

'It means you aren't dumb enough to throw away a billion-dollar acting career in order to kill a shit like Richie Stella, no matter how pissed off you think you are.'

Bobby flopped down in an art deco leather chair. 'You really think you got me pegged, don't you?'

'Well enough to know you faked that note. And well enough to know that Richie Stella is blackmailing you.'

Bobby didn't bother to look surprised. He took out a packet of French cigarettes and made a show of lighting one.

'You could just pay him,' Spandau said. 'Or better yet,

just go to the cops. They have units that specialize in this crap. I know this is Hollywood, but blackmail is still supposed to be illegal.'

'He wants me to do that fucking movie. He wants to be a fucking movie producer, the asshole.'

'Well, he's a vicious and immoral little shit. He sounds qualified to me. How bad is the movie?'

'The script is shit. Annie would never let me do it. I mean, it would be fucking embarrassing. That's what *Wildfire* is all about. It's my breakthrough, man. Annie says I could make the A-List with this one. I do his shit movie, I throw the whole thing away. What I'm doing on *Wildfire* is good, man. The best work I've ever done. Real fucking acting. I turn around and do this piece of shit and *Wildfire* looks like a fluke, you know? I can't do it.'

'Talk to the studio. Let them deal with it.'

'I can't.'

'How bad can it be?' Spandau said to him. 'You're a gold mine for them, they'll do whatever they can to protect that.'

'Oh yeah, that's exactly what I need. Get rid of Richie and then give these motherfuckers the leash. They're worse than he is.'

'What do you want me to do?'

'I want you to get him off my back,' said Bobby, suddenly animated. 'I don't care how. I mean it. I'll pay whatever it takes. You do whatever it takes, as hard as it takes.'

111

'Are you suggesting I off him?'

'He's a fucking weasel. The world won't miss him.'

'Gee, Bobby, I don't know. I have to think about it. I haven't assassinated anybody in a while and I don't know what the going rate is.'

'I want him off my back. I want him to be history.'

'It's a good thing you don't write your own lines,' said Spandau. 'You sound like a bad imitation of Jimmy Cagney.'

'Fuck you, then!' shouted Bobby. He got up and started pacing. 'I'll get somebody else, with balls. Not some fucking washed-up stunt man.'

Spandau took a deep breath. He held it for a few seconds, then let it out in a slow stream. 'Now I want you to listen to me, kid, and I want you to listen carefully. First, I'm about fed up with the way you and all the other bozos around you have been talking to me. Unlike you and all the other star-struck unfortunates in this town, I don't need them to like me. Second, I think you're a snot-nosed little prick, but I'm convinced it's mainly because suddenly you're required to act like a grown-up and you don't have a fucking clue how to do it.'

Bobby stood a few feet away, glaring at him, his fists clenched, the Gauloise dangling from the corner of his mouth like Jean-Paul Belmondo. 'You think I'm afraid of you? I used to box, man.'

'No,' said Spandau, 'you used to fart around in a gym until somebody gave you that trademark broken nose of yours. Now maybe you look like a tough guy to millions of

112

mall-rats around the country, but you've got girls' hands and you wouldn't last ten seconds in the ring with anybody except Stephen Hawking, and I'd still give him odds.'

Bobby got into what passed for a fighter's crouch. He looked at Spandau and blinked as the smoke from the Gauloise burnt his eyes.

'Jesus,' said Spandau, and rolled his eyes. 'You want to throw a punch? Come on, honey, send it home. But your feet are all wrong, and the second you throw that left cross you got cocked there you're going to be off balance before it gets anywhere near me. Meanwhile I got fifty pounds on you and four more inches of reach. And while I will try not to mess up that pretty sculpted face of yours, when I hit you it is still going to do some damage.'

Bobby thought about it and dropped his hands. Then he held them up and looked at them. 'Fuck you, girls' hands,' he said, laughing. 'Anyway, I'm not going to blow this movie because some fucking macho has-been gets lucky with a punch.'

'Good for you. At least you've learned the first lesson, which is never to fight unless you know you can win. Didn't anybody ever explain that to you? The trick is to wait until I'm off-guard and then brain me with a Louisville slugger. That's the way it is in the real world. That's the way guys like Richie Stella do it.'

Bobby took the cigarette out of his mouth and ground it into a cut-glass ashtray. 'So long and thanks for nothing. Don't let the door hit you in the ass when you leave.'

'Okay, tough guy,' said Spandau. 'You want my help or not?'

'You don't have the balls. He's not going to stop until he's dead.'

'Let me decide that. I need to know what he's got on you.'

'Then you got it too. I'm fucked no matter what.'

'Sooner or later you've got to trust somebody, sport. How bad is it?'

'It's bad.'

He walked across the room and took a wooden box out of a cabinet, and carried it back to the sofa. He sat down, crossed his legs like a brahmin, and rolled a joint. He was hesitant to begin. He lit up, took a deep hit and began talking.

'I picked up this girl . . . Really cute, man. Really hot. She had this sort of schoolgirl thing going, you know, a white blouse and a cute little plaid skirt. She even had fucking pigtails. It was, like, every dirty old man's fantasy. She knew exactly what she was doing, too.

'Anyway, I brought her back here. I'm wrecked, I don't even know how I made it up the hill without killing both of us. So we're in here, and we start making out, and she says to me, "You got anything I can use to relax, it's better when I'm high, I get wild." And I'm thinking, Fuck yes. And I've got a little rock, and she says, oh yeah, she loves rock. So we're sitting over there and we smoke a little rock and then she comes over and we start to mess around again, but

114

she says wait, she's got to go to the bathroom, so she takes this little purse she's got with her and she goes upstairs to the bathroom.

'So off she goes and I'm sitting here and then the crack hits me and I'm sort of blissed out for a while, I don't know how long. That rush, you know? So in a few minutes I'm back in the real world again, and she still isn't back. So I get worried and I go upstairs . . .

'I check the bathroom. I knock, nothing. I open the door. It's unlocked. And she's sitting there, on the toilet, sort of slumped over, her tights pulled down around her ankles and this fucking needle sticking out of her thigh. She's like fucking blue. And she's not breathing, and there's this whole set of works on the sink, man, she's been cooking up heroin and she's shot up and fucking OD'd in my bathroom. I got this dead girl in my bathroom . . .

'I panic. You know? The fucking crack doesn't help. I'm like running around the place beating my fists against my head, crying like a fucking baby . . . I don't know what I'm gonna do. I mean, this dead girl. I don't know what to do. Then I think of Richie.'

'Why Richie?'

'Because that's what Richie does, man. That's what Richie's all about. He's the champion fixer of all time. You want something, Richie gets it. You want something done, Richie finds a way to make it happen. He's fucking famous. Richie the Fixer. Half of LA uses Richie.'

'So you called Richie . . .'

'I'm on the phone, I'm like babbling, and Richie tells me to calm down, talks me down. Richie's like that, he's good at that. He's got that voice, you know. Really calm when he needs to be. You trust him. Anyway he calms me down and I tell him what's happened. So Richie tells me, "Okay, give me the details." And I tell him and he says okay, don't panic, be cool, it's not a problem, he'll take care of everything. But it's going to take a couple of hours. So he tells me to get the fuck out of the house, go check into a hotel or stay with a friend, just disappear for the rest of the night while he takes care of it. Says to just beat it and leave the door unlocked. Said when I got home tomorrow it would be like nothing ever happened.'

'Where'd you go?'

'I got in the car and fucking drove out to the desert. I checked into a motel and got shitfaced and passed out. When I finally got the balls to come back here next day, it was all gone, though the fuckers he'd sent forgot to take the set of works. Man, if the fucking cleaning lady had seen that . . . I called Richie, asked him what had happened. He said nothing. He said nothing ever happened, and that was the way I was supposed to think about it. Nothing happened. It never happened. I asked him what I owed him, and he acted like he was really insulted. "Fuck that," he said, "we're friends," he said. "This is the sort of shit that friends do for each other."'

'And you bought it.'

'What the fuck else was I supposed to do? There was a

fucking dead girl in my bathroom, then there wasn't. She was there, now she's gone. I'm sad about the girl, but I didn't fucking kill her and I'm not letting this fuck up my entire life. I didn't do anything wrong. I just wanted the whole thing behind me. I wanted the whole thing to be gone.'

'But it wasn't gone.'

'No. It wasn't gone. A couple of weeks later, Richie comes to me with this script. He wants to produce it, wants me to star in it. I explain to him I can't do it. Then he reminds me that I owe him. He says if I need to be reminded he's got photographs.'

'They took pictures of the dead girl?'

'Yeah. Says you can tell it's my place, there's no mistake. Says anybody who sees them is going to know exactly where it is and what happened. There's this cute little girl dead on my toilet with her panties down and a needle sticking out of her leg. Said a grand jury isn't going to be sympathetic, anybody is going to think I killed her. That I gave her the dope, that I was taking advantage of her . . .'

'How well did you know the girl?'

'I told you. I'd just met her.'

'At Richie's club. That's convenient. What's the girl's name?'

'I don't know. Sally something. We didn't exchange a lot of pleasantries.'

'Anybody see you leave with her?'

'One of the guys let us out the back door, behind the VIP room.'

'You get the crack from Richie too? Is that one of his other services?'

'Yeah.'

'You sure you didn't bring home a little something else? Like a small bag of bad smack?'

'Fuck no, man. She brought it herself. I mean, I didn't even know she had it.'

'But you were doing dope with her, before she got up and went to the bathroom.'

'I don't see what fucking difference it makes.'

'It makes a difference. She was fucked up before she went in there, which explains how she might have died. You do anything with her other than the crack?'

'Man, what are trying to do, make it look like I fucking killed her? I didn't, okay?'

'We got a dead underage girl, Bobby. A minor. Somebody's darling, somebody's little girl. She died in your bathroom. It doesn't make a goddamn bit of difference if you stuck the needle in or not, it'll look like you did. This comes to court and nobody on the planet is going to believe you didn't give her the dope that killed her.'

'It wasn't me, I swear to God. We were just doing a little crack, that's it. I was a little fucked, it took me a while, then I went to check on her and there she was with the fucking spike in her leg. But I didn't put it there, man. I didn't.'

'When you found her, are you sure she wasn't still alive?'

'I did that thing where you check the pulse, you know,

the fingers on the neck, but I didn't feel anything. I tried her wrist, everything, but I couldn't feel anything. I'm not a fucking doctor, man. She looked fucking dead. What do you want? I dunno, fuck, but she looked fucking dead to me. She was fucking blue and cold and she wasn't breathing.'

'You think about calling an ambulance?'

'Yeah. I thought about it. I picked up the phone and was about to call.'

'But you didn't.'

'She was dead.'

'But you're not sure, are you? You weren't sure then, either, right? A little case of career anxiety got to you.'

'You fucking bastard!'

He came at Spandau, but it was half-hearted. Spandau pinned his arms in a bear-hug and Bobby went limp and began to cry. Spandau let him pour it out then placed him back on the sofa.

'You think I'm proud of this? You think I don't feel like I killed her?' said Bobby.

'How'd you meet the girl?'

'Richie sent her over.'

'That sounds about right. You think the girl got the heroin from him?'

'I don't know where she got it. Like I said, she brought it with her, I didn't even fucking know she had it. Yeah, I guess Richie could have given it to her. He could get you about anything you want. Sometimes you'd have to wait a

119

few days, maybe. But he always had a steady supply of rock. You just call and he could get you as much as you want in about fifteen minutes.'

'He ever say where he got it?'

'You're joking, right?'

'So you got no idea where he got it from, who supplied him.'

'This shit doesn't come with a fucking money-back guarantee. All I know is that, if you wanted it, Richie could get it. The crack was fast and it was cheap. He had a pipeline somewhere. Richie just fucking loved to hand it out, like fucking candy. The fucking crack king of West LA.'

Bobby stopped talking, suddenly, as if he'd hit a wall and could go no further. Then he said: 'You think maybe she wasn't dead? That maybe I just let her die? You think maybe that's what happened? You think maybe she was still alive?'

Spandau felt sorry for him. 'No. I think she was dead.'

'But you don't know, do you? And I don't either.'

'No,' Spandau said to him softly. 'You don't.'

Six

Pookie was painting her nails black when Spandau got into the office on Monday morning. She looked like a vampire today. Normally chestnut hair dyed black. Low-cut tight black dress that showed a distracting amount of youthful and faultless breast. Artfully shredded sleeves that took someone half the night to do. Makeup somewhere between kabuki and Forest Lawn corpse. And still she made the heart skip a beat. An expensive education could do a lot, but never underestimate the value of good genes. Her mother looked like Grace Kelly.

'You in mourning?' Spandau asked her.

'I have a gothic ball tonight,' said Pookie, finishing her left ring finger. 'Everything is black, black, black.'

'I didn't know you were into that.'

'I'm not. But there's this very cute musician who invited me. He looks like Marilyn Manson, if Marilyn Manson looked like Tom Cruise and didn't have the eye thing.'

Spandau nodded to the office. 'Is he in?'

'Unless you've got your mileage logs, I wouldn't go in there. He's on the warpath today.'

'Let's see. First of the month. Ex-wife. First or second?'

'Mrs Second. He refuses to pay the alimony and she's taking him to court again. Meanwhile you got a message from somebody named Frank Jurado.' She gave him the note. 'Is he as important as he thinks he is?'

'Nearly,' said Spandau. 'He is more important than you think he is, but less important than he wants to be.'

'You're really deep today,' Pookie said.

'It's the medication,' said Spandau. 'Vicodin always brings out my philosophical side.'

'All Vicodin ever gave me,' she said, 'was a yeast infection.'

'Thank you for sharing that with me,' said Spandau. 'I shall treasure it throughout the day.'

Coren was on the phone to an ex-wife when Spandau walked in. Coren's face was purple and he held the phone with one hand while trying to negotiate the cap on a bottle of blood pressure pills with the other. Spandau took the bottle away from him, opened it and handed it back. Coren swallowed a pill while managing to talk around it.

'Look,' Coren said into the phone, 'I pay you three thousand a month already. I bought you that fucking beauty shop, which makes more money than I do. I'm not kicking in any more money to keep you supplied with

horny Zen Buddhists on day-trips down from Mount Baldy.
Why can't you fuck cabana boys like every other middle-
aged divorcee? . . .Yeah, yeah . . .'

She hung up on him. He put down the phone and
looked up at Spandau haplessly.

'She's fucking a Zen Buddhist monk, for chrissake,'
Coren told him. 'The guy comes down from the monastery
on Thursdays and goes to see her. The next-door neighbor
saw the guy sashaying in the front door in his fucking
kimono. Can you believe this?'

'Maybe he's just her spiritual advisor,' offered Spandau.

'Yeah, and maybe the next-door neighbor didn't hear
him moaning like a Holstein. What the hell do you want?
You got your fucking mileage logs?'

'We're working for Bobby Dye now. I just thought I'd
tell you.'

'Great. What are we doing for him?'

'He's being blackmailed.'

'I thought his life was being threatened.'

'That was yesterday,' said Spandau. 'Today he's being
blackmailed. You know showbiz.'

'You want to tell me about it?'

'No.'

'Good,' said Coren. 'I've got my own problems. Be sure
to file a report and turn in your goddamn logs, will you?'

On the way out, Pookie was removing the paint from
her nails.

'What's wrong?' Spandau asked her. 'Is the date off?'

123

'It really is an ethical decision, you know. I can't do this. It's too Columbine, if you know what I'm saying. I called him and said I wasn't coming.'

'I'm sorry,' said Spandau. 'Will you stay home and reheat a chicken pot pie?'

'I'm going to the opera,' she said. She held up both hands palms inward and wriggled her fingers. 'What color for *Madame Butterfly*, do you think?'

Seven

The office of Guttersnipe Productions was in a beautiful old building on Melrose. A great deal of money had gone into restoring it to its 1920s glory, and inside the place was done up in period antiques. Nothing proves success like a roomful of old furniture you're afraid to sit on. The only things out of time were the thoroughly modern Apple computer and the beautiful girl behind the Napoleonic-looking desk. She stood up when Spandau came in. She was nearly as tall as he was, physically flawless, the sort of girl Spandau, as a lustful teenager in Arizona, believed he would never meet. Here, they were everywhere, and it always took some time to get used to it. Her hair was long and blonde and danced like a perfectly choreographed companion, never missing its mark. A model. An actress. Hometown beauty queen waiting for the big break that was hers by right of her virtual perfection. One day some-body would walk in here and discover her. Let's forget the million and a half in town just like her, or the curious fact that some of our most successful actresses look like pizza waitresses when you meet them. If it were just about beauty, plastic surgeons would charge even more. What you really needed was soul – or, even better, the ability to convince a camera you had it, whether you did or not. Spandau looked into the perfectly proportioned face, the pale-blue eyes. She didn't have it, even if she clearly had everything else, and the tragedy was that no one was ever going to tell her. Not when you could get so much use out of it.

'Mr Spandau?'

'That's right.'

'I'm Marcie Whalen. Frank is busy at the moment. If you'd like to have a seat, I could get you something.'

'Do you have any absinthe?'

'We just drank the last of it,' Marcie said without missing a beat. 'Will a Perrier do?'

She smiled beautifully and fetched a Perrier from the kitchen.

'Nice place. Whoever restored it did a beautiful job.'

'This is all Frank. All these used to be apartments back in the thirties. Bing Crosby used to stay in this one when he came to town.'

The desk phone buzzed. She picked it up and said, 'I'll send him right in.' She turned to Spandau. 'Frank says to come on in.'

She knocked on a large oak door and pushed it open.

Frank Jurado was lying on a table, naked, partially covered in a thin sheet and being pummeled by a giant Samoan. Marcie went out and closed the door. Except for a desk large enough to land a Cessna, the rest of the room looked like someone's apartment. There was even a fireplace.

'Nice place, huh?' said Jurado between blows. 'This used to be Bing Crosby's in the thirties.'

'So I've heard. Me, I live in Rin-Tin-Tin's old kennel.'

'Thanks for coming. Sorry to meet you like this, but it's a long day for me. I don't get my massage, I seize up like an old car. You want a massage? You ever had lomi-lomi? It's traditional Hawaiian massage. Fidel here will fix you right up.'

'No thanks. I get too relaxed I start crying.'

'I know just what you mean,' said Jurado, though Spandau didn't think he did.

Fidel went to work on Jurado's glutes. Jurado lay there with his eyes closed and allowed Spandau to watch his ass being massaged. Then he said, 'You're working for Bobby now, I hear.'

Spandau didn't reply.

'Oh come on,' said Jurado. 'You can talk to me. *Wildfire* is my picture. Bobby is a friend.'

'I'm sorry, but if you want to know anything you'll have to talk to Bobby.'

Jurado waved Fidel's hands off his ass and sat up on the side of the table. Wrapped in the sheet he looked like a Roman senator. He hopped off the table and went across to a small refrigerator and took out a green smoothie. Fidel packed up the table and crept away. Jurado drank at the Soylent Green milkshake and walked around for a minute, ignoring Spandau, pretending he was looking for something on his desk. Spandau figured he just liked wearing the sheet. Finally Jurado said:

'Look, we all want what's best for Bobby, right? I can't help him if I don't know what's going on. Tell me about the note.'

Spandau said nothing.

Jurado said, 'I'll pay you whatever Bobby is paying you. All you've got to do is keep me informed. It's all under the table, cash, you don't even have to tell your boss about it. All I want is to stay in the loop, that's all. Nothing else.'

'It doesn't work that way.'

'*Wildfire* is my picture,' said Jurado. 'Bobby is my star. I don't think you have any idea of what is at stake here. I have a right to any information that might affect Bobby or the picture. I will do whatever I have to do to protect my picture and my star. Are you understanding this?'

'I think so. I'm being threatened somehow, right?'

'Nobody is threatening you. I'm just stating the facts as they present themselves.'

'Okay,' said Spandau.

'Okay, what?'

'Okay, I think I have a clear picture now of what you're saying.'

'Good,' said Jurado. 'I'm glad we understand each other. Now you want to fill me in?'

'No. But I really do have a clear idea now of what you're saying.'

For a moment Spandau thought Jurado might choke on his smoothie. He spilled a little of it on the sheet, where it made a lovely color.

'Do not fuck with me, Mr Spandau. I didn't get where I am by letting pissants like you get in my way. You fuck with me, you are going to think the wrath of a vengeful God has fallen down upon your shoulders.'

'That's a good line. You do that very well. I think the vengeful God thing is overdone by Tarantino, though.'

'I could hire somebody to follow you.'

'That would make Bobby mad. And it would make me mad too, come to think of it.'

'You're putting your dick in a wringer, guy. I'm telling you.'

'Why is it everybody this week is talking like an old Ronald Reagan movie? I'm almost homesick for some genuine hoods. They don't talk so much, and when they do, they know when to stop.'

'Suit yourself,' Jurado said to him. 'But understand me on this one. If anything happens, if there's even the slightest hiccup that interferes with my movie, you can bet your life I will make you the fall guy. I will ruin you, I will take everything you own, I will put your fucking children and their fucking children's children into abject poverty. And that's just me. There's also two hundred lawyers, a major film studio, and an entire fucking media empire just waiting to help me. Think about that. These people shift entire governments around like office furniture. Imagine what they'll do to you.'

Jurado appeared to be looking around for his pants. 'You mind if I get dressed?'

'Sorry. I wasn't sure you were done. I got kind of caught up in the moment.'

Spandau went over behind a chair where Jurado's pants had fallen. He picked them up and handed them to Jurado. 'You really are cute,' said Jurado.

'I could look for your socks,' offered Spandau.

'You keep out of my way,' Jurado said. 'You get in my way and I will cut you down.'

But the threat seemed rather thin, coming from a man wearing a bedsheet, and they both knew it. Spandau smiled at him and went out the door. As he closed it he could hear Jurado cursing. Spandau couldn't tell if it was at him or the missing hosiery.

Richie Stella lived in a nice old house in Echo Park. The place was full of yuppies and faggots nowadays, but it was a good address, stylish, and real-estate prices had shot up since Richie bought it. His ambition was Brentwood, of course. It seemed grossly unfair that a murderous spear-chucker like O.J. Simpson should live there and he couldn't, but that would be remedied soon enough. Richie sat in the back of the big black Audi as Martin wheeled it through the neighborhood and onto his street. The Audi pulled into the drive and rolled to a halt. Richie took another look at the screen of the laptop he always carried with him. He smiled and got out of the car before Martin did. Martin started to get out but Richie told him drive around the block a few times.

'Why?' asked Martin.

'Because I fucking told you to, numbnuts.'

Martin slumped behind the wheel, looking forlorn. Richie went up the steps, unlocked the door and went inside. He tossed his keys into a bowl in the entrance hall and went into the living room. Spandau was sitting in one of his chairs.

'What the fuck are you doing in my house?' Richie asked him.

'Don't you want to know how I got in?'

'I'm more interested,' said Richie, 'in how you think you're going to get out. This is B and E. People get shot for this.' Richie went over to the bar and poured himself a glass of white wine. 'You change your mind about working for me?'

'I want you to lay off Bobby Dye.'

'You definitely got some cojones, my man. I'll give you that.'

'I know you're blackmailing him, and I know what for. I want it to stop.'

'Look, I appreciate your effort, I really do. But I'm the wrong guy to try and strong-arm. Hasn't anybody explained this to you?'

131

Richie climbed up on a barstool and sipped his wine.

'This is just between me and Bobby and it has nothing to do with you,' he said to Spandau. 'Frankly, the only reason you're not in some garbage can bleeding from every hole is because Bobby seems to like you. I just want us all to be friends.'

'How much would it take?'

'It's not about money.'

'He's never going to do your picture,' said Spandau. 'You know as well as I do it's not even his decision. At this point he's nothing but a meat-puppet for his agency, the studio and Frank Jurado. They're never going to let you anywhere near him. So maybe they'll buy you off. Is that what this is about? Look, just say so and I'll go to Jurado and pimp the deal for you. They don't want any trouble and they'll make it worth your while. Take the money and buy yourself an entire cast.'

'You really don't get it, do you? You think I'm just some cheap little hood from back east, looking to score. I got a chance to do something I always wanted to do. Everybody's got a dream, right? This is my dream. I'm going to make a movie.'

'All I'm saying is make a movie with somebody else. Take the fucking money and move on.'

'I can't. I gotta have Bobby. Bobby *is* this fucking movie.'

Spandau laughed.

'You know, what's so goddamn frightening is that I

believe you. What the fuck happens to people in this town? Perfectly normal, rational people from all over the world, they come here and go crazy.'

'It's the magic, baby. The magic of making movies. Like Orson Welles said, it's the world's biggest electric train set.'

Spandau threw his hands up, as if pleading with heaven.

'Jesus,' he said. 'There *is* no magic! It's a business, like manufacturing toilets seats or something. Only the people who aren't actually *in* it think it's magic. That's why they call it the motion picture *industry*, get it? It's not a fucking fairy tale.'

'You're bitter, man,' Richie said to him. 'The system chewed you up. You couldn't deal.'

'That's right. You think you're any different? The system gobbles up everybody. That's what it does best. The only magic is that people keep coming back.'

Stella looks at his watch.

'Are you gonna be around for a while? Martin will be back in a couple of minutes and he's dying to stomp your ass. I wouldn't want to miss it.'

'As enticing as that sounds,' said Spandau, 'I'm afraid I'll have to pass.'

'By the fucking way, I don't like you coming to my house. I don't like being strong-armed. You proved your point. You think you can get to me, okay, you're here. But you still got to get back out that door.'

Richie pulled a .25 caliber automatic from his jacket

pocket and fired it. Spandau took a dive onto the floor though the bullet hit the sofa a foot away from where he'd been sitting. Richie put the gun back in his pocket.

'Relax,' said Richie. 'I could have shot you when I came in. I got little video cameras hidden all over this place. I watch 'em on my computer. Fucking modern technology. You think I'm stupid? I don't like surprises. Now leave me alone or I'm going to get really pissed off.'

As Spandau came out of the house, Martin was pulling in with the Audi. He saw Spandau and no Richie and he jumped out of the car and went at Spandau. They both went down on the lawn. Richie came out onto the steps, angry.

'You guys want to do this in the backyard? I got fucking neighbors watching!'

Spandau and Martin got to their feet. Martin looked confused and sheepish.

'I'm sorry, Richie. I wasn't thinking.'

'You want to stomp him I'm fine with that,' Richie said to him. 'Just don't do it in front of the neighbors. I got a good reputation here. You know the guy across the street won an Oscar? I think it was for Best Sound or one of those shit awards or something. It's a nice neighborhood.'

Spandau dusted himself off, started down the hill toward his car.

Richie called after him, 'You come back here, I'm going to shoot you, I don't care if it is my goddamn front lawn!'

*

134

When Spandau phoned Meg Patterson, she was at her desk in the *LA Times'* reporters' bullpen. She'd been with the paper twelve years, had won a Pulitzer in her second, and now commanded one of the choicer cubicles, near a window and safely tucked away from the entrance doors and the managing editor's office. She was a small, dark-haired beauty in her early forties, who'd gotten rid of an alcoholic screenwriting husband eight years earlier and now lived in Los Feliz with dogs, cats and any other lost animal – two- or four-footed – that needed mothering. She liked men and men liked her, but the match nearly always proved fatal. The greatest compliment she'd ever received had been the previous year, from a well-established madam she interviewed. The old girl looked Meg up and down and said, 'You know, a couple of years ago you and me could have made a lot of money.' It was the nicest thing anybody had ever said to her and Meg was trying to think of some way to get it carved on her headstone.

'How would you like to have lunch with an extremely good-looking cowboy type?'

'Am I speaking to George W. Bush?' she asked him.

'No,' said Spandau. 'I'm taller and I can find France on a map.'

'How are you, handsome? Still getting thrown off ponies?'

'Yes, and now I've managed to rope my own thumb. It looks like an eggplant. I'll show it to you if you'll have lunch with me.'

'That's practically an irresistible offer, but I'm swamped right now. And something tells me this isn't a social call anyway.'

'I need whatever you've got on Richie Stella, the guy who owns the Voodoo Room on Sunset.'

'You got a few days? There's a lot on him, but it's all just talk, nothing anybody could print. Otherwise he'd be in San Quentin by now. He's like Teflon. Nothing ever sticks. What the hell are you doing with Richie Stella? He's not a nice guy.'

'Just a job I'm working on. Strictly routine.'

'Routine, my ass. I'm going to be on your side of town. Meet me at Barney's in an hour. We'll make a trade.'

'There's nothing to trade.'

'We'll see.'

Barney's Beanery is yet another LA institution, like colonic irrigation and cruising Sunset on Friday nights. The chili is good and they serve around three hundred beers. Breakfast is ample and also not bad, one of those rare spots where you can create or wear off a hangover with equal dexterity. There's no question about it being a dive, but nobody would go there if it wasn't. It was a great place to play pool and pretend you were Jim Morrison, who used to hang out there. Spandau liked it because it he liked pretending to be Jim Morrison.

He was sitting at a booth when Meg arrived.

'Do I look like Jim Morrison?' Spandau asked her.

'No, but you do look like Morris Cochrane, my chiropodist.'

'You're never going to mate successfully until you learn to pick up on these little cues.'

'If I'm going to be pumped for information, I really should have insisted on someplace more expensive,' she said.

'You suggested it.'

'Only because I know you like pretending to be Jim Morrison. Anyway I'm too easy. I'd probably sleep with you if you'd offered ravioli. As it is, I'll barely contain myself when the hamburgers get here.'

'Tell me about Richie Stella and I'll throw in a milkshake.'

'I have one word of advice about Richie Stella: don't. He's a little worm, but he's ambitious and has some nasty friends.'

'Such as?'

'Connections with a lot of Latino and biker gangs. They run errands for him and help with the dirty work. But the one I'd worry about is Salvatore Locatelli.'

'The mafia boss?'

'The very one. Stella isn't made, but he works for Locatelli and is under his protection, otherwise somebody would have offed the little shit before now. That's what's kept him safe with the gangs, even they're not stupid enough to piss off Sal, and Richie has jockeyed this little safety net into a lucrative relationship with them.'

'Any arrests?'

'Nah. Been rousted a few times. It's common knowledge he's dealing, but Sal has a long arm. Anyway, he needs Richie clean to run the clubs. He gets busted and they take away his license.'

'How many clubs?'

'Three. There's a popular gay club downtown, another club in the valley. Richie's name is on the lease, but they're owned by Locatelli. Richie owns the Voodoo Room outright, but you can bet Sal takes a healthy cut. Richie's doing well, but he's not getting rich. Locatelli will never let him, and word is that Richie is champing at the bit.'

'What about the drugs?'

'Locatelli looks the other way, as long as Richie doesn't get too ambitious and cut into his own territory. Who knows how far Sal will let it go before he cuts Richie off at the knees. And he will, sooner or later. Sal didn't get this far encouraging competition. Sooner or later, Sal is going to reel Richie in, and Richie knows it.'

'You think Richie's building some kind of power-base to challenge Locatelli?'

'Christ, no. As far as the mob is concerned, Sal Locatelli owns Los Angeles, lock, stock and stinking barrel. Look, not even the Feds want to go after Sal. They're scared shitless of what they'll find. The arrangement has always been that Sal gets to do whatever the hell he wants, provided he does it quietly and doesn't rub anybody's nose in it. Richie is never going to be in his league.'

'Why not?'

'Because Richie isn't made and he's never going to get full support of the mob. To them he's just marginal, somebody they can use. On the other hand, Locatelli inherited the family business. His old man was like something out of Mario Puzo all through the forties, fifties and sixties.'

'So what is Richie after?'

'Richie is star-struck. He's like some kid. He loves movies, loves movie stars. He's got a goddamn home cinema in his basement, he invites people over for screenings of classic movies. He longs to get his face in *People* magazine next to some hot actors. Richie wants to be a player. I think he wants to make a big score and get out of the business. He wants to make movies. He knows he'll never be made, he'll never have mob support, and at some point the big guns are going to move in and take it away from him. But if he can buy enough time to get his own little empire going, then he can either sell it to the mob or auction it off piecemeal. First, though, he needs to be strong enough to convince them it's less trouble to buy him out than to kill him.'

'A dangerous little game he's got going.'

'No one ever said Richie didn't have cojones. And behind that ferrety little mug of his, there's a razor-sharp brain, always calculating the odds. Meanwhile he's trying to edge his way into the movies. He's got a couple of scripts he's hawking around town.'

'Is anybody taking him seriously?'

'This is Hollywood, sweetie. Anybody can be a producer if Uncle Herman dies and leaves them enough money. Rumor has it Richie's tied in with the Chinese. Cash provides its own veracity. You've got money, nobody cares who the hell you are, 'cause you got the one thing everybody in this town needs. Richie's also known as a guy who gets things done, no matter how unpleasant. I don't even want to think about the number of people who owe him favors.'

'So you think he's got a shot at it.'

'Did you just fall off a turnip truck? You've worked in the business. How do you think half the people in town got their start? You think all you've got to do is go to USC and people are going to throw money at you? Jesus, where the hell do you think money comes from? Half the independent movies in the seventies were financed by the yakuza, when the Japanese were willing to pour money into anything that would get them a foothold here. You need to know how to make deals. Richie Stella is very good at making deals. Does that answer your question?'

'You truly are a princess. I take back all the horrible things I've said about you over the years.'

'I want the story,' she said.

'There is no story. I am only, as they say, making inquiries.'

'You're a lying cowpat. At the end of this thing I want the exclusive.'

'I'll give you what I can.'

'Exclusive, Roy Rogers. The whole schmere, or I start making inquiries of my own.'

'That would be awkward.'

'Oh, I just bet it would.'

'I'm hurt,' said Spandau, giving her his sad Walter Matthau face. 'I always thought there was this chemistry between us.'

'Oh, darling, there is!' she said, reaching over to give his hand a gentle squeeze and gazing into his eyes. 'To me you'll always be the mildly retarded brother I never wanted.'

'Spinsterhood is making you bitter.'

'Spinsterhood is giving me plenty of time for my work,' she said, looking at the menu.

'Okay,' he said. 'It's yours. If there is a story.'

'That's all any honorable journalist could ask for,' Meg said. 'Unfortunately you're dealing with me and you'll have to take your chances. Now are you going to buy me a hamburger or what?'

At the Ventura Harbor marina, Spandau squeezed the BMW into a restaurant parking lot and walked out to the boats. It was a small but pretty harbor where people seemed to like boats, as opposed to someplace like Rio del Mar, which has become like St Tropez in its inclination toward floating status symbols. People actually sailed the boats here.

Terry McGuinn owned and lived aboard a thirty-foot

Catalina sailboat he'd bought third-hand at a desperate price from a fellow Hibernian who'd skipped town one step ahead of the immigration authorities. The boat was called the *Galadriel*, after the Tolkien elf-queen, and Terry, a Tolkien fan, thought this a clear sign from God, in spite of the fact he knew bugger all about boats or sailing. He'd just been excavated from a cabin in Topanga where he'd lived for all of four weeks with a female singer named Gooch, who uprooted him out when he drunkenly sat on her guitar. She patiently explained that she liked sleeping with Terry and all that, but he was a drunk and he couldn't pay his share of things and the guitar was just the last straw. Now she didn't have the rent or a guitar. Goodbye, goodbye.

Terry sold his car in Woodland Hills and hitchhiked out to the boat, where he paid Boylan in getaway cash, took up rental on the slip and moved in. He lined up his hardback collection of J.R.R. Tolkien on the small shelves above his rack and taped his poster of Gandalf on the bulkhead above. He talked a drunken old sailor in a rickety scow at the end of the harbor into teaching him to sail. Terry turned out to be a pretty fair sailor and picked up a cruising license. He was very sorry to hear when the old man fell overboard one night and drowned, though Terry fully expected the same thing to happen to him one day. There were worse ways to go.

Terry McGuinn was five feet six inches tall. He had bright-blue eyes and brown curly hair, and J.R.R. Tolkien was one of the few things in life that made sense to him. People indeed sometimes said that he looked like a hobbit. Depending on Terry's degree of drink, people sometimes got their noses broken. He came to Spandau's attention through a friend, another private detective, who'd witnessed Terry in operation at a roadhouse near Wrightwood. Terry had been shooting pool, minding his own business, when three drunk loggers down from Oregon decided he looked funny, and took umbrage at the peculiar way he stuck out his ass when he leaned over to shoot. Terry did an admirable job of being cool about it, until one of the loggers made the mistake of goosing Terry with a pool cue as Terry lined up a shot. Without bothering to turn around, Terry brought the end of his own pool cue back into the guy's stomach. Then Terry proceeded to beat the shit out of all three of the guys in a flurry of samurai-like spinning pool cue. All three had to be helped to their trucks. An amazing performance, considering that all three were at least a foot taller than he was and not one hand was ever laid on Terry. The detective had offered him a job on the spot.

Spandau watched a similar incident on the set of a music-video shooting in Compton. The young director had decided to shoot 'on the streets' but had no idea the complexity of such a thing. The star was Raissha Bowles, a small and painfully shy girl who'd hired Coren's to keep an aggressive ex-boyfriend off her back. The boyfriend showed up with several compatriots one afternoon, demanding access to Raissha. Normally it wouldn't have been much of a problem, but the boyfriend was vocal about it and his friends began stirring up the crowd, who started chanting, 'Show us Raissha! Show us Raissha!' Things were about to turn ugly, and inside her trailer Raissha was having a meltdown. The boyfriend boldly pushed through the security picket as guards looked toward Matt Kimons, the guy in charge of the security group that day. Spandau asked Matt what the hell he was going to do now, and Matt laughed and said, 'Watch this.' Matt looked over at Terry McGuinn, who'd been standing quietly and inconspicuously in a corner, reading a book. Matt motioned to him and Terry went over. Matt said to him, 'Don't hurt him,' and Terry nodded and went over to the boyfriend just as he crossed the cordon. Terry stood in front of the boyfriend, looking up at him. The boyfriend had at least a foot and a hundred pounds on Terry. The guy looked like a wall. He looked down at Terry and laughed, and then looked at the crowd and the crowd laughed. Great fun. The boyfriend took another step forward, as if to brush Terry aside. The moment he touched Terry, Terry grabbed his shirt and his belt, and, in the neatest little aikido move Spandau had ever witnessed, magically waltzed the boyfriend in a circle and back on the other side of the cordon. The boyfriend had no idea what had happened. In fact, hardly anybody did. It was done so fast and smoothly it looked like magic. The boyfriend tried it again, and again the same thing happened. Then he took a couple of swipes at Terry, all of which would have brained him if they'd connected, but somehow they never did. The blows seemed to move right through the little bastard somehow. The boyfriend did this over and over with the same results. By this time, the crowd was laughing at him now. It looked ridiculous. The single retirement-age cop standing by had called for backup and sirens were heard. His friends grabbed Raissha's boyfriend and swept him into the crowd. By the time the cops arrived it was history.

'Where the hell did you learn to do that?' Spandau asked Terry.

Terry just said, 'Misspent youth,' and went back to his corner, where he pulled out a paperback copy of Tolkien's *Unfinished Tales* and began to read as if nothing had happened.

'Beautiful, ain't he?' Matt said to Spandau. 'Anybody else had tried to do that, we'd've had a fucking riot. It's weird, but the little shit's size is actually an advantage. He goes up against a 250-pound bruiser and when the guy can't lay a glove on him, the bigger guy looks like a fucking idiot. I know real hard-asses who won't mess with the guy because he embarrasses 'em. They'd rather get the crap beat out of them by somebody their own size than dance around with Terry. It's like fucking ballet.'

It was a point well taken, and Spandau used Terry often. Or at least whenever Terry felt like working. Coren didn't like him, however. 'He's a liability, that drunken little bogtrotter,' Coren said to Spandau. 'You want him, then he's your fucking responsibility. But it'll come out bad one day, I'm warning you now. The little bastard likes trouble.'

'I've seen him go out of his way to avoid it.'

'Yeah, but he's always right there when it starts, isn't he? Those three guys he clobbered in Wrightwood, does it ever occur to you he could've just walked out of there? That he waited until one of them touched him and he could claim self-defense? Did you ever think maybe he wanted them to start something? No,' said Coren, 'there'll be some shit to pay yet, you mark my words. Meanwhile keep him out of my sight.'

Spandau was approaching Terry's sailboat when he heard a woman yell inside, then come stomping out onto the deck. She was beautiful and young. Terry liked actresses. This one was half-dressed and trying to pull on her clothes. She was unused to the boat and kept stumbling over things. Finally she tried climbing onto the dock and couldn't make it. She glared at Spandau.

'Well, are you going to stand there like an idiot or are you going to help me?'

Spandau helped her up and she finished pulling on her clothes.

'I take it Terry is home?' he asked her.

'Are you a friend of the miserable little son of a bitch? Or maybe a fucking bill collector. He owes everybody in the county. I hope you break his goddamn legs. Let me watch, will you? No, Jesus, don't tell me. All I can say is, if you already know him and you're coming back, you deserve whatever happens to you.'

Terry popped up on deck.

'Eve, my darling girl,' he said in a thick Irish brogue, 'you can't be leaving me?'

Eve looked around for something to throw. She took off her shoe again and threw that at him. He ducked, but she rapidly threw the other one and hit him.

'Ouch!' Terry grabbed his forehead, where the shoe had left a mark.

'Ha! I'm sorry I didn't blind you.'

Eve hobbled barefoot down the splintery dock toward the parking lot.

'A minor domestic dispute,' Terry said. 'Accused me of sleeping with her best friend. Can you imagine.'

'Did you?'

'Oh, of course. But it strikes me as damned bad manners that the bitch should have told her.'

Spandau made his way onto the boat and sat down in a lawnchair. Terry scratched his bare chest and watched Eve walk off into the sunset. Terry was a romantic and fell in love easily and frequently. Women loved him as well, though they never quite managed to like him. He seemed to collect them the way he collected belts in various obscure martial arts.

'I've got a job for you,' Spandau said to him.

'I don't want one,' Terry said. 'Last was that fellow with

147

the baseball bat. Had to have the cap on my left molar replaced.'

'That was your fault. I warned you.'

'Yes, but your timing was imperfect. One somehow expects a warning before and not after.'

'You broke his arm.'

'Well I had to take the bloody bat away from him, didn't I? No, David, me lad, you hang around with the wrong type of people. I think it's skewing your world view. Have a drink anyway and then run along home. Eve's girlfriend is due in the next little bit.'

Spandau followed Terry down into the cabin. Spandau was a big man and he didn't like boats. He fumbled around looking for a place to sit where his head wasn't in danger. Terry darted about like a water sprite and fetched up a bottle of Jameson's. He scurried about a while longer and located two Waterford crystal glasses. Terry took his drinking seriously.

'How the hell do you live in this place? It's like a shoe-box.'

'It's paid for and cheaper than an apartment. And one can put to sea at the first sign of irate husbands or over-aggressive creditors. Slainte!'

They drank.

'I have a client who's being blackmailed.'

'Someone juicy, is it?'

'Bobby Dye.'

'Bloody hell,' said Terry, delighted.

'I need your help. You ever hear of a guy named Richie Stella?'

'Heard but never made the acquaintance of. Is he blackmailing Dye?'

'There's a roll of film we need to get back.'

'My suggestion is that you find a polite way of throwing your client to the wolves. Stella is connected to the mob. But of course you already know that, hence that melancholy look you get.'

'You're the only one I can trust.'

'Which means you need some stupid mick to get his head bashed in for you.'

'The money is good.'

'What good is money without peace of mind, I ask you? This sounds neither peaceful nor healthy. You find yourself in a rare and ugly situation.'

'Uh-huh.'

'You're as likely as me buggering the holy Pope himself to get all the copies back.'

'Uh-huh. Double your last fee, by the way.'

Terry smiled. 'Is it the effects of drink or did the conversation suddenly become more interesting?'

'And perhaps a healthy bonus if we can pull this off.'

'Do you have any idea what you're going to do? Or should I be contrite for asking?'

'Well, I do have the seedlings of a cunning plan.'

'Ah. And would this cunning plan involve the pride of the McGuinns?'

'It would.'

'I suppose I might as well hear it, before I politely refuse. I'm a gentleman of leisure, after all.'

'As you say, good luck getting all the copies back. On the other hand, Richie is onto a gold mine here and he's not interested in showing them around. He's not about to surrender them all, but he's not likely to let anybody else see them either. Stop me if I'm not making sense.'

'Oh dear heart, if I was held to that you'd fain utter a word.'

'Anyway, it's only Richie who can tie Bobby to the dead girl, right?'

'There's a dead girl?' Terry asked.

'A very dead one.'

'How Dashiell Hammett,' said Terry. 'Pray go on.'

'So we need to think of some way to discourage Richie from ever using the film.'

'Ah, grand. It's murder and mayhem you're up to now. And me sitting here starting to get bored.'

'What if we blackmail him in return.'

'Sure,' said Terry, 'and you've pictures of him having carnal knowledge of the family dog?'

'Not yet. But he's got his fingers into all kinds of grungy little pies. There's bound to be some dirt we can use.'

'If you'll pardon my suggestion,' offered Terry, 'why don't we just kneecap the filthy cocksucker, wrap him in baling wire and drop him off a bridge? Call me sentimental, but that's the way we'd do it back on the Old Sod.'

'That was my backup plan.'

'You Yanks lack all sense of proportion. You've no sense of efficiency or political necessity. It's the fatally cold beer that does it.'

'Be that as it may, we need to dig up something on Richie Stella.'

'And this would involve someone sticking their nose into his potato patch?'

'It would.'

'I begin to see the drift of this conversation. And the minute someone starts asking the questions, wouldn't our Mr Stella know about it and become perturbed?'

'Is that a bad thing?'

'Only if you don't mind getting just a wee bit kneecapped and tossed off a bridge yourself.'

'Nah, Richie's no killer. At least not until the last resort. He doesn't want that much heat, and, anyway, it's not his style. He'd have somebody lean on them first.'

'But what if he's pushed? He might panic.'

'One could but hope.'

'Oh, but it's a dandy plan, isn't it? Throw Richie into a snit and hope he does something stupid that we can nail him on? Aggravate him until he tries to kill you? David, me old son, there's no career for you in diplomacy.'

'Actually I was thinking more along the lines of letting him try to kill you. While I pursue other avenues of inquiry.'

'That's right, sacrifice the bloody little bogtrotter. History only repeats itself.'

'Erin go bragh,' said Spandau.

'Get stuffed, you miserable gobshite. Where am I supposed to initiate this suicide mission?'

'There's a girl who manages the club. You might start there.'

'You think she'll talk to me?'

'No, but it'll certainly put a bug up Richie's ass when she tells him about it.'

Terry raised his glass in a toast. 'To the blessed St Teresa of Ávila and the souls of all fallen warriors!'

'Here, here!'

'And to the filthy swine Richard Stella, may God not grant him any more wit than he has at this moment.'

They drank.

Eight

Terry and Eve stood in line outside the Voodoo Room.

'Why am I here? Tell me again,' Eve demanded.

'Because you're gorgeous, me darling. And you'll meet lots of important folk once we're inside. You'll be free as a bird to fly about, charming all the royalty of Hollywood and finally becoming the star you deserve to be. I'm doing this because I'm mad for you.'

'You're doing this because you're an ugly little hooligan and they wouldn't let you in otherwise.'

'That cuts me to the bone, though I couldn't fault your suspicions,' he said.

'As long as you know that if I meet a director, I'm leaving your ass.'

'And won't I treasure the fleeting moments we have left.'

'I cannot believe I fall for shit like this.'

'Saints be praised. And show a bit of cleavage, would you, we're approaching the door.'

The place was packed as usual. Terry bought drinks and he and Eve stood near the bar, checking out the room. Terry was looking for the blonde Spandau had described. Eve was looking for a golden career opportunity. Eve was having better luck.

'Oh my God,' she said. 'I think it's Russell Crowe.' She turned to Terry. 'How do I look?'

'Like the golden apples of the sun,' he said offhandedly, not taking his eyes off the crowd.

'Fucking right,' she said, and went forth to bag her prey.

Terry had only been to the Voodoo Room once before. It was exactly the sort of place he hated: loud, impersonal and utterly pretentious. Full of showbiz types and wannabes, and underneath the music and the perfect pulsing bodies was a sense of desperation. Like the line outside, even here you were In or Out. It was so important to be In. Terry sipped his Jameson's and wondered how long this would take. Maybe she wasn't here. That would involve coming back again. Or again. Jesus, he thought. I should never have let that bastard Spandau talk me into this.

He kept his eye on the office. Staff came and went all the time. He didn't see anyone who fit Stella's description, and he didn't see the blonde. A small raven-haired beauty came up to the bar and ordered a drink. She gave Terry a smile. No ring, she was ordering a drink for herself. Unaccompanied or at least available. Terry smiled back. No you bastard, he thought, you're working.

'Wow,' said the girl to him, 'this place is crazy!'

First time, he thought, out of town, she's not holding out for Russell Crowe, she just wants to meet a nice guy. I could do the 'I'm-a-stranger-here-myself' approach and discover we are kindred spirits. She won't feel threatened, she'd be scared shitless of a player. Romance in the City of the Angels. Take her to see the La Brea Tarpits tomorrow and by evening we're conveniently at the marina restaurant near the boat. And then.

He'd done this so many times that everything immediately fell into slots, like punchcards in an old computer. The girl waited for him to speak. Oh he wanted to speak. He thought about what they'd talk about, what she'd be like in bed. Thought about how her skin would feel and taste. And in the morning or earlier she'd bugger off back to the motel and catch the afternoon flight to Nebraska. Back to her high school sweetheart, her fiancée, her parents, her fat little sister with braces. Five years down the road she'd get drunk on wine and tell one of her girlfriends about Terry. They'd giggle.

The girl's drink came. Terry still hadn't said anything. The girl looked hurt. If you only knew, thought Terry. Horrible it was, knowing everything about her at a glance. One day there would be the mystery again. Or so he prayed daily. The girl picked up her drink, smiled awkwardly again, and disappeared into the crowd.

It was after midnight when he saw the blonde come out of the office. She stopped at the top of the steps, took a managerial glance around the room, then made her way to the bar. She spoke to the bartender, inquired about stock, about sales. She made a circle of the room and spoke to the waitresses, looking to stop or anticipate any problems. She was good at her job. Serious, never smiled. Tough. And smart. She wasn't gorgeous but there was something under the skin that you wanted to get at. Spandau had mentioned Stella's hand on her hip. Stella's woman? Spandau didn't think so. But Terry could imagine a man like Stella wanting something he couldn't have, something he couldn't understand. Class, thought Terry. That would be just what Stella wanted most.

He watched her make her rounds then go back to the office. Okay then, she was here, when would she leave? The place closed at 2 a.m. She'd do some paperwork, maybe. Then drive home. Or maybe a boyfriend would pick her up? A husband? No, Terry hadn't spotted a ring. Probably a boyfriend somewhere, but he wouldn't pick her up. Stella wouldn't like that. She'd drive home herself. She was that sort.

Shortly after last call Eve returned. She was angry.

'It wasn't him, the son of a bitch,' she said.

Terry was half-listening. 'What?'

'It wasn't Russell Crowe. It was some goddamn set carpenter. He lied to me, the bastard.'

'He told you he was Russell Crowe?'

'Well, not exactly. But he never said he wasn't.'

Terry laughed. 'It's a vale of tears we live in, as me old

mother used to say. It could be worse. You could've let him have his way standing up in the lavatory.'

She gave him an angry look, since this was exactly what she'd done. Suddenly Terry said, 'Let's go.' He took her elbow and moved her toward the door.

'What the hell is this?' said Eve. 'I want a drink.'

'You'll be in mourning for your lost honor, and I would-n't presume to intrude upon it,' Terry said to her.

He took her outside and led her to a taxi stand down the street and folded her into the car.

'You men are all shits, you know that? And the fucking Irish are the worst of the—'

The cab pulled away. Terry waved to her as he watched her lips move.

The blonde didn't come out until nearly 3 a.m. He'd been sitting in his dark car, parked down the street in the shad-ows, for over an hour, watching patrons, drunk and sober, paired-up and alone, stagger out of the club. He passed the time listening to his iPod and trying to think of the raven-haired girl instead of the blonde. It kept coming back to the blonde. He peed into a plastic jogger's flask and, not for the first time, questioned the sanity of doing any of this.

He brought his mind round to Ravenhair naked and lying in his bed, but his mind slipped gears and he found himself curled up with the blonde in post-coital tender-ness. This was a bad sign. It was almost comforting that, in all likelihood, she probably had a boyfriend at home. An actor or musician. Hung like a Clydesdale and a degree in physics. And he'd be tall. She'd adore him and Terry wouldn't stand a bloody chance in hell. Terry could just approach her and ask his bloody questions and she'd report back to Stella and Terry could collect his paycheck and go off and get shitfaced somewhere. Oh yes, thought Terry, I should have spoken to little Ravenhair.

It wasn't hard to follow the blonde. She drove an old bright-yellow VW Beetle and stopped at all the lights, stop signs, railroad crossings and was generous in granting the right of way. Terry could have followed her on a bicycle, and was able to keep a safer distance behind than usual. It wasn't far. She pulled up in front of a bungalow in West Hollywood and left the motor running. She walked up to the porch and knocked instead of rang. In a moment a woman in her fifties answered the door. The blonde didn't go in. They spoke. The woman seemed to be scolding her, but gently. The blonde kept shaking her head. Finally the blonde went inside. A few minutes later she came back out carrying a sleeping child, a boy it looked like, maybe three or four years old. She put the boy in the back seat and strapped him in, talking to him all the while. She got in her car and drove away. The woman in the house stood at the door the whole time and watched. When the VW disappeared the woman closed the door.

Terry followed her down Sunset and north onto the 405. He kept at least a quarter mile behind her. She turned off at Ventura Boulevard and Terry slowed so he wouldn't

creep up on her at the light. He came down a good ways
behind her when she'd just made the turn onto Ventura
and he eased in again a safe distance behind. There was no
hurry. It was like following a yeti but he had to be careful.

Her house was in Sherman Oaks not far from Sepulveda.
A place much like the one she'd just left: old, small, reasonably affordable. A backyard for the kid. She parked in the
drive and carried the boy up to the porch, fumbled for her
keys, dropped them and had to juggle the sleepy kid while she
knelt to grab them. Terry had to resist the impulse to run up
and help her. *I was just passing by, saw your plight, would you
have dinner with me?* She got the door open and went inside.

Right, he'd done his job, he could stop off and have
breakfast somewhere and then go home and crash. But
what about the boyfriend? No other car parked in the
drive. Nobody greeted her at the door, rushed out to help
her with the child or the keys.

This, Terry admitted to himself, is where the insanity
begins.

The street was dark and deserted. Terry got out of his
car. He walked in the opposite direction then crossed and
walked back until he reached the house. He clung to the
side of the house and made his way toward a lighted room
in the back. The kid's bedroom. Terry watched her tuck
him in, sit on the side of the bed. He couldn't get back to
sleep, he said. She sang, quietly, an old song. 'Raglan
Road', for sweet Jesus' sake. She kissed the boy, turned off
the light and left the room.

In the living room she poured herself a drink from the small table in the corner. She sat on the couch – collapsed, really – and turned on the TV. The TV played for a few minutes but she never watched it, didn't acknowledge it existed. Maybe the sound itself was some sort of company. She drank and stared into space and when she finished the drink she got up to get another. She stopped at the bar table but didn't pour the drink and Terry thought, Good for you girl, it's the path to hell. She set the glass down and went back to the couch, where she put her head back and closed her eyes and cried silently. Before Terry got back to the car he'd decided to phone Spandau in the morning and tell him to shove the whole case up his ass.

Nine

Bobby was ripping somebody a new asshole when Spandau came up to the trailer. You could hear him yelling halfway across the lot.

'Yeah, shit, come in!' Bobby said when Spandau knocked.

Bobby was in costume, sitting in a chair. May, his makeup artist, was leaning over him, making some adjustments to his hair extensions. Ginger was in the back talking on a cellphone. He waved to Spandau when he came in.

'Shit!' Bobby jerked in the chair.

'Sorry,' May apologized. 'But this has got to get done. Otherwise they fall off in the heat.'

'My fucking head is raw from these things.'

'I know, sweetie, I know. Everybody complains. It's not me. I'm being as gentle as I can.'

Spandau took a seat on the couch.

'Look at this,' Bobby said to Spandau. 'Fucking hair extensions. My own fucking hair isn't good enough. I look like a goddamn pansy.'

'Hey,' Ginger called out from the back, 'I'm a pansy, so watch it.'

'You're a fucking vicious little bullfruit, that's what you are,' Bobby said to him.

'Well, I've been called everything else. Bullfruit I kind of like.'

Ginger waited on the phone. Bobby jerked a few more times as May fixed his head.

'And?' Bobby said over his shoulder to Ginger.

'Honey, I'm trying.'

'You talk to the manager?'

'He's not there. I've got a call in to him.'

'I can't goddamn believe it. Do these fucks go to movies? I can't believe it, I can't even get into a goddamn restaurant.'

'Well, no,' said Ginger, 'you can't just drop into the fanciest restaurant in town with twenty people. Jack L. Warner on the best day he ever had couldn't do that.'

'It's been a shitty day, I thought I'd invite everybody out, you know? Everybody's tired, nobody wants to go home and cook.'

'Dearest, no one is going home to cook. Do you honestly think Sir Ian is dragging his ass home to fry up some Spam over a hotplate? No, I don't think so.'

'It's a fucking gesture.'

'Yes, and it's a very nice gesture. But if you think you can just show up with twenty-plus people – it's way more than fifteen, honey, I don't know where you come up with that number – then we have a problem. On the other hand, if you want to show up with a couple of people I can get you in anywhere. Everybody loves you, you're the flavor of the year, they'll feed you and you can sleep with the maître d' if you want.'

'Just get me in somewhere then. Me and Irina.' To Spandau Bobby said, 'You want to come? Bring a date? Or no, shit, we could invite Heidi. Heidi would love him.'

'Oh God, no, not Heidi. What did this poor man ever do to you?'

'Who's Heidi?' Spandau asked.

'No, Heidi would be all over him.'

'I know, honey, but give the poor man a break. Not everybody is after instant sex.'

May said, 'I think Heidi is busy. But he's just her type.'

'Everybody is Heidi's type,' said Ginger.

Bobby laughed. 'I'm telling you, let's fix him up with Heidi.'

'Who's Heidi?' Spandau asked.

'Don't worry,' said Bobby. 'You'll love Heidi.'

'You'll hate Heidi,' Ginger said to Spandau.

'For fuck's sake, don't queer this, it'll be great.'

'Queering things is just my nature, I'm afraid,' said Ginger.

With a flourish May put the finishing touches on Bobby's hair extensions.

'Done,' she said to Bobby. 'You're gorgeous. You look like Lord Byron.'

'Except for the club foot,' amended Ginger.

'Did Lord Byron have a club foot?' asked Bobby.

'Oh, honey,' said Ginger, 'it was like a sheep's hoof.'

'Jesus,' said Bobby.

'Who's Heidi?' asked Spandau.

The mobile rang. Ginger answered it. May waved to Spandau and left the trailer.

'Oh, hi, Benny!' said Ginger into the phone, clear enough for Bobby to hear. Ginger looked at Bobby. Bobby vigorously shook his head no.

'He's on the set right now. They're working the poor thing to death. Can I have him call you when he gets off? . . . Oh sure, I'll tell him. Bye.' Ginger held up the phone. 'That's the third time he's called today.'

'I don't want to get into this shit,' Bobby said. 'It's like I got nothing fucking better to do than straighten out his fucking life.'

'He says your mom is doing well.'

'He wants more money. How much is it this month?'

'He didn't mention money.'

'You ever known him to call me and not have it be about money? Fucking-A it's about money. I bought him a fuck-ing house. In Ohio it's a fucking mansion, it's like the fucking Taj Mahal. All he's got to do is see that Mom doesn't fall down the stairs fucking drunk and kill herself. That's it. For that he's got a goddamn mansion and a salary like a fucking CEO.'

A PA knocked on the door and stuck her head in. 'It's time.'

'Yeah, yeah . . .'

The PA left. Bobby said to Spandau, 'So you want to come to dinner tonight? With me and Irina?'

Spandau looked at Ginger, then back at Bobby.

Bobby said to Ginger, 'Go tell them I'm coming.'

Ginger rolled his eyes but he left.

'You heard anything from Stella?' Spandau asked him.

'Nothing, not a word. You think maybe he's given up?'

'No. He's not in a hurry.'

'Look,' said Bobby. 'Come to dinner. I'll feel better.'

'Sure. No Heidi.'

'No Heidi,' Bobby repeated. He stood up. 'Off we go. You want to come and watch me emote?'

The *Wildfire* set was in fact a series of smaller sets inside a cavernous soundstage. They were to shoot here and complete the interior shots, and in two weeks move to Wyoming for the exteriors. The shoot was on schedule so far and the producers and the director were anxious to keep it that way. The weather in Wyoming was tricky and everyone suspected they'd lose time there but no one was stupid enough to actually mention it. Meanwhile it was important they stay on schedule or under schedule if they could manage it.

165

It was particularly important to Mark Sterling, the director. Sterling was English and had made a name for himself with a series of moderate-budget Britcom films. This was his first large budget film, his first that wasn't a comedy, his first using mainly American actors, and his first shot in the States. And it was, for God's sake, a Western. In fact nobody wanted him for this film and he knew damned well he got it only because the previous director quit at the last minute, and Sterling's agent practically offered him up as an indentured servant. He was working for half the salary of his last picture, and even if the film did well (God be with us!) Sterling's cut was going to be virtually nil. Its success, though, would mean that Sterling had made it to the A-List at last and the option of never having to film again in the damp, dismal and asthma-inducing studios of Shepperton. Hollywood was better, and Hollywood is where Mark Sterling wanted to stay if he could manage it.

They'd been shooting for two weeks already and things had gone well, though the studio bean-counters were still hovering around, waiting to pull the plug at a moment's notice. Nobody trusted him. The bastards hung about in corners of the set like Battersea wharf rats, forever at the edge of his vision, whispering to each other. Sterling was anxious to make everyone happy, or at least happy enough to cut him some slack if things went slightly pear-shaped in Wyoming. There were, however, distant rumblings that all was not well.

Today's set was the living room in the large ranch cabin of a successful Wyoming land baron circa 1900. The carefully authenticated room sat in a pool of heavenly light from above, as if it were being beamed by God into the middle of an aircraft factory. Around it were the clumsy but inescapable accoutrements of filmmaking: cameras, giant lights, sound booms, endless snaking cables, technicians, hangers-on, money-people, nervous staff, and, of course, actors. Between takes everyone ran around and tried not to trip or knock anything over. This took up far more time than one might imagine.

Bobby and Spandau walked onto the set. Bobby'd been shooting since 6 a.m. already and his hair hurt. He walked over to his chair and sat down. Spandau stood next to him and looked around. All this was familiar to him and he missed it a little. When you worked on a movie everyone became family for a time, and whether it was functional or dysfunctional, it was still family. Then the film was done and everyone scattered to the four winds until time to do it again with a different family. It was better for him, working with Beau and his crew, always having that thread no matter what film you worked on. But even if he wanted to go back he was too goddamned old now, too brittle inside and out. And Beau was gone. It would never be the same without Beau. Beau was the last of the old-timers, the real cowboys, the ones who'd stand up to a director or the Suits if a stunt was too dangerous or they tried to rush him. Every gag was all about risk, but Beau knew when the risk

167

was worth it and when it wasn't. When it wasn't Beau had no qualms about walking his boys off the set. Beau never yelled, Beau never argued, Beau never told anybody to kiss his ass. Beau just said no and walked away like the last of the gentlemen. 'It ain't a pissing contest,' Beau once told him. 'It's either shit or get off the pot. Simple as that. Most things are.' But Beau was dead, and these days you'd likely find yourself working with some hotshot who'd cave-in to an under-the-table bonus, or had an eye on his own shot at directing. Your ability to keep people from getting killed had less value than who you lunched with. Nowadays everything was a goddamn career move, even falling off a goddamn building. Spandau missed the days when people just worked for a living.

Bobby looked nervous and bored. The assistant director came over.

'We're waiting for Sir Ian,' said the AD.

Bobby nodded. The AD walked off.

'We're always waiting for Sir Ian,' Bobby said to Spandau. 'Sir Ian likes to be the last one on the set. Sir Ian likes to make a fucking Entry. Man, thank God I never did theatre. You think movie actors got egos.'

Bobby absent-mindedly lit a cigarette. The AD scurried over again.

'Bob, um, we talked about the cigarettes. The whole safety thing, and the fucking union thing, you know.'

'Right,' said Bobby.

'Sorry, it's not me.'

'Yeah, yeah.'

Bobby threw the cigarette on the ground, and made a show of stomping it out.

'See?' he said to the AD. 'Bobby make all dead.'

'Thank you,' said the AD and went away.

'Prick.'

'He's just doing his job.'

'He enjoys the power. He's fucking dreaming of the day when all this will be his.' Then impatiently to himself, 'Come on, come on . . . Jesus, somebody flush the old bastard out of his trailer.' Then he said, out of the blue, 'I want you to move in with me.'

'A bit sudden, isn't it?' said Spandau. 'I mean, we've never even kissed.'

'Fuck you,' said Bobby. 'I mean it. I got lots of room, you seen the place.'

'Why?' said Spandau. 'Do you know something I don't know?'

'It would make me feel better. I got a weird feeling. I feel like something's about to happen. If some shit comes down I want you there.'

'Like what?'

'How the fuck do I know? Maybe Richie decides to off me. Who knows?'

'You're his meal ticket. Richie would sooner off his own mother. Richie loves you.'

'Richie's a fucking pernicious little cockroach. Who knows how his fucking mind works?'

169

At that moment there was a flurry of activity on the other side of the set. Sir Ian Whateley had arrived.

'His Grace has arrived,' Bobby said.

Sir Ian and a few members of his entourage stopped at the edge of the pool of light bathing the stage, as if it were indeed a pond and they weren't sure of the water. Sir Ian, and his entourage, waited.

'You see that?' said Bobby. 'He won't go over to Mark, he's waiting for Mark to come to him. Fucking power play.'

'What about you?' said Spandau.

'Hell, there's no way I can walk over there first now.'

'You're kidding.'

'Hell no. Look, this is a fucking major scene. This is the shit that Oscars are made of. The father and the son, hammering at each other, trying to break each other down. Fucking gorgeous scene. Well, the old bastard knows I'm going to fight to hold my own with him. He's going to try to walk away with it, but he knows I'm going to fight him, and he wants every advantage he can get. He'll fucking try to take it over the top the way he does, and I'm going to play my own game and he knows it. It's fucking war, man. Now look at Mark, he's shitting himself, trying to figure out which one of us to talk to first.'

Mark went over to Sir Ian. It was like a meeting with Prince Albert. They talked. Or, rather, Mark talked. Sir Ian just nodded. Sir Ian went over and took his place on the set.

Mark crossed the set to Bobby.

'Do I need a Border collie for you two?' Mark asked him.

'I have no clue what you're talking about,' said Bobby.

'Of course you don't. Look, he's going to try to eat the scenery on this. I don't want you to follow him. I want you to set the pace. If he starts to go off, I want you to play it nice and slow and reel him in.'

'That is not my job. You're the director.'

'You know as well as I do it's like directing a stampede of elephants. I need your help. I want you to take the moral high ground on this one.'

'Moral high ground,' repeated Bobby. 'Right, got it.'

'Will you help me on this, please? And maybe we can get out of here before the senile dementia kicks in. Mine, I mean.'

Bobby nods. Mark patted him on the shoulder and went back to Sir Ian.

'Makes you wonder what he said to Sir Ian about me, doesn't it?' Bobby said to Spandau, and walked over to the set.

Spandau wandered back over to Bobby's trailer. Ginger was there, brewing tea.

'Couldn't stand it, could you?' he said to Spandau. 'People always think of movie sets as such romantic places. My impression is that, except for about two minutes once an hour, everybody is generally bored, and sweltering or freezing their asses off. I'll take Cabo, thank you. Want a cuppa?'

'Sure.'

Ginger set out two china cups and poured tea from what looked to Spandau like an old low-fired Staffordshire teapot.

'Biscuit?'

'Thanks.'

'As long as one can have a civilized cup of tea, the Empire will never die.' He sipped his tea and rolled his eyes heavenward. 'I need this. Young Master Robert is going to come through that door a little bit angry as hell.'

'How do you know?'

'Because,' said Ginger, 'Sir Ian has fallen off the wagon and he's going to be impossible to work with. Inside information. Us personal assistants are like nannies, we get together in the park and talk about our wee bairns. In this case, news has arrived via the *Sun* that Sir Ian's nubile young wife has been seen catting around all over London with a certain young actor who shall remain nameless. Sir Ian is not a happy camper, and he's been at the Macallan's. A refuge for which he is somewhat infamous, though he's supposed to be clean and sober these days. That's what young love will do.'

As if on cue, a quarreling Bobby was heard approaching the trailer. The door flew open and Bobby stormed inside and slammed the door several times, hard, until it caught. Ginger and Spandau looked at each other and Ginger closed his eyes and took a last sip of tea.

'Fuck him, fuck this whole piece of shit!'

'What's wrong, darling?'

'He's fucking drunk! Like those fucking breath mints are going to hide about half a quart of scotch. His fucking eyes are like swimming around. What the fuck am I supposed to do with that? How am I supposed to act to that?'

'Calm down, you'll give yourself a stroke. Anyway, it's not your problem, it's Mark's problem. Let him deal with it.'

'Who the fuck are you?' said Bobby, suddenly turning on him. 'Lee fucking Strasberg, you know so much about acting? Go clean the toilet or something.'

'Well, pardon me.'

'Fuck, fuck, fuck!' chanted Bobby. 'I'm going to go home, I'm going to get so fucking shitfaced, I'm going to puke and pass out and I'm fucking going into a coma until this all disappears.'

'That's the mature way to handle it,' said Ginger.

'Are you fucking still here?' Bobby said to him. 'Go earn your money. Go do something. Pretend you fucking work for a living.'

'Have a cup of tea.'

'I don't want any fucking tea. I want a fucking six-foot heroin needle. I want death.'

Ginger handed him a cup of tea. Bobby took a sip from it. And another. He put the cup down. He closed his eyes. He leaned his head back.

'Fuck. Fuck me, fuck me . . .'

173

'You want a hot towel? I can put one in the microwave,' said Ginger.

'I'm still in makeup. I actually have to go back out there. Can you believe that?'

Annie knocked at the door.

'What is this?' Bobby asked her as she came in. 'Fucking Macy's Thanksgiving parade?'

'Did I come at a bad time?' she said, looking around for help. None came.

'Whatever it is it can wait,' said Bobby.

'I heard he was drunk,' Annie said. 'Is that true?'

'His eyes are sort of rolling around,' said Bobby.

'I'll talk to Mark,' said Annie.

'No, don't fucking talk to Mark.'

'Well how are you supposed to work like this?'

'All I need is Mark pissed at me.'

'Sweetie, Mark is supposed to be doing his job.'

'Just fucking leave it alone. We're going to be here all fucking night.' To Ginger he said, 'Call Irina. Tell her I'm going to be fucking late. No, screw that, shit, tell her I don't know when I'll be there, tell her just to go and have dinner without me.'

'You don't want me to talk to Mark?' Annie said again.

'No.'

'Look, there's something else . . .'

Bobby closed his eyes and threw back his head, moaning at the ceiling. 'Oh fuck me, fuck me, fuck me . . .'

'It's nothing major,' Annie continued, 'it's just that

174

Jurado is coming over here in a minute and he wants you to do him a favor.'

'Tell him it will cost him,' Bobby said with a demented gleam in his eye. 'Tell him I want an arm and a leg, I want to be paid for it, I want a fucking villa in Tuscany . . .'

'It's the head of the local Teamsters union. His daughter wants to meet you. She's a huge fan.'

'You're kidding.'

'You make nice to her for thirty seconds, they take a picture, it's all done.'

'No,' said Bobby. 'And by the way, you're fired.'

'Look, Jurado's having union problems, he needs this.'

'Fuck Jurado. And fuck that smegma-stained little girl.'

'She may be legal and gorgeous for all you know.'

'I'm dating a supermodel. I'm not interested in the daughter of some fat guinea gangster.'

'Jesus,' said Annie. 'You didn't say that. Tell me you didn't say that, please. You want us all never to work again? Or dead? These are not the people to piss off.'

A knock and Jurado entered, smiling like Burt Lancaster.

'Greetings,' he said.

'We have a problem,' Annie said to him.

'We've no problem,' Bobby contradicted.

'About what?' said Jurado.

'Can we postpone the meeting with the union guy?' Annie asked him. 'It's been a really hard day. I heard Sir Ian is under the weather.'

'That's not true,' Jurado said sharply. 'I just spoke to him.'

'He's smashed,' said Bobby.

'That is exactly the sort of thing we don't need,' Jurado said to Bobby. 'You say stuff like that and you're going to have his attorneys all over you for slander. It's patently untrue.'

'Do we have your word on that?' Bobby asked him.

'Can we postpone?' asked Annie.

'No,' said Jurado, 'he's on the set.'

'You ever think about asking me?' said Bobby.

'I don't have to ask you,' Jurado said, angry now.

'Frank—' Annie started.

'Look,' said Jurado, 'he's not the only one with a hard day. I'm tired. I want this thing done.'

'Kiss my ass,' said Bobby.

'Tell him to read his contract,' Jurado said to Annie.

'Where does it say in my fucking contract that I've got to jump up and do a minstrel show whenever you feel like it?'

'Tell him,' Jurado said again. All of the sudden he looked up and around. 'Why are all these people here? We don't need all these people. Why is he here?' he said, as if Spandau had just materialized out of nowhere.

'Because I want him here,' said Bobby. 'He stays. I may have him beat the crap out of you.'

'What about him?' Jurado said, nodding to Ginger.

'I guess I'll be the one to leave,' Ginger said breezily.

'No,' said Bobby, 'I want witnesses.'

'Bobby, this isn't helping,' Annie said to him.

'Helping? I'm not trying to help. I'm trying to get some respect.'

'Jesus,' said Jurado. 'Tell him, Annie.'

'It is in your contract,' Annie said.

'Bullshit.'

'It comes under publicity and actively supporting the film. I knew you'd be pissed so I ran it by Robert. He says it's not worth fighting, and it isn't.'

'Whose side are you on?' Bobby said to her.

'Your side, honey, but that's what it's all about.'

Jurado said, 'In about five minutes, okay? I'll send them over here.'

'When that little girl walks in the door,' Bobby said to him, 'I am going to flash her. I am going to wave my dick in her face. I swear to you.'

'Right,' said Jurado, 'great. Five minutes. I really appreciate this, guys.'

'Appreciate this,' said Bobby, and grabbed his crotch and shook it at Jurado.

'I thought that went well,' said Annie when Jurado had gone.

Bobby stood up and announced in an oratorical fashion, 'I am going to go take a massive shit. With luck, when they get here, this place will smell like the inside of a camel's ass.'

Bobby locked himself in the bathroom. Annie looked at Spandau.

'Are you getting all this down?' she said in an attempt at sarcasm. 'You did sign a confidentiality agreement, didn't you? What happens here stays here.'

'You want to check my references?' said Spandau. 'This isn't the first time I've done this. This isn't anything new.'

'I'm just saying, a word of this leaks out, one word, and you get buried in a pauper's grave.'

'You and Jurado ought to get some new material.'

'You and Bobby are awfully close, all of a sudden.'

'I'm supposed to be his bodyguard. That usually entails close.'

'And why the hell does he need a bodyguard, I'd like to know? Particularly you. You sure you're not feathering a little nest for yourself?'

'It would look that way to you.'

'What's that supposed to mean?'

'It means I don't need to explain to you a goddamned thing. It means even if I did, the likelihood of your understanding it is about nil. There's a whole fucking world outside of Hollywood, lady. Not everything on the planet is run by jackals. Not yet, anyway. You want rid of me, then talk to Bobby. It's his call. In the meantime, back off. I told you before, I've had about all of your crap I'm going to take.'

Annie smiled at him coldly, then went back to the bathroom and knocked on the door.

'I'm leaving, honey. You don't need me here for this.'

'Yeah, yeah,' said Bobby tiredly, on the other side.

Annie walked past Spandau and out the door. A minute later there was a flush and Bobby came out of the toilet.

'You two making nice-nice?' Bobby said to him.

'Oh, you bet.'

Another knock. Jurado was back with the visitors. He stuck his head in the door. 'Permission to come aboard?'

Bobby ground his crotch at him.

'Mind your step!' Jurado said over his shoulder. 'Now you'll get to see how glamorous the stars live, ha ha!'

Jurado came in followed by a thirteen-year-old girl and her father. The father was grinning from ear to ear and the girl was practically apoplectic with excitement.

'Bobby, this is Mr Waller, and this is his daughter Tricia.'

Bobby made a nice smile. 'Nice to meet you, Tricia.'

'Oh . . . my . . . God . . .'

Mr Waller extended his hand to Bobby. They shook.

'Nice to meet you, Mr Dye. My daughter Tricia here is your biggest fan. We all like your movies, including Mrs Waller and myself.'

'Thank you.'

'Oh, my, God,' repeated Tricia.

'How are you, Tricia?'

'I can't believe it's you.'

'It's me okay. Everybody being nice to you? Showing you around the set?'

'I've been on movie sets before. They're gross.'

'It's what's on the screen that counts, right?'

'You're not as tall as I thought,' Tricia said to him.

'Did you get a chance to meet Tiffany Porter?' Bobby asked her. 'She's in this movie too. And Sir Ian Whateley, wow.'

'He's, like, way old. He looks like my grandmother.'

'How about an autographed picture?' Bobby suggested. 'I've got a picture around here someplace.'

Mr Waller pulled out a camera. 'We were thinking, if you wouldn't mind . . .'

'No, sure, that would be fine.'

Bobby moved over next to Tricia and put his arm on her shoulder. Tricia put her arm around his waist and pushed in close. Very close. Practically humping his leg and smiling at the camera.

Click.

'Can we get another?' asked Mr Waller.

'Sure,' said Bobby.

Bobby tried to keep his distance from the girl this time but she moved in under his arm and hooked her finger in a front loop of his pants so that her hand rested on his fly.

Click.

'Well that was great!' said Jurado.

'Thank you,' said Mr Waller to Bobby.

'No, no, any time.'

'Will you sign my shoulder?' Tricia said to Bobby.

'Tricia!' said Mr Waller.

'Well it's, like,' said Tricia, 'just a shoulder.'

Bobby looked at Jurado for help. Jurado looked sympathetic but he shrugged.

'Gee, Trish,' said Bobby uncomfortably, 'maybe we should ask your father.' There were in fact a thousand headlines involving pedophilia buzzing around in his head.

'Well,' Mr Waller said, 'anything she wants . . .'

Tricia bared her shoulder and gave Bobby a felt-tip pen. He signed.

'How come you dumped Shania Fox for this Russian babe?' she asked while he was signing.

Bobby said, 'It's been real nice meeting you, Tricia. Thanks for coming to visit.'

Jurado said, 'Well, we have to let Bobby get to work now. We can't hold up a big movie like this.'

Jurado hustled them out. As he left he turned to Bobby and mouthed 'I'm sorry'. Bobby gave him the finger.

'Did you see that?' Bobby said to Spandau. 'Can you believe that?'

'Your biggest fan,' offered Spandau.

'Fuck me, fuck me, fuck me . . .'

Knock. It was the PA.

'You're needed.'

Bobby said to Spandau, 'I am going to blow my fucking brains out. You just watch me. This isn't worth it. None of this is.'

And he went out.

181

Ten

It was around ten in the morning when Allison Graff and her four-year-old son, Cody, went into Denny's Restaurant in Sherman Oaks. The restaurant was busy but there was a small booth in the front and they snagged that one. They were regulars and, anyway, Cody liked to look out the window. A waitress came by and smiled at Cody and gave them menus.

'I want the Grand Slam,' said Cody. He knew the menu.

'You won't eat all that,' said Allison.

'I will,' he said. 'I'm hungry.'

'You'd better eat every bite.'

The waitress went away with their orders. Cody drew on the paper place setting with crayons and Allison stared out the window at the traffic. Terry came in. A booth had just opened up behind Cody and he took that one.

This was going to be Terry's second breakfast. He had already stopped and eaten at six o'clock that morning at a similar all-night diner in Newbury Park, where he had sat for an hour and a half wrestling with his soul and that small sliver of brain where common sense resided. The sliver lost, and not for the first time. Terry drove back to Sherman Oaks and parked around the corner from her house. He listened to Lightnin' Hopkins on his iPod and every so often he got out of the car and looked down the street at her place or drove a circuit around the block. He did this for three hours until he saw her come out of the house with the boy and get in her car.

Terry ordered his second breakfast and Allison said to Cody, 'You wait here, I'm going to go get a paper,' and she stepped out of the restaurant. Cody watched his mother leave and then stood up on his knees and peered over the back of his seat at Terry. Terry smiled at him. Cody looked at him suspiciously. Terry stuck his tongue out at him. Cody turned around and sat down. Allison came back with her paper and Cody whispered something to her. Allison looked over at Terry and smiled at him.

'Well, maybe you're bothering him,' she said to Cody.

Allison was reading the paper and Cody turned around again to look at Terry, this time sticking out his own tongue. Terry made a ridiculous face at him and Cody laughed.

'What are you doing?' she said to Cody. 'Leave the poor man alone.' To Terry she said, 'Is he bothering you?'

'It's fine,' Terry said to her. 'It's nice to have someone my own age to play with.'

Allison laughed. Perhaps Terry would have been able to walk away, if she hadn't done that.

'You talk funny,' Cody said to him.

'I'm Irish. You know where Ireland is?'

Cody shook his head.

'Well, imagine a country where everybody talks funny and goes around making faces at strangers. That's Ireland. You'd fit right in.'

As Terry said this, Rosie Villano came by with another girl on their way out. Rosie was a bartender at the Voodoo Room and had been working the night Terry was there.

'Hey, Allison,' said Rosie, 'welcome to Chez Denis.' To Cody she said, 'Hey, Cody, my man.' She smiled at Terry, who smiled back quickly and turned to look out the window.

Allison was friendly enough but the politeness on both sides had a cold edge to it. It was clear they didn't like each other. 'Hi, Rose. Yeah, God, we're in here practically every day. I should be ashamed. I should be home making him oatmeal or something.'

'Oatmeal?' said Rosie. 'Yech! Got to have them hash-browns, right, Cody?' To Allison: 'You working tonight?'

'Yeah, I'll be there.'

'Take care,' Rosie said. 'You be good now, Cody.'

Rose glanced again at Terry, gave him a brief smile, and left with her friend.

The food came and no one spoke to Terry again. Allison seemed to avoid looking at him. They ate and at the end of their meal Allison and Cody got up, smiled in passing at Terry, paid the tab and left.

Terry had made contact and that was all he had wanted. To press it any further would have put her off. He knew where she lived now, and knew enough of her routine to be able to find her when he needed. If Rosie had not turned up things might have progressed a little further but probably not by much. Now he was a familiar face, no longer an instant threat. Next time he saw her in here he'd greet the kid and work up a conversation with her. Terry would turn on the charm, make her laugh. Guys trying to pick up women came on like James Bond. Truth was, in this fucking world everybody is afraid of everybody else and all anybody really wants is to feel safe. A woman like Allison – he knew her name now – feels vulnerable all the time. You make her feel safe, you make her laugh, and you're at the head of the line. A woman once told Terry he had a face like five miles of Kilkenny roadway but he was the only man she'd ever met who knew how to laugh in bed.

Terry left a couple of minutes after they did. In the parking lot he saw her standing next to her car with a tall blond guy. The guy was buff, looked like someone who worked in a gym or an athlete. He had her backed up against the car and was up in her face about something, angry. Cody was sitting in the car, watching all this through the window.

'I got a note from your goddamn lawyer,' the guy was saying to her.

185

'I have nothing to say to you, Lee. Just go away and leave me alone.'

'Well, I got plenty to say to you. You think I'm going to roll over for this shit? Where do you think the fucking money is supposed to come from?'

'Gee,' Allison said, 'maybe it'll come from the same place you got money to screw half the teenyboppers in Santa Monica.'

She tried to move past him to get in the car but he grabbed her arm.

'The idea of a restraining order isn't quite penetrating that pea-brain of yours, is it?'

'We're still married,' he said. 'You can't keep me away from my kid.'

'I'm trying to fix the married part of it,' she said. 'Now get out of my way.'

She tried to open the car door but Lee grabbed her arm and threw her up against the car. She struggled to get free but he squeezed her arm hard enough to make her wince.

'Excuse me,' said Terry, 'but do you have the time?'

'What?' said Lee.

'The time,' said Terry. 'My watch has stopped.'

'No,' said Lee.

'But you're wearing a watch,' said Terry.

'Look,' said Lee, 'fuck you and the time. I'm busy here.'

'Is that an Omega? Damned fine watch,' said Terry. 'That's the James Bond watch, right? The Seamaster. Or is that the Rolex?'

'Look, you fucking Irish dwarf,' Lee said to him, 'I don't have the goddamn time and I'm not interested in talking about my frigging watch. Now beat it.'

'Leprechaun,' said Terry.

'What?'

'I don't think you meant dwarf, you probably meant leprechaun, didn't you? Little fellows in cute hats. Like the Lucky Charms adverts, right? People often get them confused. Dwarves are in *The Lord of the Rings*. D-W-A-R-V-E-S. No F there.'

Lee looked at Allison. 'Is this a friend of yours?'

'No,' said Allison, and gave Terry a warning look.

'Fuck off,' Lee said to him, and turned back to Allison.

'I couldn't help noticing your size,' said Terry. 'Considerable upper-body development. Do you lift weights?'

'What are you, some kind of homo?'

'I was just thinking, because of your size, I imagine this young woman is frightened of you. Bloody hell, I'm frightened of you. I think we're all frightened of you.'

'Well, you better be frightened, you little Irish fart. Fuck off, I said.'

'I hate to belabor a point, but, as I say, you're frightening this young woman and this child. I believe you should desist.'

'What?' said Lee. 'Desist?'

He looked at Allison, who started laughing.

'It means stop,' she said to Lee. 'He's telling you to stop.'

Lee stared at Terry. 'Is this guy a boyfriend of yours?' he asked Allison.

'Look, I don't know him, he's just trying to help. Leave him alone.' To Terry she said, 'You should just go.'

'Oh, of course. But he needs to let go of your arm first.'

Lee let go of her arm.

'There. See. The pissant asks me to let go and I let go. You want anything else?'

'No. Thank you. Not for the moment.'

'Not for the moment,' Lee repeated. He said to Allison, 'Is this what you want to leave me for? This fucking runt? Are you that fucking desperate?'

She tried to get in the car but Lee grabbed her and slammed her hard against the car again. This time she started crying.

'Back away from her,' said Terry.

'Fuck you.'

'We can be gentlemen about this,' Terry said. 'I don't want to hurt you in front of the boy.'

'Hurt me? You?'

'In ten seconds,' said Terry, 'I'm going to paralyze your right arm.'

'You're kidding, right?'

'. . . Eight . . .' said Terry.

'Who is this guy?' Lee asked Allison. He was fascinated now by Terry, who was looking down at the second hand of his own watch.

'. . . Six . . .'

'Lee, let go of me,' Allison said, 'I think he means it.'

'Oh yeah, I'm scared.'

'. . . Three . . . two . . .'

Terry moved toward Lee, who turned Allison loose and spun to face him. Terry got in close but just out of Lee's arm length, then stopped and moved back a few paces. Lee came after Terry and Terry moved him away from Allison so she couldn't be hurt. Terry backed up a little more with Lee following then Terry stopped abruptly, moved low and forward again, underneath Lee's swing. He grabbed Lee's left wrist, twisting it and grinding one of his knuckles into the nerve junction behind Lee's left elbow. Lee howled and Terry let him go and moved back a few paces. Lee stood slumped over, holding his dead arm.

'I lied about which arm it was,' Terry said.

'You son of a bitch . . .'

'What the hell did you do?' Allison asked, shocked.

'I compressed a nerve in his arm. It'll go away in a few minutes. I think.' He turned to Lee. 'It hurts, but you'll be okay. The point is, I can do this all day. There are spots like this all over your body, most of them hurt a hell of a lot more. What you want to do is back off now. You don't want to look stupid in front of the boy, right? Right?'

Lee nodded.

'Good. We're going to go now. Also, for future reference: beware of leprechauns. Lying little buggers. You'd know that if you were Irish.'

Cody was crying. Allison had opened the car door and

189

Cody had come out and climbed into her arms. Cody was looking at Terry and Terry felt like shit now and started to say something to the boy when Lee's good right hand clouted Terry in the face. He staggered backwards, stunned, his nose bleeding.

The blow had the dangerous effect of setting Terry's instincts in motion. His mind cleared and he forgot about Allison or the boy and his entire being focused on Lee. He didn't wait for Lee to move again but dropped to the ground and, spinning, swept Lee's legs from under him. Lee fell backwards onto the tarmac striking his head. Terry, suddenly standing over him, brought his foot down hard inside Lee's right elbow crippling the other arm. Then he sat down on Lee's chest. He grabbed Lee's hair and lifted his head and pinched his esophagus with his fingers and squeezed. Lee gagged and struck at him with his useless hands and Terry squeezed harder and smiled down into Lee's panicked eyes. He stopped when he felt Allison pulling at him, hitting him on the shoulders. *'You're killing him for God's sake let him breathe let him breathe . . .'*

Terry remembered where he was now and the familiar sick regret filled him once again. He got off Lee and backed away. Lee was clutching his neck and hoarsely trying to pull air through his bruised throat. Allison had put Cody in the car and was bent over Lee, who was breathing now and lying there more shocked than damaged. Terry watched her and again felt the revulsion at who and what he was. He expected her to turn on him now or to

190

run from him but instead she said to him, 'Quick, get in the car before he recovers,' and Terry followed her into the car. Allison hastily shoved the VW into gear and drove out of the lot. Cody was in the back still crying.

'Talk to him,' Allison said as she drove. Terry didn't know what she wanted. 'Talk to him about what happened, goddamn you. Explain it to him.'

Terry turned to face the boy. The boy's eyes were red and full of tears and snot ran from his nose. Looking into Terry's face set off a new bout of crying and Terry reached back and put his hand on the side of the boy's face. The boy didn't pull away and Terry said to him, 'He's okay, I didn't hurt him, it just looks worse than it is. Okay? Look at me now, look at me.' The boy looked into Terry's eyes. 'He's okay. I didn't hurt him.' Terry left his hand there and could feel the pulse in the boy's neck, throbbing rapidly. The boy sniffled and stopped crying.

'Go on,' said Allison. 'You owe it to him.'

'I was afraid he might hurt your mother,' Terry said to him. 'I'm sorry. I know he's your father. I should have done something different but I didn't know what else to do. That's the way I was raised, you know. It's not a good thing and I'm sorry for it. You want to forgive me?' he asked the boy. 'I'm asking you to forgive me and not be too mad at me. Can you do that?' The boy said nothing but he wasn't crying now. Terry said, 'Jaysus, look at that, a huge green slimy great godawful slug has climbed up your nose! Argh!' Terry pretended to retch several times. The boy

191

laughed. 'Dear God, woman, pull the car over, me pan-cakes are coming up! Look at it! It's climbing up to feast on his brain! Argh!'

Allison looked in the mirror and frowned. She rum-maged through her purse and handed a tissue to Terry, who took it and wiped Cody's nose. Cody laughed and tried to blow more snot out onto his lip.

'Enough of that,' Allison said to the mirror. 'You do that again and I'm the one who's going to be sick.' Cody kept huffing through his nose and soon they were all in on it, pretending to gag and Cody laughed all the harder.

Allison drove to her house. They went inside and Allison washed Cody's face then took him into the living room and put a cartoon video on for him and settled him on the sofa. She led Terry into the kitchen and closed the door and said, 'You want to tell me what that shit was all about?'

'I'm sorry,' said Terry. 'Truly.'

'I thought you were going to kill him. Jesus, I've never seen anybody do that before. I mean you see this crap on television, but I've never seen anybody do it in real life. What are you, some kind of martial arts instructor?'

'No,' he said. 'I used to be a soldier. I mean, you learn this shit and it never quite goes away.'

'Look, there was no chance you were going to hurt him, right? Not seriously.'

'No,' lied Terry. 'Not seriously.'

'You've got blood all over your shirt.' And he had. Blood clotted in his nose and he wiped at it and could feel fresh blood spill warmly onto his fingers. 'You're still bleeding like a stuck pig.'

Terry sat in a chair. Allison put ice cubes into a plastic bag and told Terry to hold it on the back of his neck and to lean forward and pinch his nose with the other hand. Terry did as instructed.

'He got you pretty good,' she said. 'You must have a head like concrete because I've seen him cold-cock big guys with less. He used to box. He was lousy at the thinking part of it but he could still punch.'

'Now you tell me,' Terry said, sounding like Underdog.

'You think your nose is broken? Not dizzy or anything? You don't need to go to a hospital?'

'No,' Terry said, still making that ridiculous noise. 'This will be fine.'

'Yeah, that was some show you put on. I suppose I should thank you. Is that what you want? Me to thank you, you being the knight errant and all?'

Terry let go of his nose. 'Okay, it wasn't any of my business.'

'No, it wasn't.'

'It struck me that he'd done this sort of thing before.'

'Often enough,' she said. 'He broke my jaw once.'

'So you won't mind if I save the hypocrisy and stop apologizing.'

'It was still none of your business.'

'I'm not clear on a couple of things,' Terry said. 'Are you thanking me or yelling at me?'

'Both, I think. You're right. He was liable to have hurt me. He was pissed off enough and he's done it before.'

'The other thing is, I'm not sure why I'm here.'

'What do you mean?'

'I expected you to take off.'

'Oh that,' she said. 'That was my initial reaction. But Lee hit you pretty hard and I was going to drive you to a hospital and leave you there. It was the least I could do. Also I was afraid the cops were going to show up and I didn't want to deal with that.'

'So why didn't you just drop me at a hospital?'

'Are you complaining, for chrissake?'

'No, just curious. Nothing you did was what anybody else would have done. It was all out of character.'

'So okay, you did a really stupid, but sort of nice, thing. Even if you did scare the shit out of all of us. And there was the other thing. When you started to fight him. I saw you lead him away from me. That's what you did, wasn't it?'

'Yeah.'

'And if you'd really wanted to hurt him badly, you could have. I could see that. But you didn't. Granted you got a little postal there for a second, but you could have killed him if you'd wanted, couldn't you?' Terry didn't answer. 'So that means you're not a homicidal kung-fu maniac or whatever that stuff is you did. And you were good with Cody, in the car. The explanation was better coming from you. He knows his father is a shit but nobody likes to see their dad get his ass kicked.'

'Have I made things worse?'

'Between me and Lee? No, they were already as bad as they could possibly be. There's a restraining order but Lee's not great about listening to people. Anyway, I haven't had anyone fight over me since the third grade. If I were a better human being I'd be ashamed, but I have to say I'm kind of flattered. You were trying to impress me, weren't you?'

'Did it work?'

'I haven't decided. At any rate it won't happen again. Will it?'

'No.'

'You're right about one thing, though,' she said.

'What?'

'In the restaurant. I wouldn't have spoken to you if you hadn't been nice to my kid. You're not the first guy who's thought of that approach, by the way. Children and dogs. I think it's in the *Singles Handbook*.'

'Seen it all, have you?'

'I'm not ugly and I have a pulse. And you're a man.'

'He was going to hit you,' Terry said.

'Maybe.'

'No.'

'Maybe you're right,' she said. 'And maybe I should be fluttering my eyelashes and thanking you and swooning a little over the testosterone of it all. The truth is that I do thank you, sort of, but I'm afraid there's no reward for you at the end of it. I'm sick of men at the moment and you

happen to fall into that category. When you've finished
bleeding all over my kitchen I'm going to have to ask you
to leave.'

'My car's at Denny's.'

'It's three blocks, for God's sake.'

'Not even a cup of tea?'

'Not even that. Sorry. And I might suggest less violent
ways of picking up women.'

'Usually I throw myself under a train, but this was the
opportunity that presented itself.'

'You're really cute and all, but you're wasting your time.
You seem like a nice – if potentially lethal – kind of guy.
But I'm not really into the whole dating thing right now.
My life is too complicated.'

'I'm the most uncomplicated guy you'll ever meet. I'm
Mister Simplicity himself.'

'This would have to be a lie, I'm thinking.'

'Do you like seafood?'

'Yes, but I'm not going to go out with you. You just beat
up my ex-husband. Although this isn't necessarily a bad
thing.'

'I know this great little place in Ventura, near where I
keep my boat. Do you like boats?'

'Yeah, I like boats, but as I was saying—'

'We don't have to see the boat, unless you want to. It's a
thirty-two-foot mono-hull sailboat. Great for sitting on
deck and having a drink while the sun goes down. You'll be
perfectly safe. You'll love it. Kids love it too. It's a great

thing, sunshine, a picnic lunch. Get them out of the smog and some fresh air into their little lungs.'

'Christ, you don't miss a trick, do you?'

'Just dinner. You can meet me there, if you want. If you begin to doubt my sanity, you can drive right home.'

'I already doubt your sanity. What I'm not sure of is mine.'

'It seems like a win–win situation to me.'

'Okay, but on one condition. I don't want you to come here again. I mean it. We go out one time, but that's it, right? And I'll be honest, the only reason I'm doing this is out of curiosity. I've never met anyone quite like you. Do not jump to the conclusion that this is a compliment.'

'If that's what you want.'

'This isn't going to go anywhere. I want you to know that.'

'Okay,' said Terry.

'I mean it,' she said. 'Ah God, this is going to be a huge mistake.'

'That was a huge mistake,' said Allison.

She had climaxed for the third time, actually screaming at that last one and the world went dark for a little while. She was gripping Terry's hair in her fist and couldn't quite manage to let go. 'Again?' he said.

'Oh God. Oh God no, please.'

'It wasn't good?'

'I don't know how you managed that but most men don't even know that place exists. And if you do it again

I'm not sure I could deal with it. I mean it.' Allison lay on her back and Terry propped himself up on one elbow beside her. 'This is awful,' she said.

'Why?'

'Look,' she said, 'do you mind if I don't talk for a couple of minutes? I think I'm going to pass out.'

She closed her eyes and smiled contentedly. Terry kissed her.

'This is all wrong,' she said. 'This wasn't supposed to happen. I'd swear you drugged me but I know you didn't. And I'm not even drunk. There was you talking about playing in the streets of Londonderry and there was that lobster and the next thing there was this.'

They were on his boat. The water lapped at the hull a few inches from her head and the sex had been amazing even with that poster of Gandalf staring down at them. She truly liked this little Irish bastard but she knew she had to find some way of getting herself up and going home and never seeing him again.

'I mean, I promised myself this wouldn't happen. You don't know how screwed up my life is right now.'

'Maybe I can help unscrew it.'

'You're in way over your head, here. Look, we can't do this again. I don't want to see you, I don't want you to come anywhere near me, okay?'

'The sex was that bad?'

'I'm serious. I like you, but I don't want to see either one of us get hurt. Just trust me on this.'

She started to leave.

'Don't go yet,' he said. 'Just a few minutes longer.'

He took her in his arms. She lay close against him, her eyes closed, breathing softly. Not asleep but safe.

Her cellphone rang. She reached out and grabbed her purse, fished it out and looked at the caller.

'Shit, I have to take this.'

She gave him a look that said she wanted privacy.

'I'll go out on deck,' Terry said.

Terry pulled on a pair of shorts and went up top. He lit a cigarette then eased over to the side of the boat where an open window allowed him to hear what she was saying.

'No, I'm out . . . No, goddamn it, with a girlfriend. With Rima, you know Rima. No, look, for God's sake, you've got to stop this . . . I'm telling you, this is not what I want, you're putting too much pressure on me . . . Yeah, okay . . . Okay. Look, I'm going home now. I can't talk, Rima is waiting for me, I'm in the bathroom, for God's sake . . . Yeah . . . Yeah . . . Bye.'

When Terry came back into the cabin Allison was dressing to leave.

'If that's your ex, you don't have to let him push you around,' Terry said to her.

'No, it's not my ex. I wish it was. Him I can handle.'

'Whoever it is, I can help.'

'Trust me, you can't. Is there a bathroom on this thing?'

Terry pointed to the head. When she went in he took the phone from her purse and checked the last received call. RICHIE. When she came out he was sitting on the bunk.

'I'm sorry, I have to go. It was nice. I want you to know that. Really nice.'

'He's not going to let you go,' Terry said to her. 'Not without help.'

'What are you talking about?'

'I know Richie Stella. I know what he's like when he gets his hooks into someone.'

Allison stared at him. Her mouth was open as if to say something but she didn't. Finally she shook her head and gave a small sardonic laugh. 'What are you,' she said finally, 'a cop?'

'I'm not a cop, but I can help you. I can get him off your back.'

'Who are you working for?'

'Somebody like you. Somebody Richie is trying to hurt.'

She sat down at the table across the cabin from him, as far away as she could in the tiny room. She put her face in her hands. 'You're really good,' she said. 'You're the best. I've met some lying bastards in my time, but you are without a doubt the king of them all.'

'He won't quit. You know that. He'll end up owning you.'

'He owns me already,' she said wearily. 'Anyway I don't see the difference in him or you. You're both vicious shits. You use me for one thing, he uses me for another.'

'He's just a two-bit punk. He's not invulnerable. You can help bring him down.'

'No. You do your own fucking dirty work.'

'He doesn't have to know it was you. He'll never find out. He'll never connect you to it. You know I'm right, don't you? This won't end until Richie goes down. You know that.'

'And if I don't help you what happens? What leverage have you got? Everybody's got leverage, right? Richie's got leverage on me. What's yours? What have you come up with?'

'Nothing,' Terry said. 'Nothing at all. But nothing changes. You think he owns you now, just wait. Wait until he gets bored with you, maybe. You know what I'm talking about. You've thought about it already. Maybe he wants you to run some errands for him. Maybe he'd like you to be nice to a friend of his. I'm not telling you anything you don't already know.'

'I can't lose this job. I've got my baby, I've got the house.'

'You think you've got some sort of future, just doing nothing? You think he's just going to leave you alone? You want your kid to see you, what's going to happen to you? You think Richie is going to be such a swell role model? One way or another, Richie is coming down. I don't know how deep you're in, but I can keep you out of it. You can walk away.'

'You're as bad as he is.'

'You know I'm not.'

'What's your interest in this? I know it isn't me. Why go to all this trouble? Why are you after Richie?'

'Richie Stella has hurt a lot of people. Aside from the drugs and his connection to the mob, he's responsible for the death of a young girl and he's blackmailing the guy I work for. All this is going to continue unless Richie is brought down.'

'Who are you working for?'

'You know I can't tell you that. But I can tell you that Richie has struck the wrong victim this time. My friend has the money and the power to bring him down. Richie has over-reached himself this time. He's weak and he's vulnerable. He's gotten arrogant and he can be brought down. I need you to help me.'

'You can protect me? You can protect my baby?'

'Yes. I promise you. You can walk away from this thing free and safe and with a new life. My friend can help you. Money isn't a problem.'

'Maybe you're lying,' she said. 'Maybe I can't believe a thing you say. Why should I?'

'Because,' said Terry, 'in the end it all amounts to the same fucking thing, doesn't it? What are your choices? You stay with Richie and he is going to use you up and pass you onto somebody else or worse. You think he is going to let you quit? Richie has made his life never letting anything out of his grip. You're waiting to ask him for a job reference while you stock groceries at Safeway? He's got you, baby, and he's going to keep you and you fucking well know it. He's fucking sweet to you now, but what happens when he gets bored? Maybe he wants you to shove a kilo of cocaine up your arse and take a stroll across the border? Or you'll wind up in a hotel room blowing some spick drug supplier Richie needs to keep happy for a while. The longer you stay the more he has on you, and the more he has the harder it's going to be. What happens to you and Cody then?'

'If he finds out I helped you . . .'

'He won't find out. I've no connection to him. There's no link. All this goes to my friend. I'm nearly out of it myself. I'm just helping to set the wheels in motion. After that we're both out of it.'

'You can protect me?'

'Yes.'

Allison thought. She sat at the small table and lit a cigarette and smoked it through and she thought. Finally she turned to Terry and said: 'You fuck me over again, you put my child in fucking danger, and I will crawl through broken glass in order to kill you. I mean that. Do you understand me? I never imagined I could say this but I will kill you if you fuck me over. I swear on my father's grave.'

Terry got up to sit next to her but Allison pushed him away. 'Don't fucking touch me,' she said. 'Don't you fucking come near me. You ask your fucking questions and when this thing is done I never want to see you again.'

Eleven

So there was Potts, in the fucking grocery store.

Potts was in Safeway, walking up and down the aisles, pushing that fucking stupid little cart around, the cart with the inevitable bad wheel, the one they always saved for Potts so he could feel even more of an asshole than he normally felt in these places. Potts hated it here, hated all the bright lights and the clean people and the smart-assed high-school clerks who looked at him like he was shit when he piled up his fucking Cheerios and his fucking Hamburger Helper and his fucking helpless-looking rolls of three-ply toilet paper on the counter to pay for them. What Potts longed for was one of those little mom and pop Mexican stores in El Paso, some dark little place where you didn't have to have a fucking college degree to figure out which processed foods were least likely to kill you, where there were maybe two choices you had to make, you want the black beans or the pintos? Where you could go in and get out fast and you didn't have to worry about some Starbucks-sipping yuppie cunt on a cellphone killing you with her fucking SUV before you even made it across the fucking parking lot.

Potts was not happy.

He was looking for the canned peaches. Lately he'd had a craving for canned peaches. It was the thing he loved most as a kid, his favorite treat. His old lady would dish out some dismal supper – chicken or hamburger, both cheap in those days – then Potts would sneak outside in the dark where he'd cached a tin of peaches in syrup he'd boosted from some grocery. He carried a knife with a can opener on it and he'd pry open the peaches and sit in the dark drinking the syrup first and then spearing the sliced peaches like guppies with his knife and forking them down his throat. Jesus, thought Potts. The shit that makes us happy. There comes a point when you realize you can never be that happy again and it's all fucking downhill from there, brother. What do they call it? Diminishing returns.

The other thing was, they always kept moving fucking things around in these places. Potts couldn't find the goddamn peaches, and you ask one of these bastards and it's like you interrupted brain surgery or something. Or else you follow around some dumb fuck who didn't know any better than you did and before long there was a big fucking production with half a dozen assholes including the manager trying to locate one goddamn can of peaches. On the other hand you could just leave all this shit in the same goddamn place day in and day out so that it was right where you fucking left it the last time. There was clearly some reason, some money-making reason, why these bastards played with our heads like this, why they needed to keep us off-balance. There always was. Potts just couldn't figure it out.

So, anyway, here was Potts. Standing with his limping gimp cart in the middle of the aisle trying to figure out where he'd be if he was a can of peaches. Potts felt someone was behind him and he turned round to see a small, pleasant-faced woman waiting with her cart behind him. He was blocking the aisle. The woman smiled sweetly at him.

'Oh. Shit,' said Potts. 'Sorry.'

'Sorry,' the woman said also, continuing to smile.

Potts dragged aside his cart to let her pass. He went back to his search for peaches and found them, except everything was either whole peaches or low-sugar peaches or diced peaches or peaches and something else. Potts gave up. Nothing made sense to Potts anymore. The world was joyless and there was nothing you could do about it.

Potts saw the woman again in Dairy products. She was buying yogurt, those little containers you saw healthy people slurping on TV. She was around Potts' own age. She wore a pale-blue button-up dress and as she reached up to get the yogurt Potts realized she had a pretty good figure and nice legs. She was small and tight and she had this face like a grade school teacher. Potts didn't think anymore about it. She wasn't his sort of woman. But she reminded him of all those teachers he'd had the hots for as a kid, the series of not-gorgeous women in plain dresses who still managed to give him a hard-on every time they bent over his shoulder to correct his work. Potts stood in the Meats section and tried to figure out how much fat he needed in his ground beef.

He passed her once again buying toilet paper. She nonchalantly picked up a big package of toilet paper and dropped it in her cart, like it was the most natural thing in the world, which of course it was. Potts on the other hand couldn't pick up a roll of tissue unless the whole goddamned aisle was clear and even then he'd bury it under whatever was in his cart. Like nobody in Potts' universe ever had a bowel movement. She smiled again at Potts and passed him with her big package of ass-wipe paper and Potts admired her, admired that ease in the world that he would never have. Potts sniffed some kind of perfume as she passed or maybe it was soap. Potts saw her bending over his desk, gently pointing out what a fuck-up he was in math, inhaling her scent and having his ear brushed by the cloth of her dress and praying, praying, she wouldn't call him to the board because of his small but proudly distinct nine-year-old's boner.

He didn't see her again in the store. He looked for her at the checkout but she'd already gone. Potts paid and lugged his peachless few groceries outside, two small bags. There was a Starbucks next door. Potts hadn't eaten breakfast and he wanted coffee. Normally he wouldn't be caught dead in the place. It was always full of teenagers from the high school and the girls were cute and wore revealing clothes and Potts always felt like a pervert. I mean, it was only human to look but still you felt like a pervert and what's more you were convinced they knew you were looking and that you were definitely a pervert. Potts went in anyway because he'd forgotten to buy coffee. What Potts really wanted was a simple goddamn cup of Folgers but he submitted to a fucking coffee-Nazi interrogation and wound up with something from Sumatra and a triangular maple thing. Where the fuck was Sumatra? One more place designed to make you feel like you didn't belong. He looked for a seat and saw the woman sitting alone at a table in the corner. She was reading a book. The available table was near hers. She gave him a big smile. Potts sat down. She said:

'How do you get those groceries home on your motor-cycle?'

Potts was surprised. How did she know about the bike?

'It's a trick,' he said.

'I'll bet. You strap them on the handlebars in some way?'

'I've got panniers – saddlebags. I'll just take them out of the bag and put them in the panniers.'

She laughed. 'Not much of a trick. I didn't notice the saddlebags. People always want to make things more complicated than they are.'

'I guess,' said Potts. 'You like motorcycles?'

'My brother liked them. He used to put me on the back of his sometimes. I was a kid. It was the most exciting thing in the world then.'

'It still is. Maybe. What happened to your brother?'

'You're thinking: tragic motorcycle accident. But no, he just got married and got responsible and stopped riding. I think I liked him better when he was wild and irresponsible.'

'Not all bikers are wild and irresponsible,' said Potts, although he clearly believed that he was.

'Oh God, I'm sorry. I didn't mean that. I've put my foot in my mouth.'

'No, it's okay. I know what you meant.'

'Thank you for being a gentleman about it.' She looked at her watch. 'I have to go. It was nice meeting you.'

'You too,' said Potts.

She gave him another of her smiles. Potts watched her walk out into the sunlight. He imagined, as he did with practically every decent person he met, what her home life was like. Whatever it was, it was not something Potts would ever have in common.

Twelve

A TV screen. Bobby Dye is being interviewed.

> BEV METCALF
> (*to camera*)
> Hi, I'm Bev Metcalf, and today we're on the set of
> *Wildfire*, the new movie starring Bobby Dye, Tiffany
> Porter and Sir Ian Whateley. And we're talking to
> Bobby Dye – Bobby, we've managed to catch you and
> pull you aside here. Wow, it's a busy time for you,
> huh?

> BOBBY
> Yeah, I'm in a lot of scenes, and the days are long, but
> you know, it's going to be worth it. It makes a difference,
> as an actor, to be working on a film you're really proud
> of. You want to give it your all.

BEV

Can you tell us what the movie is about?

BOBBY

Well, it's the sort of movie they don't make anymore, at least not since David Lean. It's an epic, a big movie, about a Montana ranching family at the turn of the century. I play Chad Halliday, a rebellious son, and Sir Ian plays my father, a powerful rancher who's fighting to keep his ranch not only from crooked land developers but a massive forest fire that's threatening to wipe him out.

BEV

It sounds symbolic, the forest fire raging . . .

BOBBY

Oh yeah. That was one of the things that really attracted me to the script, the whole environmental side, the encroaching of industry on nature, and the destruction of a whole way of life. I mean, we're seeing that now. Look at the rainforests.

BEV

Wow!

BOBBY

And of course Tiffany plays my half sister, with whom I fall in love . . .

211

BEV

What? Ooh, this sounds pretty racy!

BOBBY

Well, I can't give away the plot. But everything works out okay in the end. I mean, there's nothing to really offend anybody. So, you know, you can bring the kids. Something for everybody.

BEV

What's it like working with Tiffany Porter? This is her first serious acting role, after her fabulous career as a pop star.

BOBBY

Tiffany is a doll, a real sweetheart. I mean, the press has always been so hard on her, so unfair, that you expect some prima donna, and she's absolutely nothing like that. She's absolutely professional, on time and knows her lines, and she's got these great instincts. I just love working with her. And when people see the movie, they're going to get an insight into a whole different character than the one in the press. I mean, you can't carry off a role like hers and be some sort of flake. It requires real concentration and real dedication. She's got both.

BEV

And Sir Ian Whateley . . .

212

BOBBY

What can I say?

BEV

Were you nervous?

BOBBY

Oh my goodness. Nervous doesn't even touch it. Petrified, maybe. Rigid, I was afraid to speak. There he is, this . . . legend. I grew up on his films. I wanted to *be* Ian Whateley. So I'm, like, unable to speak, and he comes over and starts talking to me in that amazing voice he has – you know, that rich plummy British accent –

BEV

Unmistakable . . .

BOBBY

And he's like the kindest, gentlest guy on the face of the earth. He makes you feel so relaxed, you forget all about the whole 'Sir Ian' business. And he's funny as hell. He has this raunchy sense of humor – oh wow, maybe I shouldn't say that – but he's, like, hilarious. We sit around and laugh. We're like two schoolkids, Mark –

BEV

Mark Sterling, the director –

BOBBY

Mark has to get us aside and scold us. We'll be doing a scene and start giggling and it's like 'time out' and Mark makes us sit at opposite ends of the stage until we stop giggling.

BEV

It sounds like a dream.

BOBBY

Oh yeah, it is like a dream. Working with all these great people, and there's this amazing script – Denny Kessel, who won an Oscar for *Lowdown* – and Mark Sterling, a wonderful director . . . Yeah, it is like a dream. Sometimes I want to pinch myself.

BEV

So this performance, does it have Oscar written on it? The buzz is amazing.

BOBBY

Oh gosh. I don't even want to think about that. You know, you just go out there and do the best you can, just give it what you've got with all your heart. I mean, an Oscar . . . It's nice people like my work, but in the end it's about pleasing the fans, right? and trying to make a good movie.

BEV

Thank you, Bobby Dye, for taking the time out to talk to us.

BOBBY

My pleasure, Bev.

*

Bobby and Spandau were at Bobby's place. They were sitting in front of a giant plasma TV and eating Buffalo chicken wings washed down by an expensive bottle of Napa Zinfandel.

'She's hot,' Bobby said around a chicken wing. He backed up the DVD and played it again. 'There, you see that? The way she laughs and leans forward there, that little jiggle. She wasn't wearing a bra. You can't tell it on screen but those babies were on display. She gave me her phone number.'

'Your life is hell all right,' said Spandau.

'You think this wine is okay with the chicken wings? It's a Zin.'

'It seems pretty good to me.'

'I didn't think a French wine would be up to it. I got about a hundred French wines in the basement. I'm like an addict now. Or maybe we should have gone with beer? You think wine with chicken wings is fucking pretentious, don't you?'

215

'Look, it's fine. I don't know what the current snobbery is for wine and chicken wings but it seems pretty good to me. I wouldn't worry about it.'

'Jesus, you know, my mother worked in a fucking factory. She made can openers for thirty years, you know, those kind you turn the wing around and around? I drink a nice bottle of wine and I can't get past that.'

'You're a success. Enjoy it.'

'Nouveau riche. I think everybody's watching me, waiting for me to make a mistake. Order the wrong wine, eat with the wrong fork. Hell, they are watching me. I can't eat soup with crackers in public, you know that? I can't have a fucking bowl of chili anymore, in case I get fucking crumbs all over the place and it winds up in a newspaper someplace.'

'That's the price. You're not so naive you didn't know what it was.'

'Not like this. And now with cellphone cameras, I'm afraid to take a shit in public, somebody'll shove the thing under the wall and take off running. A big picture on the internet of me on the shitter, my pants down around my ankles.'

'There are laws.'

'You going to sue some fourteen-year-old? By the time you find the goddamn thing is out there it's too late.'

'You ever been to Mexico City?' Spandau asked him. 'Take a drive along the outskirts. There are people who have to shit in public because there's no place else to go.'

216

Bobby threw down his chicken wing. 'Jesus, what are you supposed to be? The fucking voice of moral authority? My fucking conscience? I tell you how I feel and you fucking try to put it down, make it less than what it is?'

'Calm down.'

'Fuck you, man. I thought I could talk to you. I don't get to do this with anybody. I can't even talk to my fucking mother anymore, or my own fucking brother. This is exactly the sort of shit I hear. You think I don't know how lucky I am? But you think that somehow increases the number of people I can trust? How many people you think I can trust? How many friends you think I got these days?'

'I didn't mean to belittle it. I was just trying to put it into perspective. You're not the only one with problems.'

'Yeah, but those people in the slums of Mexico City, they got problems. But they got one set of problems and I got another. At least they fucking got each other. This place I'm in, it's like a fucking shark tank.'

'I'm sorry.'

'I don't want you to be sorry, I just want you to listen.'

'Look, maybe I'm the wrong guy for this.'

'Why? You're not fucking interested? You just want to do your job and go home?'

'You're talking to me because you think I'm safe, because you know I can't tell anybody, because I'm tied up the wazoo with the same fucking confidentiality clauses everybody around you signs. Why me? Look, you want a sycophant, I'm not it. You want somebody to tell you how

great you are and absolve you for being the occasional priv-
ileged asshole, it's not me.'

'I thought we were friends.'

'I'm not your friend, I'm the fucking hired help. I'm like
the maid or the gardener. I'm bought and paid for. And
frankly I resent your pretending it's otherwise. It's insult-
ing.'

'What do you want me to do? Fire you, and then maybe
we can be pals?'

'Yeah. Fire me and let's see how long this lasts.'

'No.'

'Why not?'

'Because I need you. I need you to help me get through
this.'

'Through what? This business with Richie? A thousand
people can do what I'm doing. I don't even know that I'm
accomplishing anything, except wasting your money.'

'Fuck you, then. Quit.'

'No.'

'Why not?'

'Professional pride. I'd look like an asshole.'

'Bullshit. You think that's better than getting fired?'

'Fuck you, then. I quit.'

'Fine. You know where the door is. But you really think
the next guy I hire is going to be as good as you? Be any
better than you? And the next guy, am I going to be able to
trust the next guy? The next guy might get me fucking
killed.' Spandau didn't reply. 'I fucking got you there, sport.'

'You really are a pain in the ass.'

'Admit it. We're pals.'

'No, fuck you, and fuck this whole male bonding fantasy of yours. I'll stay until we get this crap with Richie settled one way or another. That's it.'

'Sure,' said Bobby. 'You want some more wine? I think this Zinfandel is working out okay.'

Terry and Spandau sat in Pancho's Mexican Grill on Olympia. They drank beer and Terry picked compulsively at a bowl of nachos. Terry hated Mexican food. He was nervous about something, and in turn that made Spandau nervous. He kept hearing Coren's words in the back of his head. *Shit will happen one day.*

'You spoke to the girl?' Spandau asked.

'I did.'

'And?'

'Are you sure you want to involve her in this?' Terry asked him.

'She's not involved in this,' Spandau said. 'Her function is to tell Richie you were asking about her and that will be that.'

'Yeah, but what if she doesn't?'

Spandau was starting to get worried and you could tell it in his voice. 'What do you mean, what if she doesn't? She works for him, she'll look out for her own ass. Of course she'll tell him.'

'And suppose she neglects to tell him, for some reason?

219

Suppose Richie finds out? And suppose Richie doesn't believe she kept her mouth shut?'

'Look. She'll tell him. Of course she'll tell him.' Spandau looked at him. 'Shit.'

'Don't look at me that way,' Terry said.

'Ah God. You pathetic Irish bastard. I know that face. Not again.' Spandau wanted to throw the beer bottle at him. There was an ugly little tug somewhere in his chest, like the first unraveling of a tightly woven sweater.

'You should see her, David. It's poetry in motion, she is.'

'You don't even know her.'

'She's an old soul. I can see that much.'

'You didn't sleep with her, did you? Oh for Christ's sake, you did, didn't you?' His mind raced for a way he could explain this to Coren, though he knew the only course of action was not to.

'It was overcome with passion, I was.'

'Yeah, and it's overcome in a shit-storm we're all going to be if Stella finds out you were there. What the hell were you thinking? You know the position you've put her in?'

'Jesus and Mary, it's all I can think of.'

'Well, thank you. That effectively makes you pretty fucking useless, doesn't it?'

'She wants in,' Terry said to him.

'In what? What are you talking about?'

'I had a talk with her. I told her about wanting to bring Stella down. She wants to help. It's the only way she's going to get free of him as well.'

'Fucking Christ, Terry, what have you done? How much have you told her?'

'She doesn't know about you or Dye. She just knows I have a friend with money who's after Stella and setting all this up. She's inside, David. We need her. She can help us.'

'Jesus.'

'You wanted to know about the crack. Stella gets the shipments brought in on Thursday nights, to get ready for the weekend. He sends that big guy, Martin. Martin goes to fetch it.'

'What else, Terry? What did you fucking promise her?'

'That she'd be safe. That when we brought Stella down she'd be free of him.'

'You promise her money?' Spandau asked him. 'You promise her a motherfucking Rolls-Royce and a villa on the Riviera? We stand about as much chance of delivering on those promises.'

'I'm sorry, David.'

'You're out of this ballgame. Just keep a low profile while I go ahead and try to dig something up. And stay the hell away from her, right?'

'On my honor.'

'In that case we're royally fucked,' said Spandau.

Thirteen

Potts saw her again the following week, at the bank in that same shopping center.

Potts had a checking account at the bank but he was afraid to go there. When he'd opened the account they'd made him feel like shit. Potts and his piss-trickle of money, hardly enough to justify all the goddamn paperwork. And they knew it. Potts sat there in the leather chair, waiting for the pretty girl with the stiff hair and enormous tits to call him over and 'assist' him. Potts watched the solid citizenry walk past as the solid citizenry watched Potts sitting in his chair. They knew Potts was the sort of guy who was liable to break into their houses. They were right, of course, but this wasn't what Potts held against them. Potts hated them because they didn't bother to hide it. Potts wasn't important enough, Potts was beneath the line of civility. They walked past and glanced sourly at Potts and wondered what the world was coming to, this used to be such a nice bank, maybe it was time to put their money elsewhere. The girl with the big tits 'assisted' Potts nervously and quickly, wanting to have done with it, while the security guard kept looking across the room at Potts, waiting for him to pull out an Uzi and start killing people. All his life people had told Potts he was going to kill somebody but Potts couldn't see it. Potts was essentially a peaceful man but maybe he panicked too easily. He sometimes wondered if there was some core of hatred other people saw in him that he didn't get, but in the end he thought that was stupid. Potts didn't hate anybody, he didn't want to kill anybody, never had killed anybody. Mainly he just wanted to be left the fuck alone and get his daughter back. He didn't think killing anybody would fix that.

Every now and then Potts had to go to the bank to pull out cash. They'd given him one of those goddamn little cards for the machines, but Potts could never remember his code and the machines scared the shit out of him. So he'd have to go into the bank and write a check and get pocket money with them eyeing him like a mad dog. He got sick to his stomach every time he had to do it so he tried not to do it very often. On this particular day Potts had gone to the bank to pull out money and as usual emerged feeling like crap. He got on his bike and cranked it up and gave it a nice roar, which drew looks and made him feel better. He saw her pull into the parking lot and he rode over. She smiled at him through the car window and waved and Potts, feeling playful, circled her car a few times with his bike, like an Indian circling a covered wagon, close enough so she couldn't open her door. Inside Potts saw her laughing and it made him feel pretty good. He stopped the bike and she got out of the car.

'Now I know how Custer felt,' she said.

Potts made an Indian *woo-woo* sound by flapping his fingers over his lips. She laughed. It did something to Potts whenever she laughed. The bank security guard came over and glared at Potts.

'Everything okay, Miss Carlson?'

'Thank you, Mark, everything is fine.'

The guard gave Potts a warning look and went back to his post.

'I'm sorry,' she said to Potts.

'Nothing for you to be sorry about.'

'I've lived here most of my life. People get protective. I went to high school with Mark. It's nice, sometimes. But lots of times it just gets in the way. Sometimes I'd like to be anonymous, be somewhere nobody knows me. Where are you from?'

'Texas.'

'Oh, I should have guessed by the accent. You sound like a cowboy.'

'I'm no cowboy,' said Potts.

'My name is Ingrid Carlson, by the way. What's yours?'

'Potts.'

'No first name?'

'I don't like it,' said Potts.

'I bet it's religious,' said Ingrid.

'How'd you know?'

'That's just the way it works. Ezekiel or something, right? You could be an Ezekiel.'

'Yeah, close.'

'Obadiah?'

Potts laughed. 'You ain't going to get it out of me.'

'I never give up, even if I have to work my way through the Old Testament.'

Potts looked over at the guard, who was still watching him.

'Well,' said Potts, 'I reckon I ought to go. Your friend there is getting nervous.'

'We could have a coffee. That would give me time to worm that name out of you.'

'Yeah, sure, I guess.'

Potts parked the bike next to her car and they walked over to the Starbucks while the guard seethed. Potts could tell the guard liked her and he wondered if maybe they ever dated or something. But he'd called her 'Miss Carlson' so probably not. Potts liked the idea of him being jealous though.

Potts and Ingrid ordered coffees and sat at a back table.

'So what do you do?' Potts said, just to be saying something.

'I'm a teacher. I teach music.'

'Yeah, you look like a teacher.'

'I suppose I do.'

225

Fuck, thought Potts. Wrong thing to say. 'No, I mean, that's real nice. You look, I dunno, nice.'

'Nice and dull.'

'No, not that at all. I mean . . .'

'It's okay. I know I'm not the most glamorous creature in the world.'

'No, you're . . .' Potts was starting to sweat. 'All I'm going to do is say all the wrong things.'

'You can just say what's in your mind. It's okay. You're not going to hurt my feelings.'

'It's nothing bad, it's just the opposite . . .'

Ingrid smiled. She liked playing with him. 'You mean a compliment?'

'Yeah.'

'Oh, I could use a compliment,' she said. 'Now I'm not going to let you off the hook. Now you have to tell me.'

'You're laughing at me.'

'You're just incredibly nice to tease. Now what about my compliment?'

'You ain't going to make this easy.'

'Nope.'

'I like talking to you. I wanted to talk to you the first time I saw you, in the grocery.'

'Why didn't you?'

'A guy like me . . . you know. Kind of rough. I figured you'd start screaming or something.'

'Would it surprise you to know I wanted to talk to you too?'

'Yeah?'

'Rough is nice, sometimes. Attractive. Everybody I meet is so, what's the word, genteel. Let me see your hands.'

'No, they're—'

'Come on.'

Potts held out his hands. She ran her fingers over his palms. Potts felt like somebody'd stuck an electric current up his ass.

'My old man's hands,' Potts told her. 'Dumb Bastard's Hands, he used to call them. Dumb bastards who got no choice.'

'I think they're beautiful.'

'Yeah, they sure are.'

'I mean it.'

Potts pulled them away.

'Your friend Mark there, I bet he's got smooth hands, like a goddamn baby.'

'You're angry.'

'No, it's just I get around people like you and I realize who I am. I get put in my place real fast.'

'That's not what I meant and you know it.'

'I'm a motorcycle mechanic. It's an honest job. I worked hard all my life. You work hard like that, these are the kind of hands you get. There's nothing pretty about it. Look . . .'

He took her arm and ran his callused index finger down along the inside. A pink mark was left on the soft flesh. She shivered a little and Potts mistook it for disgust.

227

'That ain't pretty,' said Potts. 'That ain't what a woman wants.'

'How do you know what a woman wants?' Ingrid said.

Potts stared at her, confused. Ingrid looked at her watch.

'I have to go,' she said. 'I have to get back to my mother. I can't leave her for very long.'

'Sure,' he said, and believed he had run her off.

Then she said, quickly, 'I want you to come to my house for dinner. Will you?'

Potts wasn't sure he understood her correctly. It took him a moment to reply. 'I'm not the sort you want to socialize with. I ain't going to be some entertainment for your fancy friends.'

'No one else, just you and me. And maybe my mother, though she usually eats in her room. Will you come?'

'You serious?'

'I'm a good cook. I'll make you a pot roast. You look like a man who appreciates a good pot roast.'

Potts believed with all his heart that this was a mistake, that it would end badly, that he'd wind up in the shit somehow because of it. Everything his old man ever said about screwing around outside your class, about wanting things above your station, came roaring through his mind like a freight train. Things this good just didn't happen in real life, not to guys like Potts. If they did it was a fucking trick or a joke by God designed to take some of the starch out of you. That's what his old man always said. But Potts was a fool, Potts was a fucking idiot, Potts was going to do it again, Potts said:

'Yeah, sure. Okay.'

Ingrid took out a notebook, scribbled down her phone number and address, and handed him the note. 'Seven o'clock Tuesday night. The address and phone number are there. You won't stand me up, will you?'

'No,' said Potts, though he wasn't sure.

'Then I'll look forward to seeing you, Mr Potts,' she said.

'Potts,' said Potts. 'Just Potts.'

Fourteen

They wrapped for the day at 6.30 p.m. and by 8.00 Bobby was out of makeup and climbing into the car. He'd been on the set for fourteen hours and, in spite of the money and the Victoria's Secret girlfriend and the fame and the cars and the fancy house on a mountaintop, Spandau almost felt sorry for him. Truth was, he often felt this way about actors. Their lives were nothing like people thought, and whatever they got it was always in extremes. Either not enough or too much of everything, and both had clever ways of killing you in the end. It was ugly to starve and struggle to do your craft well and not have anyone notice or give a shit. On the other hand it was perhaps even uglier to be glutted by fame and money like some Strasbourg goose and isolated by the people around you to the point where you lost touch with whatever it was that made you an actor.

It had been a rough day. Not as rough as some, since things had gone well on set, but Mark was being a bastard about getting his number of shots in. So the days were long. Some of the actors bitched about feeling rushed but everyone knew it would have been worse if they'd started to slip over schedule. It was cheaper and easier just to go into overtime a few hours a day than eat up additional days. They'd built this into the budget but Mark was still pushing it. Mark wasn't the sort of director who'd tell the producers to go fuck themselves and he was already jumpy and looking over his shoulder at the Suits whenever they came on set. The Suits knew this and as a result spent more time irritating the hell out of Mark than they would normally. Anyway it wasn't inspiring and now everyone was dreading Wyoming where they suspected Mark was going to have a meltdown. Directors can't afford to be nervous and even when they are they can't afford to show it. It's like blood in shark-infested waters. By now it was commonly understood that there would be a face-down at some point in Wyoming when cast and crew got fed up and told Mark to kiss their asses. And Mark was going to freak because he was scared to death of the Suits and by now the Suits had his number and were happy to make him the patsy for getting this thing in well below the budget, which was actually $15 million more than they'd told Mark or admitted on paper. Hollywood films operate on a 'need to know' basis and Hollywood producers never think you need to know anything.

With the makeup off you could see the fresh lines in Bobby's face and the darkness under his eyes. He was unusually quiet and slow moving, seemed to drag himself out of the trailer and into the waiting car. Acting isn't like digging ditches for a living and most of what you do is sitting on your ass, except whenever you're sitting on your ass you're aware of what's at stake and what will happen if you can't manage to do whatever magic it is they expect you to do. Nobody is shy about telling you you're fucking up an $80-million picture. Conversely, you can't believe a word they tell you if they tell you you're good. In fact you can't believe a word anybody tells you until it's either a success or it collapses suddenly around your ears, and it is precisely this sort of anxiety that wears you down. Which was why at the end of the day hot new star Bobby Dye was slumping around like an old man.

Spandau himself was mind-numbingly bored and antsy from standing around with nothing to do all day. Yet Bobby wanted him there and Spandau didn't feel comfortable leaving him alone. Nobody was going to try to kill him, so the bodyguard part of it was a joke, but Richie Stella had been unnaturally quiet and things were bound to heat up the minute Stella found out Spandau was asking around about him. It was a dangerous game, but whatever Stella did would weaken his position and make him vulnerable. Stella operated by moving in the shadows, and whatever he did now would draw him into some degree of light. Bobby wasn't in any danger but there was a very good chance that Spandau might meet with an unfortunate accident. Spandau was far safer with Bobby – Stella would never do anything around Bobby – and this was one of the reasons he stayed close to him. That and the fact that the kid was so goddamn lonely, and Spandau liked him in spite of the dictates of common sense.

Bobby and Spandau sat in the back of the car. Duke, the driver, climbed in and looked at Bobby in the mirror. 'Where to?'

'Home,' said Bobby. 'I just want to go home.' He sat back and closed his eyes.

'I can do that,' said Duke, and started the car.

Crusoe was about to be released and showed every sign of doing far better than expected, and the studio, wide-eyed with glee, had upped their promotion to fan the flame. Bobby was locked onto the set of *Wildfire* all day and couldn't make the rounds of the talk shows, but the studio had made him accessible between takes. Bobby was furious but contractually there was nothing he could do but go along. This meant that instead of working on his lines or just chilling in his trailer, Bobby endlessly had some hair-helmeted bozo shoving a mike and camera into his face and asking him the same goddamn stupid questions. As the studio anticipated, Bobby found himself in the position of simultaneously promoting *Crusoe* and *Wildfire*, and on his own time. Half the time he didn't know which questions were being asked about which movie and he answered the wrong ones, which made him feel like an idiot. If there is an actor's idea of hell, this is it. In truth it didn't make a goddamn bit of difference what

233

he said as long as he didn't say anything negative and he got the names of the films and the stars right. Except for key words, no one is actually listening, his publicist once explained to him, only watching. Imagine your audience out there trying to heat up their frozen entrees and swatting at children. As long as he could keep smiling and looking good, everything would be fine.

The lot was quiet and everything was fine until they rolled through the gates. The guard said to Duke, 'You got some fans out there,' and Duke took it to mean a few desperate autograph hounds, which was normal. Instead the car came off the lot and was instantly engulfed in a swarm of screaming bodies.

Nobody was prepared for this. It was 8.00 at night on a weekday. But the extra publicity had worked okay and either the studio or somebody inside had leaked when Bobby would be coming off the lot. They were waiting for him. Duke stopped the car, unable to move without running over someone. Once the car stopped it got worse, and they were all around the car, on the car, trying to get in the car. The heavy vehicle lurched from side to side as faces and hands pressed up against every inch of glass surface. The screaming itself was maddening and the contorted faces just inches away behind thin glass was like a Francis Bacon-designed nightmare. Inside the car they heard 'We love you Bobby we love you' but there was instead something malevolent about it, as if they'd hurt him if they could, rip him apart and devour him in their affection, ingest him to make him part of them. Sometimes through the spaces between the bodies you could see the flash of cameras. A photo op. Crazed Fans Eat *Crusoe* Heartthrob. How many more tickets would this sell? How many more tickets do you need?

Spandau had been through this before with other actors, but usually at premieres and other planned events where it was expected and could be controlled. Even then you felt vulnerable, you always felt vulnerable, but after a very long couple of minutes it was obvious no one was coming to help them.

'Jesus, Duke, get the fucking car going!' said Bobby.

'I don't want to kill anybody. They're hanging on the front and back.'

'Well do something!'

'Maybe if you went out there and signed some autographs or something.'

'I'm not going out there, are you crazy?' Bobby yelled at him. 'Call security, for chrissake!'

Spandau was laughing in spite of himself, though now he was nervous as well.

'What the hell are you laughing at?' Bobby said to him.

'The absurdity of this never ceases to amaze me.'

'You're my goddamn bodyguard, why don't you go out there?'

'Are you nuts?' laughed Spandau. 'Look at those faces. Anybody opens a door and they're all going to be sitting in your lap.'

Bobby started laughing too. 'This is ridiculous.'

Duke called lot security on his cellphone. 'Hi, this is Duke Slater, I'm Bobby Dye's driver. We got a problem out at the Pico entrance. We were just leaving and we got swarmed by fans. They're all over the car and I can't move it. I don't want anybody to get hurt, can you guys send somebody out?'

Duke listened, then hung up.

'That's just great,' said Duke.

'What?' said Bobby.

'They're sending some security guys to the gate but it's not likely they're going to do anything. We're not on Fox property. Technically it's a job for the Beverly Hills PD.'

'You're shitting me. I'm making a goddamn movie for these people!'

'Fox has no authority, and if they try to break up the crowd and somebody gets hurt, they get sued.'

'So what the hell are we supposed to do? I can't fucking wait here all night and they're going to be in the fucking car in a minute.'

'If I move the car, I'm going to hurt somebody.'

Spandau is laughing. Bobby is laughing. Duke starts to laugh. They all just sit there.

'What the fuck do we do?'

'We just sit here until the cavalry comes,' said Duke.

Bobby looked out the window at the faces. Many of them, male and female, kissed the windows.

'This is surreal,' said Bobby.

'Yeah,' said Spandau, 'but one day it won't be there and you'll miss it.'

'Nah,' Bobby said to him. 'I mean, this is what it takes for now. But eventually I don't want to do this. This whole star trip is bullshit. I'm going to direct my first film, did I tell you? I've got it all set up with Jurado. I finish *Wildfire*, I'm going to do a small film. Something like Cassavetes? You know Cassavetes? Cassavetes is the fucking shit, man. Cassavetes is my hero. Maybe I'll stop acting altogether. You know, get into a position where I got some control. Produce, direct. Stop being a meat puppet.'

Spandau tried to stop thinking about the number of actors who'd said this to him. Big ones, little ones. In the beginning all they want to do is be loved as actors, and after a while all they want to do is get out of it and manipulate somebody else for a change.

A very pretty girl, maybe eighteen, wrote her phone number in lipstick on the window. She smiled at Bobby and kissed the window next to the number, leaving the sexy imprint of her lips.

'She's kind of cute,' said Bobby.

'She's not bad,' agreed Duke. 'Too bad we can't think of some way to get her into the car. Well, you've got her number.'

About that time another female fan pushed the pretty girl away. She smeared the phone number and tried to replace it with her own. This one wasn't as hot.

'Too bad,' said Duke.

'Get away, you scurvy bimbo,' Bobby said to her quietly through the glass. 'Bring back the other one.'

The crowd began to thin away from the car, and it became obvious that somebody was doing something. Security guards from the lot wedged themselves between the car and the crowd and pushed them back.

'We catch you guys at a bad time or something?' Duke said through an inch of open window.

'We can't just run onto the street and start shoving people around,' said the guard. 'We got it under control now. You can roll.'

'We can roll,' Duke said to Bobby as he closed the window.

'We're rolling,' said Bobby. 'Oh boy.'

The car inched forward until it was clear of the crowd and Duke pressed the gas.

'Fucking unreal,' said Bobby as he turned to look at the crowd.

'You're a star, man,' said Duke. 'They love you.'

'They love me,' repeated Bobby. 'Right. I need to remember that.'

Fifteen

The guy on the skateboard was in his early twenties. He didn't do any fancy tricks but he was fast and he pushed the board along at a good click. He came sailing down the sidewalk on Richie Stella's street when, for some reason, he decided to hop off the sidewalk into the gutter and then hop back onto the sidewalk. He almost made it, too, but the back wheels didn't quite clear the curb and he went down just behind Richie Stella's black Audi parked in Richie Stella's driveway. The board went sailing on past the car but the skate-rat didn't.

Richie himself happened to be standing near the front window and saw all this. He went quickly out the door not with the intention of helping the skate-rat but with the intention of breaking the kid's legs if he'd damaged the car.

'Hey, you little shit!' Richie called from the front porch.

The skate-rat staggered up from behind the car, holding his elbow.

'Stay the hell away from my car,' Richie said to him. 'You and your goddamn skateboards, you're gonna dent it!'

'Hey mister, I'm okay,' said the skate-rat. 'I've just lacerated my fucking elbow, thanks for your concern.'

Richie said, 'Just stay the hell away from my car, you little faggot,' and went back inside.

The skate-rat flipped him off, then limped over to his board and skated away. Terry was sitting in his own car down the street and around the corner. The skate-rat whizzed up to Terry's car, did a skid-stop, flipped the board into the air and caught it, all inches from Terry's window.

'Charming,' Terry said to him. 'But at your age don't you ever want a real car?'

'Man,' said the skate-rat, 'I deserve to get compensated for this shit. Look what I did to my arm. This falling shit, I should get hazardous duty pay or something.'

'Nobody told you to fall. How do we know you did it on purpose? How can we be sure you're just not a shitty skateboarder? Think of it from our perspective.'

'A little something extra in the paycheck, is all I'm saying. This is above and beyond the call.'

'I'll talk to Coren,' Terry said. 'Did you attach it?'

'Of course I attached it. This is why you guys pay me the big bucks, right?'

'You turn it on?'

'Gee, duh . . .' said the skate-rat, crossing his eyes. 'Talk to Coren. Get me some extra bread or tell him I ain't doing this shit no more. It's fucking dangerous.'

'You're bleeding on my door. Now go away like a good boy and bleed elsewhere.'

'And tell Walter we're in the twenty-first century now. This Victorian Radio Shack shit he's using is an embarrassment. That thing was big enough to have tubes in it. Tell him to pony up some bucks so we can look like pros, for chrissake.'

The boy skated away. Terry sighed and thought about his own youth. Nobody had skateboards in Derry in those days. Nobody knew what a fucking skateboard was, and wouldn't have cared if they did. Terry's youth was about smoking and trying to get laid and drinking until you puked and trying to see if you could clout a Brit greenie with a brick without getting caught or shot. Life was so innocent in those days. Terry sighed again and looked down at a laptop computer sitting in the passenger seat. He typed in the Internet address Spandau had given him. A map appeared with a small dot blinking in the middle of it. Terry settled back in his seat to wait. It was Thursday. The car would be moving soon. Terry didn't trust technology but he was all for anything that made his life easier.

The dot began to move a couple of hours later.

Terry watched the dot move almost imperceptibly toward him and glanced up to see the Audi, with Martin behind the wheel, glide past. Thankfully Martin was in his own little world and didn't notice him. Or at least

Terry hoped like hell he didn't, or things were liable to get complicated. Terry gave him a good lead and then followed.

The system was remarkably easy to use, except for Terry having to watch the screen and still drive the bloody car. A couple of times Terry overshot a turn – you couldn't really tell the distance to a turn, just that a turn was coming – and had to backtrack. It was worse through town, since Martin apparently had his own unique shortcuts, but once Martin turned onto the interstate life got easier. Terry had his iPod jacked into the car's sound system and listened to Bach's *Goldberg Variations* as the flashing dot led him out of LA and east toward the desert. Martin stopped twice, and both times Terry thought Martin was making a pickup, but it was only at gas stations to pee. Poor Martin had something wrong with his plumbing, or maybe the whole business just made him nervous. Terry drove past and found a discreet place to pull over and wait until Martin caught up again. It was like playing leapfrog, and it amused Terry to think that you could probably do a decent job of tailing somebody even if you were ahead of them. There was a lot about this job that Terry found amusing. He had no great hopes for human nature and was rarely disappointed or shocked by what he saw people do. He took these occasional jobs for Spandau and Coren as much for the entertainment value as the money. Terry didn't like being bored and would complicate his own life unnecessarily if he wasn't amused. Then again, the whole of fucking Ireland was like that, so he came by it honestly.

Martin took highway 10 out through Rancho Cucamonga and Redlands to just beyond Cabazon. Terry was a mile or so behind him when he noticed the dot veer to the right and off the highway into a blank area. Martin was either flying or he'd driven onto a road too small for the chart. Terry sped up and missed the road the first time. The dot was heading south and Terry was still going east. He turned around and found the road, hardly more than a dirt path. In the distance he could see the cloud of dust kicked up by the Audi. There was no cover to speak of and Terry's own dust-cloud could be spotted as well. Whoever had picked the location knew what he was doing. Terry waited for the dot to stop moving. It did finally, about three miles in. The Audi had disappeared around some hills a mile ahead. Terry decided to take his chances and moved his car at a snail's pace down the dirt road, kicking up as little dust as possible. He was reasonably safe anyway until he rounded those hills. Then it was anybody's guess. Meanwhile he prayed Martin wasn't in a hurry to follow the road back. Meeting Martin head on would be interesting to explain, and there was no place to hide.

Terry was lucky. The road turned around one set of hills and then, about a mile on, around another. Terry decided not to push his luck. He pulled off into the second hills and parked the car where it wouldn't be seen. From the trunk he took a knapsack he always kept packed – goodies for all occasions – and a pair of strong Zeiss binoculars. He climbed up into the rocks and from there could see, half a mile on, a small house trailer sitting in the open. An SUV and the Audi were parked in front. Terry looked around him to make sure he wasn't putting his ass down on a scorpion or a rattlesnake, then made himself comfortable. The contents of the knapsack included a thermos of coffee, bottled water, toilet tissue, snacks, and a paperback of *The Silmarillion*. Terry popped the iPod buds into his ears and listened to Enya while he read, for maybe the ninth time, about the history of wizards and orcs. Every now and then he glanced at the trailer. It wasn't going anywhere.

Martin was inside for just over an hour. He came out of the trailer carrying a brown paper grocery bag, and followed by a tall, skinny geeky-looking fellow in a knitted cap. They talked for a moment at the car, then Martin drove away and the geeky-looking guy went back inside. There didn't seem to be anybody else around.

Terry had decided to let Martin go. Terry'd done his job, he'd followed Martin to the source, and he knew where Martin was going next – right back to LA and Richie. Terry wanted to see what was inside that trailer. He was pretty sure he knew already. Terry didn't think the geeky guy lived inside the place. The trailer was small and rusty and dented and the windows were covered from the inside with cardboard. It was no palace. It was the sort of place you got out of as soon as you could. At least Terry hoped so. He didn't fancy sitting here all night. It would get cold and windy and he couldn't use a book light to keep reading.

It was dusk when the Geek came out of the trailer, locked the door, and climbed into the SUV and drove away. Terry waited until the sun went down, then, shouldering the knapsack, picked his way toward the trailer. He checked the perimeter of the place. A propane tank attached at one end and a tiny gas-run generator but no electrical wires or plumbing running in. The place was completely off the grid and could be moved or abandoned in a heartbeat. When Terry was satisfied there was no alarm system, he took out a small crowbar and jimmied the door. He waved his flashlight around. The place was as much of a shithole inside as out. A rickety kitchen table and a couple of chairs. An old refrigerator, damp and empty except for some cans of beer, a loaf of bread and some dubious lunchmeat. A small, new and efficient-looking four-burner stove. Lots of pots of various sizes and pans with their inside bottoms well darkened, three cases of bottled purified water, and ten boxes of baking soda. Plastic Ziploc sandwich bags. He looked into cupboards and nooks and crannies, then ran his hands over the surface of the countertops. As clean as a hospital. They were careful about the cocaine. Cocaine was expensive. Terry got out his digital camera and took a lot of photographs. Not much legal proof of anything, though maybe you could scrape the pots if you cared to get scientific. There was no point. Spandau didn't need legal proof, he wasn't a cop. Terry had found the source and that was all he needed. Terry felt very proud of himself. Spandau would be happy.

He would have been significantly less pleased with himself, however, had he noticed the tiny red dot in an upper corner of the trailer. This was a camera, and Terry was starring in his own reality TV show.

Sixteen

The disreputable Potts drove his disreputable pickup truck to Ingrid's house. It was exactly the sort of place he'd imagined she would live. A nice, quiet street with postage-stamp green lawns, flowerbeds and wooden houses. A Leave it to Beaver neighborhood, about as familiar to Potts as the far side of Jupiter. He drove past her house three times, afraid to pull in, waiting for the Neighborhood Watch to call him in to the cops. No mob with axes and clubs blocked the street. He parked in front of the house. He had a box of candy and some flowers. He thought about bringing wine, he knew people did that, but he knew shit about wine and you could make a moderately smaller ass out of yourself by bringing the wrong candy and the wrong flowers. He'd resigned himself to the fact that whatever he did would be wrong, and that the evening was never going to be repeated. Still, you had to try. Potts knocked on the door.

Ingrid wore a blue flowered dress. Potts was surprised by the amount of skin showing. She opened the door and the first thing Potts took in was her bare arms and the V of a neckline that lost itself, as did Potts, in the shadow between her breasts. In truth it was nothing she couldn't have worn to a church social, but Potts had always seen her looking so prim and so proper and so, well, covered. Potts had imagined her a kind of old maid. She wasn't. Potts realized his eyes were ranging up and down her body and he felt himself going red. Ingrid didn't seem to mind.

'Mr Potts,' she said, giving him that smile. 'You've indeed showed up. Please do come in. And flowers and candy! How gallant!'

She ushered him inside. The house was dark and cool. Old heavy furniture. Some lace, some knick-knacks. Books. A goddamn baby grand piano. The smell of food cooking. A woman's place. No hint of a man in sight. An old maid could live here. Potts looked at her shoulders, the back of her long neck, her hips. He couldn't get one vision of her to merge with the other.

'I was waiting for the sound of the motorcycle,' she said to him.

'I drove the truck.'

'Don't you look handsome!' she said, looking him up and down. Potts had worn his one suit, the one he'd bought for the custody hearing over his daughter, the custody hearing that never happened. 'Come into the living room.'

Potts sat down on a rose-covered sofa. Rounded copper tacks outlined the frame, held the upholstery on. It felt solid, old, full of history and class. Potts took comfort in nervously rubbing the tacks at the end of the armrest with the tops of his fingers.

'The flowers and candy, thank you, they're lovely.'

'I was thinking maybe I should have bought wine. But I didn't know, like, if you drank wine, and, anyway, I don't know anything about wine, I'd a brought the wrong stuff anyway, probably.'

'No, you did well. These flowers are beautiful.'

'Ingrid,' called a woman's voice from the back of the house.

'It's Mother,' said Ingrid. 'She's curious about anyone who visits. She may join us for dinner. I hope you don't mind.'

'Ingrid,' the voice said again.

'She has Alzheimer's,' said Ingrid. 'She goes in and out. It can be distracting. Clear one minute and off the next. It's sad. She was a college professor. She's published books. She was an expert on Brahms.'

'Ingrid.'

'Excuse me, please,' Ingrid said and left the room. Potts had no idea who Brahms was.

Ingrid brought Mrs Carlson into the living room. She looked like a perfectly normal old lady to Potts. She was nattily dressed and had a string of pearls around her neck and her gray hair was done up neatly. She had lipstick on and her eyes were bright and she greeted Potts with a smile and her hand extended palm down. She looked kind of regal and Potts wondered for a second if he was supposed to kiss it but, no, it was for shaking. Potts shook it.

'Mother, this is Mr Potts. He's having dinner with us. I told you about him.'

'Potts?' repeated Mrs Carlson.

'Yes, Mother, I told you about him. He's staying for dinner.'

'Oh good.'

Mrs Carlson went over and turned on the television. There was a show about something called a meerkat. Mrs Carlson was immediately absorbed in it.

Ingrid gave Potts an apologetic look. 'Can we turn this down?' she said to her mother.

'What?'

'The TV, Mother. Can we turn it down a little?'

'I can't hear it.'

'You can hear it, Mother.'

'There's never anything on,' said Mrs Carlson. 'I never like anything they have on anymore.'

Ingrid turned down the TV volume to almost nil. The old lady didn't seem to notice and kept watching the screen.

'Would you like a glass of wine, Mr Potts?'

'Thank you.'

'I can't keep calling you Mr Potts.'

'Just Potts is fine.'

'It still doesn't work for me,' Ingrid said.

Ingrid left the room. Potts watched the old lady, who appeared to have forgotten he existed. Her lips moved, as if she were talking silently to someone. Ingrid returned carrying glasses of wine for herself and for Potts. She handed him the glass.

'Red okay?' said Ingrid.

'What?'

'Red wine. I got it to go with the pot roast.'

'Oh, I don't know anything about wine.'

'Red usually goes with red meat. White wine with fish.'

'Yeah? I usually just drink beer.'

'I'm sorry, would you prefer a beer?'

'No, the wine is fine.'

Ingrid held up her glass in a toast. 'Especially mine,' she said, and it took Potts a second to realize she'd made a rhyme, a joke. Ingrid took a sip of her wine. Potts laughed nervously and took a sip of his. He didn't like wine.

'Maybe this was a mistake,' Potts heard himself saying.

'No.'

'I don't know about the wine, I don't know which fork to hold, I don't know any of that.'

Ingrid said, 'There's only one fork. One fork, one knife, one spoon. A plate, a glass. This isn't a test. I invited you here because I wanted you to be here.'

'Angelo,' said Mrs Carlson. She was looking at Potts.

'Who, Mother?'

'Angelo. You remember Angelo.'

'No, Mother, I don't remember Angelo.'

'Your father hated Angelo. I almost married him.'

Ingrid gave Potts a surprised look.

'Well, this is something new. You almost married Angelo?'

'You'd better get him out of here. Henry will be angry when he comes back,' she said with some gravity.

'This is Mr Potts, Mother.'

'I can't see you anymore,' Mrs Carlson said to Potts. 'I'm promised now to Henry.'

'This is Mr Potts. Mr Potts, Mother, not Angelo.'

Mrs Carlson became agitated. 'He'd better leave, I'm telling you! Henry has threatened to shoot him!'

'All right, Mother. Don't worry.'

'Oh lord,' said Mrs Carlson, 'I don't want to make him mad! I hate it when he's mad!'

Ingrid went over to her mother. She took her hand and helped her up out of the chair.

'It's okay. Why don't we just go to your room, you can watch TV in there.' She started to lead Mrs Carlson from the room.

'Tell Angelo I'm sorry, will you?' Mrs Carlson said.

'I'll tell him.'

'He was good to me. You tell him.'

'I will, Mother.'

Ingrid led her mother from the room. She came back a minute later.

'Sorry about that.'

'No, it's okay, said Potts. 'She seems like a real sweet lady.'

Ingrid sat back down, picked up her wine.

'She is. She was the best mother in the world. The gentlest woman you ever met. It's sad, all this. To watch this. It's so unfair.'

Potts didn't know what to say, sipped his wine. Which he despises.

'So it's just you and me for dinner. I'll take a plate to her room.' She stood up. 'Well the pot roast is done. We can eat now, if you're ready. I hope you're hungry. I made enough for an army.'

'Yeah, I could eat,' said Potts.

They sat in the dining room, at right angles to each other at the end of a long table. In spite of his nerves, Potts was hungry. Maybe it was the wine, which was tasting better by now. The food was excellent and Potts chowed down pretty heavily.

'Is it okay?' Ingrid asked.

Potts realized he was gobbling the food down too fast.

'I'm sorry, it's just . . . Yeah, it's real good. I don't know the last time I ever had a meal like this. I guess not since I left home. My mama could cook. Nothing this good though.'

'You come from a large family?'

'Just me and a sister.'

'Are you close?'

'We don't talk. Leastways not unless we have to.'

'I'm sorry,' Ingrid said, and meant it.

'I don't miss it.'

'No, I mean that family is important. Everyone needs somebody. I have Mama, for instance. Even the way she is now, it's something. Maybe the mind is going but it's still the same heart, isn't it?'

Again, Potts had no idea what to say. He stared down at the food.

'I don't mean to make you uncomfortable.'

Nothing. Potts wants to say something but can't. What the hell are you supposed to say?

'I wanted you to meet her,' Ingrid said. 'She's not always like this. Sometimes she's worse, sometimes she's better.'

'She seems like a real nice old lady. I'm sorry she's ill.'

'I wonder if we'll ever know about Angelo? It sounds racy. This is the first I've heard of him. Maybe Angelo is the great love of her life. I don't think my father was. He was a good man, but I don't see him as anyone's great passion. But Angelo. Ah, my mother and some dark Latin lover, some torrid affair carried out under the noses of her puritan family. They were bluebloods, and bluestockings, old back East family. Oh yes, Angelo would have driven them crazy.'

She looks at Potts, who's watching her talk.

'I'm sorry. Maybe it's the wine. And I rarely get to talk to grown-ups. Not for a while, anyway.'

'I like hearing you talk,' Potts told her.

'Oh I'm a talker,' said Ingrid. 'I'll talk your leg off.'

Potts shook his leg. 'Still attached.'

'Oh my, Mr Potts, you made a joke.'

'Yes, ma'am.'

'Could it be that you're actually relaxing a little?'

'Yes, ma'am, I guess.'

'Would you like some dessert? Apple pie. I made it myself, and I'm not shy about accepting compliments on it.'

'Yes, ma'am, that sounds real good. You want me to help you with these dishes?'

'Thank you for the offer, Mr Potts, but we have this amazing new invention. It's called a dishwasher. But you can, if you don't mind, bring the rest of that pot roast into the kitchen. I'll wrap it up before it dries out. You're taking some home. I insist on it.'

'Thank you, yeah, that would be real nice.'

Potts followed her into the kitchen carrying the pot roast. He sat it on the counter and watched Ingrid scrape the plates into the garbage. When she bent over the front of her dress opened and Potts could see the thin nylon bra with a tiny bow near the top and the darkness of nipple through the fabric. Potts watched her rinse the dishes and put them in the dishwasher. She moved as if he wasn't there, or else had been there all her life.

'*Voilà*. And now for some coffee and that pie,' she said.

She started the coffee in the machine. She sliced the pie and licked some apple filling from her finger. She was aware that Potts was staring at her, watching every move she made.

'I'm sorry, Mother always taught me I should never . . .'
Potts had no idea what she was going to say. She let the
sentence just end and hang there. She and Potts stared at
each other.

'I better go,' said Potts.

'What do you want to do?' she asked him.

'I best be going,' Potts said again, but didn't move.

'No,' she said to him. 'Do what you want to do. Do what
is in your mind.'

Potts put out his hand and touched her face. She took the
hand and slid it beneath her dress, his hand enveloping the
nylon and the tiny bow and the tip of her breast growing
hard beneath his palm. She raised the skirt and put his hand
between her legs. Potts let it rest there, cupping her, felt the
moist warmth of her fill his hand. Ingrid leaned against him,
her hands around his waist, her cheek pressed against his
shoulder. She led him slowly out of the kitchen and down
the hallway, past the room where the old lady sat watching
television, mouthing words to herself, and into the bedroom.
Ingrid undressed slowly and allowed Potts to watch. Now,
she was saying to him, this is who I truly am, and he finally
felt the two versions of her in his head come together. She
crossed to Potts who held her naked and then she began to
undress him. He let her do whatever she wanted and she
pulled him into the bed and slid beneath him and Potts was
lost, oh so lost, put one arm beneath her neck and the other
hand beneath her hips and tried not with just his cock but
his entire body to enter her, to pass through flesh and into

her core. He buried his face in her neck in a dimple where sweat gathered and he inhaled her, tasted her and ended with a violence that left him weak and helpless and not a little frightened. Potts lay on his back, her hand on his chest, head on his shoulder, and can feel the burning lines on his back from her scratches and the place at the base of his neck where she bit. She is warm and soft and he can feel every inch of her along the side of his body. Jesus.

'I'm not beautiful,' she says. 'I know that.'

'I think you're beautiful,' Potts said. 'I think you're the most beautiful thing I've ever seen.'

'I've been with other men. Too many, I think. I've done things with them, because of them, that I'm ashamed of. But I'll tell you, if you want to know.'

'I don't need to hear it.'

'I don't want you to think I'm something I'm not.'

'I already know what I need to know.'

'What's that?' she asked.

Potts propped himself up on his elbow and looked her in the eyes. 'That you're a good woman. Neither one of us is an angel. I've done time, for one thing. I did five years in Texas for armed robbery. That make a difference to you?'

'No.'

'You think you'll want to see me again?'

'I don't want to let go of you now,' she said.

Potts heard the sound of his old man's voice. He pushed it away.

Seventeen

Bobby Dye was having a barbecue at the top of the world.

It seemed like it to Spandau anyway. It was a crisp sunny day, and from the deck of Bobby's pool, LA stretched out forever and could be tolerated because you were one of the gods and above it all. Two budding culinary geniuses manned the giant grills, food was brought round by acting students going through their obligatory waitress phase and who were nearly as pretty as the models who disported themselves in and out of the water. The males were all friends of Bobby's – a few minor actors, some musicians, drinking and drug buddies from the old days. No one from the film cast or crew. It was the weekend and Bobby was letting his hair down. This was about relaxation, the kind of down-home event where you could say what you want. You couldn't, really, but Bobby enjoyed the illusion that you could. The models were friends of Irina Gorbacheva, Bobby's girlfriend, and to the utter joy of Bobby's pals were competing to see who could shove the most body into the least amount of cloth. A few had already given up and abandoned the top half. Rock music blared from the speakers and, while booze was everywhere, many were bright-eyed from other sources.

Irina was tall and blonde and perfect. She knew this as well as anybody and was generous about being stared at. She was far and away the most beautiful woman there, and had planned it that way as well as Bobby had planned his own superior presence. Only an idiot sets a stage to their disadvantage. Spandau felt guilty about watching her, but so was everybody else, and anyway she liked being watched. Irina wanted to be a movie star and as long as people couldn't help staring there was hope. She hadn't an ion of talent and sounded like a fluffier version of Natasha in the Rocky & Bullwinkle cartoons, but then so did Arnold Schwarzenegger and look how he turned out. Spandau was standing off to one side drinking a beer when Irina drifted over. She took the beer from his hand and took a pull of it and made a face.

'Russians like vodka,' she said.

'So I've heard.'

'A nice life, huh?' she said, sweeping her hand around in a grand gesture. 'Shitload better than Petersburg.' She was from Minsk but someone had told her that Minsk didn't sound as good.

'It's tolerable,' said Spandau.

'So if somebody shoots at Bobby, will you jump in front of the bullet?'

'Is that what I'm supposed to do? Jesus, nobody told me.'

'You're a very funny man.'

'It's a gift.'

'Lots of pretty girls around and you stand here drinking beer. At least one of them wants to fuck you. Are you gay?'

'I was wounded in the war. Caught a landmine between the legs.'

'That's too bad.'

She walked over to a deckchair. She looked at Spandau, smiled, and took off her top. She draped herself along the chair in the sun. Ginger appeared with a plate of food.

'Shy little thing, isn't she?' Ginger said.

'How long have she and Bobby been together?'

'A couple of months. They met on the set. Jurado introduced them. I had the pleasure of watching it. She sort of went up to Bobby and grabbed him by the ear and said, "You're mine now." He didn't have a chance.'

'He's a big boy.'

'No he's not. He's in love with her. Can you imagine that? Somewhere in his head, he imagines she's going to settle down and be a housewife like June Cleaver. No, I'm sorry, Miss Gorbacheva has other plans.'

'Which are?'

'Well, we want to be a star, darling, don't we? Why else is she here?'

Bobby popped up, looking nervous. Ginger faded away. 'You having a good time?' Bobby asked Spandau.

'The view is nice.'

'Yeah. It's like a fucking Victoria's Secret convention. How come you're not hitting on something?'

'I'm out of my league here.'

'Bullshit. You're my friend. You're in the circle now.'

'What's the matter?'

Bobby was dancing in place. 'I'm about to piss all over myself. There's a fucking mile line to the downstairs bathroom.'

'Use the upstairs.'

'I can't.'

'Why not?'

Bobby stared at him. At that moment Spandau too envisioned the dead girl.

'I'm looking for a new place. I can't stay here. It's haunted now. I fucking can't do it.'

Bobby looked around and spotted Irina topless on the deckchair.

'Fucking shit.'

Bobby went over to her and said something angry. She argued back. He said something else sharply and she shrugged but put on her top. Bobby came back over to Spandau.

'They got no fucking shame,' said Bobby.

'Bobby, there are photos of her all over the place.'

'Yeah, I know, but that doesn't mean I have to like it. It's one thing in a magazine, it's another thing her waving them around in front of my friends.' By now Bobby was looking desperate. 'This is my fucking house and I have to go piss in the bushes. Jesus.'

Bobby wandered off to find a spot to pee. Spandau found a chair at the edge of everything and finished his beer and then had another one, entertained by the beautiful in frolic. When he went into the house there was indeed a line for the downstairs bathroom. He went upstairs and knocked on the toilet door. A woman's voice said, 'Yeah, just a minute . . .' Spandau waited and heard voices coming from the master bedroom, the one Bobby was now afraid to sleep in. The voices sounded familiar and Spandau moved nearer to the not quite closed bedroom door and saw Irina and Frank Jurado having an intimate tête-à-tête. They were talking softly and Irina was pouting at him. Jurado smiled, not taking it seriously, and pinched her nipple through the skimpy bikini top. Irina laughed but didn't move his hand away.

The bathroom door behind Spandau opened and a blonde came out, sniffing and rubbing her gums with her finger. She smiled at Spandau and brushed past him while inside the bathroom yet another model was dusting off the countertop and dropping a vial into her purse. She too smiled at him and went downstairs. He looked at the toilet and the sink and remembered Bobby's description of the dead girl. Spandau saw her sitting there, limp, the spike dangling from a blue-tinged thigh. He closed the door without going in.

Irina came out of the bedroom and gave him a playful

poke in the ribs as she undulated past. Spandau went to the bedroom door. Jurado sat on the edge of the bed, talking into his mobile phone. He looked up at him but didn't interrupt his conversation. Spandau went back downstairs.

Spandau was standing in front of a large bookshelf looking at Bobby Dye's library. There were books on philosophy mixed in with movie-star bios and books on film and directing. Several books on John Cassavetes. A copy of Sun-Tzu's *The Art of War*. Spandau opened it up. Inscribed on the title page was, 'To my Shining Star / Let's make a movie! / Best wishes / Richie.' Jurado was looking over his shoulder.

'Where's Bobby?' Jurado asked him.

'Last time I saw him, he was peeing behind a rosebush.'

'Aren't you supposed to be guarding his life or something? You don't appear to be taking any of this very seriously.'

'The biggest threat to Bobby right now is getting stung on the dick by a bumblebee. Not much I can do about that.'

'You think about our little talk?' said Jurado.

'Not really.'

'Has he talked to you about the *Crusoe* premiere?'

'Yeah.'

'You're not necessary. We've got our own security.'

'He wants me there.'

'Well, he's the star, right?' Jurado said.

'That's right.'

'You better hope nothing happens to him, cowboy.' He gave Spandau a friendly pat on the back. 'Tell Bobby I had to go. Nice party though, and thank him for inviting me.' Jurado made his way, fashion model by fashion model, to the front door.

When Spandau got back to the pool, Bobby was standing at the bar knocking back a vodka. He ordered another and sank that as well.

'You have a hard time watering the plants?' Spandau said to him.

'Fuck you.'

'I'm not your whipping boy, chief. I'm here because you asked me. If you're having a hard time, take it out on somebody who likes kissing your ass, not me.'

'Fucking coke-head cunt.'

'We're not talking about me this time, are we?'

'I look around and the bitch is gone. Somebody told me she was upstairs in the bathroom doing lines. She promised she wouldn't.'

'Aren't you being a little naive about all this?'

'Don't you fucking start. Not you too.'

'I don't want to see you get hurt.'

'Mind your own goddamn business.'

Bobby motioned for a third vodka. 'You seen Frank? Somebody said he was here.'

'He left. He told me to thank you for inviting him.'

'Fucking bastard. We were going to talk about my film, the one I'm going to direct. I got this idea for a script. I want to do it in South Central. Shoot it in 16mm, handheld camera, no fucking actors, man, just real people. Fucking gritty.'

'That ought to wow them at the box office. People just love gritty.'

'What have you got a bug up your ass about?'

'All this physical perfection is starting to get to me. I'm going back to the guest cottage, unless *Cosmopolitan* has decided to do a shoot in there.'

He left Bobby drinking at the bar and went back to his room. He thought about inviting one of the girls but the idea of having sex with a stoned woman, however beautiful, didn't do it for him. He missed Dee. He thought about getting shitfaced drunk himself and calling her. Dee would talk to him and in the end he'd only say something to compromise them both. She deserved to be happy, she deserved to choose what she wanted. It wasn't him. He went back to the guesthouse and locked the door and lay down on the bed and closed his eyes. He drifted off into a fuzzy sleep and woke with a dark-haired model scratching on the window and smiling at him. But perhaps he was only dreaming. He never knew anymore.

Eighteen

'Anybody ever seen this fuck before?' Richie Stella said.

They were in Richie's basement watching his widescreen plasma TV, where a grainy but easily recognizable Terry McGuinn moved around in the crack-lab trailer. Martin and the Geek looked at each other like Laurel and Hardy.

'I dunno,' said the Geek. 'I never seen him. Got to be a cop.'

'Cop my ass,' said Richie. 'You hear any sirens? Cops find a crack lab, it's like going to the fucking circus. He was a cop, he wouldn't a waited until you left. Now it's all inadmissible, they wouldn't have shit. It ain't no cop.'

'Then who?' said the Geek, and immediately knew it was the wrong thing to say.

'How the fuck do I know?' bellowed Richie. 'Ask numbnuts here, he's the guy who brought him.'

'Hey! How do you know it was me?' Martin protested.

Richie tossed him the homing device in the magnetic collar. 'Because it's fucking always you. Because we found this on the car. You weren't my cousin, I swear I would blow your fucking brains out.' To the Geek he said, 'You close it down?'

'Burned to a cinder. Not a trace, nothing, and no way to trace it. We're set up again in the place out near Barstow. Business as usual.'

'I'm sorry, Richie,' said Martin. 'I really am.'

'You want to make it up to me? Find out who this bastard is.'

'Sure, Richie. But how?'

'Get a still of this guy made from the video, show it around. This guy don't know that we nailed him, so he won't be hiding. Ask around the club, but be fucking discreet, will you? You know what discreet means? I've seen this guy in the club. I know I've seen him in the club.'

'What then?' asked Martin.

'You just fucking find him,' said Richie.

'Why don't we go to Cabo,' Richie said to her. 'You ever been to Cabo?'

They were in the office of the Voodoo Room. It was ten o'clock at night and Richie had been hanging around all evening. Most of the time you couldn't get him in the office with a cattle-prod and the employees were just as happy, because whenever he did show up it was to rant and rave about something pointless and chew asses indiscriminately

267

and then fire somebody. Usually it was the wrong person, but after Richie had canned someone he was happy for a few weeks and nobody saw him. Allison dreaded him coming into the office like everybody else, and recently he had taken to coming in almost daily. It was driving her mad. He'd follow her around playing grab-ass when he could, making it hard for her to get anything done. Allison was good at running the place, she liked the work, and thought maybe, one of these days, she'd get away from Richie and manage a place where the owner didn't try to grab her tits every five minutes. She'd been working there for six months and so far had managed not to sleep with him. But Richie was getting antsy now, which was the reason he was underfoot.

'I don't have time to go to Cabo,' Allison said to him. 'I'm too busy running your club.'

'I can find a hundred people to run this bar.'

'Great, swell,' she said. 'Then what the hell do you need me for?'

'You know why I need you.'

'I'm not your girl, Richie.'

'Sure you are,' he said.

She was at the desk, trying to make sense of a pile of bar receipts. Richie came over and started massaging her neck. His hands on her neck sent a jolt through her body, and if the muscles weren't tense before they were now. Maybe he was actually trying to massage her or maybe it was a threat. You never knew with Richie.

'Sure you're my girl,' Richie said, kneading his thumbs at the frail point where her spine disappeared into her skull.

Allison stood up and held some papers out for him to see.

'They're fucking stealing us blind. Why don't you just let me do my job, Richie? I'm good at this, I really am. Why can't we just leave it at that?'

'Jeez, what are you going to do? You going to quit on me again?'

'Would it work this time?'

Allison had quit twice then found out that Richie had put the word out and no one else would hire her, unless she wanted to sling burgers, and even then it was doubtful. Everybody knew Richie and nobody wanted to cross him. She had a kid and a house and she needed the job. She came back both times, just like Richie knew she would.

'The thing is, we both know you don't want to quit. We both know what you want. You want the same thing I do. You want to quit, quit. I never stopped you, did I? So how come you keep coming back, huh?'

'I've got work to do,' Allison said.

'You think about Cabo,' Richie said. 'We fly down, spend a week in the sun drinking margaritas and laying on the beach.'

'I've got a kid, Richie.'

'You leave him with your mom. Hell, I'll get them into Disneyland for a week. No, fuck that, I'll fly them both to

269

Florida, fucking Disneyworld in Orlando. Don't tell me they wouldn't like that. Everybody likes that shit.'

'Can we talk about this later? I have to take care of this,' she said, showing him the papers.

'Sure, sure. We'll talk over dinner. Schedule yourself off tomorrow night.'

'You honestly don't think I do anything around here, do you?'

'Now don't get huffy on me, baby. I know you work hard. You make this place hum like a top, I know that. But you got to consider the delicate machinery of management and labor. The wheels need to be oiled occasionally.'

'And you want your wheels oiled, is that it?'

'You're taking all this the wrong way,' Richie said. 'I'm trying to be professional.'

'Yeah, I think so,' said Allison. 'And maybe a pro is exactly what you need.'

'You just got to be a hard-ass, don't you,' Richie said to her. 'You just got to make everything so fucking difficult.'

'I just want to do my job, Richie. That's all I want. Why don't you go and take your squeaky wheels to somebody else, okay?'

Allison took her handful of receipts and went down to the bar. She was relieved when Richie didn't follow. Sooner or later if she didn't give in (and even if she did, for that matter) Richie was going to get bored. Allison had no idea what would happen at that point. What she hoped was that, if she could hold out long enough, Richie would get fed up and let her quit. Then she could move on to some-place else. Her gut told her this wasn't the way it would happen, though. Richie was a shit if he didn't get what he wanted, and he held a grudge. He'd screw her over just as a lesson to anybody who followed, as an example. On the other hand, if she slept with him God knows where it would go. When he got bored then maybe he'd let her quit, or maybe he'd find other uses for her. There were rumors this had happened to other girls who'd worked at the club, though nobody was suicidal enough to elaborate.

Rose was working the bar when Allison went over to her and showed her a receipt.

'You see this?'

'Yeah?'

'How many shots do you get out of a bottle of scotch?'

'Twenty maybe,' said Rose.

'According to this, we only get sixteen. We're losing a quarter of every bottle.'

'Look,' said Rose, 'I'm not the only bartender in this place.'

'I'm just saying I want it stopped, now. Pass the word along. I see anybody handing out comps to their friends or pocketing money and I treat it like it's theft, which it is.'

Allison went downstairs to talk to the other employees, leaving Rose to steam. Martin had been watching all this and went over to her. Rose Villano was small and hot and Martin wanted her bad. A sympathetic shoulder would not go amiss.

'Did you see that shit?' Rose said to him. 'Where does she get off calling me a fucking thief? Miserable bitch. If she wasn't blowing Richie she'd be out on the street where she belongs. You want a drink?'

'Yeah. The usual.'

She poured him a large scotch.

'It's on the house. The bitch,' said Rose.

'She's not putting out for Richie,' Martin said.

'Oh yeah? I bet that makes him happy. Well, that shit won't last long. Fucking dyke, maybe. That would explain a lot.'

'Maybe,' said Martin. 'Anyway, it's not right her taking it out on you.'

'Fucking-A it's not,' said Rose. 'You're lucky you don't have to work with her. Fucking ball-buster, that's what she is. Not giving it up for him?'

'Nope.'

'Somebody ought to talk to Richie about her,' Rose said, looking him in the eyes.

'Yeah, maybe I should. It's not, you know, good for the work environment.'

'You're fucking right it's not. So you think maybe you'll talk to him?'

'Maybe,' said Martin, smiling at her.

'Oh, you're a sly one, ain't you? Maybe there's more to you than I thought.'

'There is,' said Martin. 'I got all kinds of ideas. She won't be here forever. You and me ought to talk.'

'We could talk,' said Rose. 'I'm real good at talking.'

They were both leaning on the bar and smiling and looking into each other's eyes. Rose reached down behind the bar and picked up a cocktail cherry and put it in her mouth. She moved the cherry around behind her teeth and when she pulled it back out there was a knot in the stem. She put it in his hand.

'Jesus,' said Martin, unaware he'd said it aloud, in equal admiration for the dexterity of her tongue and the way she sucked at the cherry as she pulled it from her mouth. Martin was blissfully lost for a moment in a reverie about that tongue and those lips when he remembered what he was actually there for. 'Look,' he said, 'I want you do me a favor.' He pulled out the video still of Terry and showed it to her. 'You ever see this guy?'

She looked at it carefully.

'Yeah, I seen him. He's been in the bar. And I seen him the other day with miss tight-ass bitch. They were together in Denny's. Why?'

All thoughts of love suddenly dropped through Martin's ass.

'Mind your own beeswax,' said Martin.

Rose brightened. 'The bitch been cheating on Richie? Oh my God, this is going to be sweet!'

'You keep your goddamn mouth shut,' Martin said quickly. 'I mean it, or you'll have Richie down on you, you got that? You know who this guy is, where I can find him?'

'Ask the bitch,' said Rose.

'Not a word, right?'

'Not me, baby. I'm just going to watch and enjoy.'

Martin found Richie in the office. Allison had just come back in and Richie was trying to talk to her. Allison was doing what she usually did, which was trying to simultaneously work and fend off Richie's roaming hands.

'Richie?'

'What?' snapped Richie. 'Can't you see we're doing the books here?'

'I need to talk to you.'

'What the fuck about?'

'It's important.'

'Jesus.'

He led Richie into the empty VIP Room. 'What the hell is all this about? That bitch is killing me, I don't even know why I bother sometimes.'

'You know that guy we're looking for, the guy in the trailer? He's a friend of Allison's.'

'What?'

'She knows the guy.'

'What the fuck do you mean, she knows the guy?'

'Rose said she saw them together. And you were right, she's seen the guy in here.'

'Rose fucking hates her, she's fucking jealous of her. She's a lying goddamn little spic.'

'I don't think so, Richie. She said she saw them together. I didn't even mention Allison's name, I just showed her the picture.'

'Jesus,' Richie said weakly.

'You want me to talk to her?'

'No, you stay the fuck away from her, you hear me? Anybody going to talk to her, it'll be me. You don't say a fucking word.' He sat down on the sofa. 'Jesus,' he said again.

'What do you want to do?'

'Just keep an eye on her. If Rose is telling the truth, she'll lead us to the bastard sooner or later. If Rose is lying, I want her fucking greaseball thumbs cut off or something.'

'What if she's telling the truth?'

'I'll fucking let you know, okay? Now get the fuck out of my sight. I want to think.'

Richie Stella sat alone in the VIP Room with a broken heart. No, that's a lie. Richie Stella had never had a broken heart in his life. Richie Stella had whatever it's called when you want something really bad but it fucks you over and makes you feel like an asshole and now you want to kill it. Maybe that's not a broken heart, but it's as close as Richie Stella was ever going to come.

It was after 2 a.m. the following night when Allison's phone rang. Allison got out of bed and went into the living room to answer it.

'Yes?'

'I want to see you,' said Terry. His Irish brogue was thick and slow and Allison could tell he'd been drinking heavily.

'Leave me alone,' whispered Allison. 'You got what you wanted. Now just stay out of my life.'

'I need to see you. I can come there.'

'No, for God's sake, don't come here. I told you.'

'Then meet me somewhere. We need to talk. It's important.'

'I'll call you tomorrow. I have to go.'

'Is he with you?'

She didn't answer.

'He's with you, isn't he?'

'No,' said Allison. 'He's not. I have to go,' and hung up.

'Who was that?' Richie called from the bedroom.

'It's Mom. Cody's got a temperature.'

'You want me to get a doctor?' said Richie, coming into the living room naked. 'I'll have a doctor right over there.'

'It's just a cold or something. It's not bad. Better just to let him sleep.'

'You need a doctor, anything, you just tell me. I'd do anything for that kid. You know that.'

'Yeah, I know.'

Richie put his hands on her shoulders, massaged them, massaged her neck. 'Come to bed. You got nothing to worry about as long as I'm here. You know that, right? You're my girl, aren't you?'

'Yeah,' she said. 'I'm your girl.'

They were sitting in the galley of Terry's boat. It shifted slowly back and forth against the dock, like an animal lazily trying to scratch its side. It was stuffy inside and Allison wished the windows were open, that some fresh air was moving around. No, what she wanted was off this goddamn boat. Her stomach was upset from the tension and the rocking.

'Can we go outside?' she said.

'I want you to talk to me,' Terry said, leaning across to her.

'What do you want me to say?'

'I want you to tell me you didn't fuck him.'

'Okay, fine, I didn't fuck him.'

Terry looked at her then sat back and covered his face with his hands, took them away, let out a deep sigh.

'It's not my job to make you feel better,' Allison said.

'I thought . . . I mean, I wanted . . .'

'Grow up, will you.'

She needed to get out of there. She got up to leave.

'You don't feel anything?' Terry asked her.

'Jesus, what if I did? What possible difference could it make?'

'He'll be out of your life soon, one way or another. I swear to God. I can fix everything. It will all be fine.'

'I can't tell you how sick I am of hearing this shit from guys,' Allison said. 'All my life I've been hearing this, and all they ever do is make it worse. What are you going to do? Kill him?'

'You think he deserves to live? I wouldn't lose a minute's sleep. The world would be better.'

'I don't want to listen to this. You're crazy.'

'Trust me,' Terry said to her. 'Just trust me. It will all be over. I can take care of you. Then we can be together. If that's what you want. You want to give it a try, just you and me? Is that maybe something you'd want?'

'Yeah. It would be nice. I think you're crazy, but you make me laugh.'

'I love you,' Terry said.

'I sort of figured.'

'We need each other. We're alike, you and me. It'll work. It'll all be fine. You'll see.'

'You think?'

'I know it will.'

Terry kissed her, and to her own irritation she found herself responding. He had this affect on her, pheromones or something. He wasn't tall or handsome or rich, and there was some of him that was a disaster in its own right. He didn't even live in a goddamn house or apartment, like normal people. Just floated in this goddamn little hobbit-themed watery cocoon, him and his fairy stories and his picture of Gandalf and his map of Middle Earth. Except when he was out strangling ex-husbands and talking people into shit they had no business getting into. The sort of guy who will complicate your life beyond all common sense but you can't help wanting to let it happen because it's like nothing that ever happened before. Suddenly a panel slides back and there is a new world presented for good or ill and you already know what you've got in this one. All the little bastard had to do was touch her and she wanted to hold onto him and not let go. She forgot about her stomach and the stale sea air and the resolution to never see him again and wanted to be in bed with him and fuck and laugh and forget the rest of it existed.

'Can you stay with me?'

'It's a bad idea,' said Allison, knowing that she'd think of some way to do it.

'Call your mom. Ask her to keep Cody overnight. We'll anchor out a ways, it'll be nice and quiet. The water's calm, it'll be like being rocked in somebody's arms. I'll make you dinner, we'll watch the sunset. That's all I've been thinking about. Holding you in my arms and watching the sunset.'

'I shouldn't . . .'

They kissed again. He pulled her around the table to him and she straddled his lap. He buried his face in her breast and his hands were on her hips. She kissed his dark curly hair, put her arms around his neck. She was tired, tired of it all, tired of trying to push and pull at the same time. She wanted to be swept away. He led her to the bed.

'They're on his boat,' Martin said to Richie. 'He's got a boat out in Ventura.'

Richie was in the dining room eating a steak. He carefully trimmed some fat away then set it aside. Then he cut a small square of meat and dipped it in a mixture of horseradish and ketchup and brought this to his mouth and chewed carefully. Then he did this again. He didn't look at

Martin, who was hovering over the table, waiting for the explosion to happen.

'What are they doing?' Richie said finally, still cutting and eating, mechanical-like, not looking up from his plate.

'Jesus, Richie, what do you want me to say? They're playing house.'

Richie over-masticated the last piece of meat then set down his knife and fork, took a sip of his wine, wiped his lips with the cloth napkin, and put his hands on the table on either side of the plate. Richie said, 'Two-faced fucking bitch. I'd have given her everything. She finally fucked me, too, you know that? Lying cunt.'

Martin would have felt more comfortable if Richie had set about screaming, smashing and throwing things, making vile threats, which is what he usually did. This way it felt like sitting on a bomb that might or might not go off under your ass any second.

'What do you want to do?' Martin asked him.

Richie let his hands remain still at the sides of the plate but twitched his thumbs. He sat that way for a while. Then he said:

'Call Squiers and Potts. Tell them I got another job for them. Tell them they'll get a bonus if they do it right. And ask that little weasel Potts if he knows anything about boats.'

Nineteen

Potts unlocked the door of his house. He reached in, flipped on the light, and stood aside to let Ingrid enter first.

'It ain't much,' Potts said to her.

Ingrid went in. She walked around the living room, looking at things, smiling to herself.

'It's lovely.'

Potts pulled back the patio curtains. 'Out here's the patio. I got a grill. And there's a horseshoe pitch, if you like that sort of thing.'

Ingrid came to the picture of Potts' daughter, the one taken two years before. Potts had only managed to get it from her last year. He'd practically had to beg and wound up promising her fifty dollars before she'd sent it.

'Is this your daughter?'

'Yeah, that's Brittany. Her grandparents, my wife's family, they got custody of her right now. Back in El Paso. I'm fighting to get her back. I'm going to bring her out here, give her a real home. That's what I got this place for. She'd like you. You two would get along. You'd be a good influence on her.'

'She's very pretty,' Ingrid said. 'She has a lot of character, like you. I think we would get along fine.'

'You think so? You think you would?'

'I know so. I can tell by her face. We'd get on like a house afire.'

Potts could feel happiness come over him like a cool mist.

'I got some money coming in soon, from this job I got to do. Not a whole lot. But enough to get my business started, I think. Enough to rent a garage and get some tools, hire me somebody to help. It won't take much. All I got to do is get through the first month and it'll be fine. And I can pay this lawyer, he'll get Brittany for me. And you two can meet each other.'

'I have some money,' said Ingrid. 'I could help you a little. And Mother won't be around much longer, there's that house, I don't want to be all alone in that house.'

'It's going to be good, ain't it? Everything is going to be so good.'

She laughed. 'You say that like there's something wrong with it.'

'I don't know. Maybe I shouldn't have said anything. I don't want to jinx it. Sometimes you shouldn't say a thing out loud, you know. No matter how happy you are.'

Ingrid came over and put her arms around him. 'I think

you should say it aloud especially when you're happy. I think you should celebrate it.'

'We ought to get some champagne,' Potts said, his arms around her. 'You think you could pick us out a good bottle of champagne? And we could celebrate for real. We ought to celebrate me and you. We'll get some champagne, and I'll grill us some steaks in the backyard.'

'It's been so long since I was happy. You make me happy. Do I make you happy?'

'Hell, yeah. I've never been this happy. I reckon I could get used to it.'

Ingrid kissed him, then went over to the patio door and looked out.

'Amos,' said Potts.

Ingrid turned around. 'What?'

'Amos,' repeated Potts. 'My first name is Amos.'

'I love you, Amos Potts,' she said. 'Do you love me?'

'Yes.'

'Then everything is going to be just fine.'

Twenty

Something about sex makes it better in desperation. Maybe so much of what sex is about involves forgetting. Maybe so much of why we fuck is about, for as long as we can wind it out, for as long as we can push our bodies and our senses to their extremes, not remembering who and where we are. People wonder why the poor have so many children, but fucking is free, at least in the beginning, at least until the kids come along. Fucking is like a drug, you forget where you are, who you are, don't care, as long as you're cranking up to an orgasm and then the blessed event itself – everything else goes away. Marx was wrong. Fuck religion. As everyone in advertising knows, a good shag is the Opiate of the People.

Terry had nodded off for a bit and Allison had a chance to think about this. Terry excited and pleased her in a way no one else had done before, though she was unable to say why this was true. He was a good lover but it wasn't a matter of technique. She thought maybe it was because, even though she felt safe with him, he still confused her. He was unpredictable – in making love, in everything he did, up and down the scales between tenderness and violence. The possibilities were endless, which is why it was so easy to accept his blarney. With any other guy you could write it off as just hot air, but you never knew with Terry, and that is what got to her. With Terry, the lines between reality and fantasy sort of got blurred. It made him a great lover but it also made him dangerous, she knew.

Allison and Richie had gone out to dinner that night they'd argued in the club, the night he talked about taking her to Cabo. Alison was so tired of resisting that she simply gave in, let him have what he wanted, to get it over. The worst part was that the sex wasn't bad and she'd always been a little attracted to Richie in spite of herself. Maybe this is what made him so relentless. He was nicer in bed than she'd imagined. No marathon lover and not terribly original, but he'd been uncharacteristically gentle and anxious to please. Being Richie, she'd worried about whips and chains, maybe something with razorblades. Instead he was almost boyish, uncertain. He'd climaxed and she thought it diplomatic to fake hers. He didn't appear to notice and was grateful. But there was that vacuum afterwards. Nothing to say, no warmth, no laughter, you roll apart like boxers to neutral corners. As far as Richie was concerned, she could have been anybody. And she felt the same about Richie. Did Allison feel like a whore? No. It's the twenty-first century, when sex and power are so clearly confused that nobody worries about it anymore. Allison didn't feel any better about herself, though it was one less thing to struggle against. Richie would stop hounding her now and do whatever he was going to do.

Well enough.

Except now there was Terry again.

Terry, showing up like the proverbial bad penny. As hard to get rid of as dogshit on a shoe.

If she'd known she'd be seeing Terry again, she'd never have slept with Richie. But she'd promised herself that Terry was history, that he was nothing but trouble, him and his grandiose plans for taking Richie down. She never should have told Terry, the persuasive little shit, about Martin and the dope runs. That was a mistake, even though she couldn't imagine how Terry would ever be able to use it, or that Richie would ever find out it was her. Nevertheless, she should have kept her mouth shut. Richie was nobody to fool with.

Allison lit a cigarette and watched Terry sleep and found herself wanting him again. As if the very act of worrying about it aroused her. The more she worried, the more she wanted the sex. The more sex they had, the more she'd worry. Like a drug. She stubbed out the cigarette and reached down between the sheets to wake him up. She wasn't crazy about this whole boat thing, but there was something erotic about the sound of the water and the gentle rocking, and the fact that, a mile from shore, they could be as loud as they wanted. There'd always been the child and the neighbors or guests or something. The freedom to let yourself loose, say what you wanted as loud as you wanted, was an additional spice. Now she could scream if she felt like it and no one would hear.

The skiff made its way over the water toward the sailboat. Potts sat in the stern steering the thing while Squiers sat perched up front like George fucking Washington crossing the Potomac. Squiers had even tried standing up at one point until the craft lurched precipitously and Potts told him to set his fat ass down. It was dark and they ran without lights, though the only real danger was getting ploughed by some motorboat. No one else was on the water, though, and the skiff simply followed the line between the lighted harbor and the bobbing lights of Terry's boat anchored a mile out.

The evening had started out badly and wasn't getting any better. Richie had worked out this elaborate plan involving an 'amphibious assault' on Terry's boat. Like the D-Day invasions, it sounded plausible until you tried it, then the real problems popped up out of nowhere. Like getting a boat. First you get a small boat, says Richie. Only Richie knows shit about boats, large or small. Richie has seen too many fucking commando movies. He envisioned a rubber, Jacques Cousteau-like Zodiac creeping up in the night. In reality all Potts could get was a frail, wooden piece of crap that took on water like a sieve and had an

287

engine that wouldn't blend mayonnaise yet sounded like a freighter. And even this had cost them two hundred bucks to borrow from an old smelly bastard who sold bait on the docks and wanted three hundred until Squiers leaned on him a little. Periodically Potts would bitch at Squiers to pick up the fucking bucket and bail.

Then there was the small matter of the drugs.

Potts' drug days were long behind him, though God knows he sucked down enough tequila and beer to float a barge. On this particular evening he'd felt the need for something more appropriate, however. He was a nervous wreck about the whole fucking thing, didn't want to do it, didn't know if he was actually capable of doing it, though he was desperate for the bonus Richie had promised. His stomach had been churning since Richie had laid this on him, so drinking was out, but he was shaking too hard to carry it off without aid. What he needed was a Xanax or something to take the edge off and forestall a grand case of the whirling-twirlies. Potts had rummaged through his medicine cabinet and the various drawers in his house before leaving and could find no worthy chemicals. So he hit the tequila, which only made things worse, since now he felt ready to both shit and puke on himself.

It was here he made his great mistake, from which all others would follow: he listened to Squiers. Normally he would never do this for the obvious reasons that Squiers was insane and a pathological liar and was only useful for the threat of violence, which he was good at. As they left

LA headed toward Ventura, Squiers was driving as usual and Potts was squirmy in the passenger seat.

'You nervous?' Squiers said to him, smiling.

'I'm fine,' said Potts, though clearly he wasn't. He was one short step from telling Squiers to pull over and let him out so he could puke on the side of the road and hitchhike back home. He couldn't go through with this. It was Squiers' type of job, though Squiers couldn't be trusted to do it without getting out of hand.

'You want a Xanax?' said Squiers.

Potts felt a ray of hope when he heard the word 'Xanax', like a small gift from God. Of course he knew better – this was Squiers after all – but he was desperate. 'You got any?'

'Sure,' said Squiers. He reached into his coat pocket and fished out three vials of pills. This in itself was a bad sign. Squiers liked chemicals and carried around a small pharmacy. Potts never knew if the pills explained Squiers' insanity or merely kept it from getting worse. Squiers studied the labels of the vials in the headlights of oncoming cars, then opened one, dumped out a couple of tablets and handed them to Potts. They clearly weren't Xanax.

'These aren't Xanax,' said Potts.

'Same fucking thing,' said Squiers.

Potts stared at the pills. It was like falling out of an airplane with only an umbrella. You might as well open the thing, you're fucked anyway, it couldn't hurt.

Potts, in his own moment of madness, took the pills.

By Calabassas the pills had kicked in and Potts realized,

with a certain bemusement, that he had finally crossed over into Squiers' universe. It wasn't bad, far easier to cope with than Potts' own version. The churning gut went away, as did the feeling that somebody had inflated his veins. He was hot and sweating a little and suddenly thirsty as hell. A small price to pay. Objects took on a slight aura and sounds appeared to be relayed through a third source, reaching Potts' ears slightly behind his vision. This was not unpleasant once you got used to it. Potts felt his muscles unknot and he sighed and sat back in the seat.

'Good, huh?' said Squiers. His own eyes were aglow with God knows what. The evil twin maybe of whatever Potts had taken. Potts was mellow but Squiers was amped. Squiers drove far too fast down the long, steep, snaky grade into Camarillo. Potts normally would have been hopping up and down, telling Squiers to slow down. Instead Potts studied the soft glow of the lights on the plain below. The car rocked back and forth with the curves. It was like being in a glider, sailing in for a landing. Wow, thought Potts.

Now they were on the water with the exhausted whine of the pissant motor rattling Potts' drug-addled brain. Things had been fine as long as there were no problems, and Potts was allowed to sail along padded in a fat little drug-bubble, cushioned and slightly separated from a world he did not particularly like anyway. Then came the search for a way out to the sailboat and the smelly old man and Squiers having to lean on him a little. Nothing too physical, just that looming, glaring thing that Squiers did so well, grabbing the man's scrawny wrist and forcing the two hundred bucks into his hand, take it or regret it. The old man took it but now the vibes were all wrong. It was then that Potts' mellowness took a U-turn. The pleasant bubble-wrapping against reality now felt like tying your shoelaces with oven mitts. Things were increasingly difficult to grasp, leading to confusion and not a little paranoia.

They traveled into the wind, pushing sound behind them, but Potts stopped the motor halfway out. The sudden quiet was like heaven, and Potts felt his brain cease to vibrate against his skull.

'I fucking hate the water,' said Squiers. 'My uncle drowned.'

'Will you shut up? Sound travels over water. How many times have I got to explain this?' While this was true, Potts mainly just didn't want the bastard to speak.

They got out the oars and began to row. Squiers made a great show out of banging the oars against the boat like playing a fucking kettle-drum until Potts had to take them away from him, switch positions and row himself.

Sitting in the dark water, light poured out of the sailboat as if the inside were on fire. Which it was, in a way. As Potts and Squiers rowed closer to the boat they could hear the sounds of Terry and Allison having vigorous sex.

'Shit,' said Squiers admiringly.

Terry was crying things out in short, breathless bursts, but was overwhelmed by Allison's even louder moans and exhortations. Yes, oh God, yes, do it, yes, please do it, yes yes.

Squiers was smiling widely and Potts could swear he saw his eyes glowing red in the dark. Potts himself was not unaffected. There was that voyeuristic frisson than ran up his spine, the brief clear image of what they were doing. Potts rowed harder. This was a good thing, they'd be distracted. It would make it easier. They coasted in next to the boat and the sounds were so intense it was as if they were in the cabin with them. Potts hung out a small rubber tire to keep the hulls from bumping and tied a line onto a cleat. The lovemaking continued. Potts and Squiers climbed carefully up onto the deck. The hatch was open and from the far end of the deck you could see the couple writhing naked on the bunk. Potts started forward, wanting this over quickly, but Squiers stopped him and signalled him to wait. Squiers listened to the sex and after a time his own breathing seemed to match theirs. Potts was impatient to get it done and wanted to move but Squiers glared at him and gripped his arm menacingly. They waited as the sounds got louder and quicker and Allison and Terry both cried out in a final wave when Squiers took out a 9mm pistol and launched himself down into the cabin.

'Scream and I blow your fucking brains out,' Squiers said to Allison. Terry rolled off her quickly, sat up in the bed and looked as if he might spring at Squiers. Allison grabbed a corner of the sheet and tried to cover herself.

'You lost your boner!' Squiers said to Terry. 'Damn, I never knew anybody could lose a boner that fast.'

Squiers motioned for Terry to back up against the bulkhead. 'You get heroic and I'm going to kill her first, you got that?' Holding the gun on Terry he grabbed Allison by the hair and dragged her from the bed and across the cabin. He lowered her onto her knees, still clutching a fistful of her hair in his right hand, which he jerked occasionally to remind her.

Potts said to Terry, 'Roll onto your stomach.' Terry glared at him but didn't move. Naked, tensed, he looked like a cornered animal and just as dangerous. Potts said, 'We don't want the girl, it's just you we're interested in. You do what we say and she doesn't get hurt. You're going to get fucked up no matter what. You can save the girl.'

Terry glanced over at Allison, naked and cowering on her knees beside Squiers. Squiers was smiling. Squiers gave her hair a snap and she cried out. Terry didn't move, trying to think, and Squiers twisted her hair and Allison screamed. Terry started forward but Potts put his gun in front of his face and motioned him back onto the bed. Potts nodded to Squiers and Squiers tucked the 9mm into his waistband and slapped Allison, hard, with his left hand, never letting go of her hair in his right. She cried out and Squiers pulled the gun back out of his pants. Allison was sobbing and there was a trickle of blood from the corner of her mouth. Squiers seemed to be enjoying himself. Allison looked at Terry, pleading.

'Okay,' said Terry. 'You don't hurt her.'

'Nobody's going to hurt her,' said Potts, 'as long as you do what you're supposed to.'

Potts motioned for Terry to roll onto his stomach. Potts tucked his gun into his back pocket. Under Squiers' guard, Potts took out some long plastic ties from a messenger bag and bound Terry's wrists, then his ankles. Potts rolled him over. 'Open your mouth.' Terry opened his mouth and Potts shoved a cloth into it, then sealed the mouth with duct tape. Potts got out a roll of thin wire and Terry began to panic when he saw it. Potts stepped back out of reach and nodded to Squiers, who gave another hard tug to Allison's hair, enough to make her yell. Terry quieted down and Potts moved in again and tied Terry's hands to the top of the bunk and his feet to the bottom. Terry was breathing hard through his nose, trying not to suffocate, trying to maintain some sort of control.

'You know who sent me?' said Potts.

Terry nodded.

'We're not going to kill you. We're going to hurt you, but you're gonna wish you were dead for a while. Two things I got to tell you. First, you shouldn't fuck other people's girlfriends. It's not nice. Second, when you can talk again, you tell that fucking cowboy faggot friend of yours that he's going to be next.'

Potts looked at Squiers, who pulled Allison to her feet. Squiers put one hand over her mouth and the other firmly around her waist. Potts reached into the messenger bag again and took out a short length of iron bar wrapped in tape. Terry bucked and twisted when he saw it, his shouts lost behind the cloth and the tape. Allison too tried to shout and struggle but Squiers held her tightly and didn't mind at all her writhing body. Potts pulled on a rubber glove then Potts stopped and held the iron bar in his hands and looked down at Terry and froze. There was a kind of high-pitched buzz in his head and for a moment he believed all this was just in his mind, that he wasn't really there at all. But the buzzing went on and his pounding heart and shortness of breath brought him around and, yes, he was there okay, he had to do this, everything depended on him doing this, he'd do it for Brittany, for Ingrid and their future and who the fuck was this guy anyway, some complete stranger, some guy who was fucking somebody else's girlfriend, some guy who meant shit to him, some guy who was just in the way between him and what he wanted and the people he cared about.

Potts raised the iron bar and brought it down hard, quick, onto Terry's left shin. He felt the bone give and heard the dull snap and Terry's muffled scream all at the same time. Somewhere behind him the girl was trying to scream as well. Potts rested. The iron bar had become unbelievably heavy. Potts could barely lift it. The buzzing was like a relentless siren and Potts felt his hand sweating in the rubber glove. Potts clenched his teeth and broke Terry's other leg in the same place. Then Potts went to work with his gloved fist on Terry's face. Richie had insisted. Somewhere along the way the man on the bed passed out. Meanwhile Squiers was whispering into Allison's ear. He let go of her mouth. She was past screaming and was sobbing and weak and Squiers groped her with his free hand.

Potts stood and tried to get his bearings. He could feel his body swaying. The drug was in full force now. The adrenaline gave it a turbocharge and his heart pushed the torrid mixture through his veins like a rocketing flare. He thought he might pass out but caught himself. He took off the bloody glove and dropped it back in the messenger bag then picked up the iron bar where he'd dropped it on the bed and put that too in the bag. He picked up the bag and thought things were going to be fine then had to lunge for the head, where he puked violently in the toilet. He splashed cold water on his face and when he came out Squiers had the girl pinned on a seat and was trying to open his pants. Potts stared at this and it took a moment to register.

'What the fuck are you doing?'

'Please?' Allison begged Potts. Squiers ignored both of them.

'Get the fuck away from her!' Potts told him.

Squiers was between her legs and was trying to unbuckle his Levi's. Potts yelled at him again and when he didn't respond Potts got out the iron bar again and hit him on the back, hard enough to assure his attention. Squiers grunted and turned on him.

'Are you fucking crazy?' said Potts. 'Richie said just the guy. He said to leave the girl alone!'

Potts' head was an air-raid siren and Squiers himself was beyond reason. Squiers' own bubbling chemical stew had glazed his eyes and dulled his flesh. A truck could have ploughed into him and it wouldn't have registered. Squiers hit Potts and sent him flying across the cabin, dropping the bar. When he looked up Squiers had retrieved the bar and had it raised and was coming at him.

Potts never knew how the pistol got into his hand. He'd forgotten it in his back pocket, though surely he'd fallen on it, remembered it was there, reached for it without thinking. All he knew is that suddenly it was there, and it fired, and a small hole appeared in Squiers' chest.

A 9mm pistol is not a large gun, but in a small enclosed space – like the tiny cabin of a thirty-foot sailboat – it makes a noise that is literally deafening. Potts' ears exploded and all he could think of for a few moments was the pain. The drug-buzzing had been replaced by the pain and the ringing and Potts couldn't hear a goddamned thing. Not a thing. He got to his feet and looked over at the girl, who was curled up and crying with her hands over her own ears. Potts could see she was crying but he couldn't hear it. Potts said something to the girl but it was pointless. Squiers was slumped on the floor with a small, blossoming hole in the approximate area of his heart. If he wasn't dead he was dying. Potts wasn't going to get close enough to check.

Potts sat down at the small galley table. Deaf, disoriented, plagued by the hellish raging of the drug. The sides of his face throbbed, while the sheer weight of how ugly things were came to rest on him. It was as fucked as fucked could be. Everything. All of it. His entire life. Forever.

He struggled to think of some way to recover, but he knew it didn't exist.

The plan had been this: they show up and break the guy's legs, mess up his face. Nobody touches the girl, the bitch gets to watch, but nobody touches her. At the end of it she calls the ambulance or whatever, but nobody is going to be able to pin this on Richie and nobody is going to the cops anyway, it's just more trouble. A valuable lesson in morality learned. Potts and Squiers are long gone, and Potts has enough money in his pocket to start his life, a real life, with Ingrid and his kid. End of story. Well, okay, it is a shitty little story. But life is full of shitty little stories and we do what we can, the best we can. Here we have Potts doing his best, making lemonade from lemons.

Or not.

Now we have a murder on our hands. Oh yes, it's murder. A life lost in the commission of a violent felony. Screw self-defense, Potts is going to spend the rest of his life in jail.

Potts thought. Or tried to think.

Potts had killed Squiers. Now we have this large dead body. All this now goes to the cops. They are going to question the man and the girl, who will tell them everything, all about Richie, all of it. They are going to identify Squiers and tie him to Potts. They are going to find Potts and lock him up for a very long time if Richie does not find him and kill him first.

None of this is pretty.

Potts knows what he has to do. He does not want to do it. How soon can they tie Potts to Squiers? How much time does Potts have? Can they prove Potts was in on this when they do? Oh yes. The man and the girl, they'll talk about Potts. They'll paint a lovely picture.

Witnesses, thought Potts, and the drug seemed to echo it.

Potts got up and went into the head. He tore off some toilet tissue and dampened it and stuffed it in his ears. He went back into the cabin and went over to the girl. 'Everything is fucked,' Potts said but he couldn't hear it and neither could she, then he shot her. He went over to Squiers and shot him in the head for good measure, then removed anything in his pockets that could ID him. This would at least slow things down. Potts went over to the man on the bed, the bastard who'd caused all this trouble, the guy who'd ruined Potts' life. As he stared down at Terry, Terry's eyes flickered and opened and for a few moments the two men gazed at each other like lovers. Terry saw the gun in his hand and knew what was about to happen. Potts raised the gun and Terry closed his eyes and thought about Allison, wondered if she'd be fine, prayed to God she'd be fine, and never heard the gun go off.

Potts came out on deck and nearly slipped, looked down to see the blood he'd tracked everywhere. He sat down and took off his shoes and threw them as far out as he could into the water. He looked at the gun and threw that too, far out into the sea. Potts sat there trying to remember if he'd covered everything, left prints, made mistakes. Fuck yes, everywhere. And that smelly old bastard on the dock, he'll make me. What do I do, fucking row back and whack him too? Short of building an atom bomb and nuking the whole of Ventura, Potts couldn't think of a decent alternative. Just run. Just run and don't look back, you miserable unlucky fuck. At best I've bought a little time.

Potts climbed into the skiff, and started the motor, which no longer bothered him since he could not hear it. And anyway, he had other problems.

Twenty-One

Bobby stood in front of a mirror, half-dressed in a gray Versace suit, trying to button up his pants. Spandau was sitting in a chair, reading a fashion magazine. Bobby was fumbling angrily with the buttons and finally one came off in his hand.

'Fuck! Fuck me, fuck me . . .'

Ginger came in with a collection of neckties. 'What's wrong?'

'A fucking five-thousand-dollar suit and the fucking button comes off.'

'I'll sew it back on.'

'Fucking piece of shit. I'm wearing something else.'

'You promised them you'd wear it. They had the whole thing tailored for you. You have to wear it.'

'I don't have to do shit.' He began to take off the suit.

'You're just going to tear something else,' Ginger warned him.

'Give me a pair of scissors. I'll send it back to them in a grocery bag. Fucking wop confetti.'

'Just calm down,' said Ginger. 'What else would you wear?'

'I have a fucking closet full of clothes.'

'You want to piss off Versace,' said Ginger, 'then be my guest. But good luck getting anything else from them.'

'Fuck,' said Bobby.

'Hold still while I sew it on. And be still, unless you want me to stitch your Little Soldier to the fly.'

'Is it always like this?' Spandau asked.

'Always,' said Ginger.

'I hate these things,' said Bobby. 'Man, you don't know. You watch this shit on television, it looks simple. You just get out of the car, wave, walk in. It's not like that. You fucking don't know where you are. The flashbulbs, and everybody yelling. It scares the shit out of me.'

'Jurado says the security is good,' said Spandau.

'Where the fuck is Irina?' asked Bobby.

'She called and said she's on her way,' Ginger said.

'What's she wearing? Is she okay?'

'I told her you were wearing Versace. She knows what to wear. She's a supermodel, for chrissake.'

Bobby, Spandau, Irina and Annie stood out in front of Bobby's house in front of a pair of limos. Janine, Jurado's publicist, gave directions.

'Bobby and Irina in the first limo. They pull up, get out,

walk almost to the doors. Then, Annie, you and David are in the second limo. You follow behind. I'll already be there.'

'I guess you're my date,' Spandau said to Annie.

'I am so fucking thrilled,' Annie said to him.

'You start to swoon,' said Spandau, 'just grab my muscular arm.' Annie sucked at her teeth with a hissing sound.

Crusoe was going to be a huge hit. Tonight was the official Hollywood premiere, and in the next weeks it would open in Europe, then be released in Latin America and Asia. The critics had already had their screenings, their verdicts were locked in and assured. The ones who could be bought or cajoled were taken care of. The ones who couldn't never got to a screening in the first place, and by the time their reviews came out it would make no difference. *Crusoe* was going to be a huge. The Powers That Be had spoken. This is the way the industry worked.

Like everything else about the film, the premiere had been hyped for months, so there was no surprise at the turnout. People lined both side of the street for half a block, with a screaming, roiling mass surrounding the entrance to the theatre. Guards and a tight cordon kept fans off the street and away from the cars as they approached. The cordon stretched up into the theatre itself, on either side of the red carpet leading from the street. Bobby's limo pulled up and when the door opened the crowd went wild. Spandau watched from the second limo. Bobby and Irina poured out and stepped forward, stopped, allowed themselves to be photographed, stepped forward, allowed themselves to be interviewed briefly, stepped forward again. Meanwhile Spandau and Annie's car moved forward and spat them with little fanfare onto the red carpet. They shuffled forward quickly, told by the driver that Jurado's car was just behind and they needed to free the way. They caught up with Bobby and Irina three-quarters of the way down the carpet. Bobby had a TV camera aimed at him and Bev Metcalf shoved a microphone in his face. The fans screamed and flashbursts went off and the high-standing lights were bad enough anyway. The crowd itself was one encompassing, roaring blur. You couldn't see faces, couldn't see what people were doing. You felt helpless, naked, vulnerable. Whatever animal instincts you'd been given for survival were useless. You were blind and in the open and surrounded. You hoped like hell the security people were good, knew what they were doing. Somebody could be pointing a howitzer at you and you'd never know it. It happened often enough too. This was why Bobby hated these things. This was why everybody hated these things, it was a nightmare every goddamn time. But you had to do it, you had to walk down there naked and shaking because that was what was expected.

Security looked good. Spandau surveyed the cordons. The guards were pros, were patient yet strong and not aggressive. They held the line, taking their orders through discreet earpieces, kept aware of where the stars and guests were on the carpet. Spandau had forgotten to ask who the head of security was. Whoever it was, he or she knew their job. Then it happened.

Spandau saw it purely by chance, otherwise he'd have missed it like everyone else. He happened to be looking right at one of the guards, was able to see him clearly in spite of the lights. Saw him lean his head slightly to listen to an order in his earpiece. Then saw him pretend to check his section of the cordon where it met a post, but instead he unhooked it and let it drop. It might have been an accident but it wasn't. That section of the crowd instantly plunged through the breach and onto the carpet, heading straight for Bobby. The rest of the crowd, on both sides of the carpet, all around, followed suit and simply broke through the rest of the barriers in a gigantic swarm.

Spandau ran toward Bobby before the crowd closed between them. Three guards assigned to Bobby tried to form a circle around him, but one of the guards went down and they couldn't close the circle and kept getting pushed apart, so that Bobby was wide open. Fans reached forward, some trying to talk to him, some trying to touch him, some just wanted to be acknowledged by the movie star, some were as much victims of the crush as Bobby was. The guards tried to push Bobby toward the doors, but it was a case of pushing him deeper into the crowd, no one had yet started forcing a path from the inside toward him. Spandau ruthlessly knocked and elbowed people aside. He was big and he put his shoulder down and ploughed through like a linebacker. Through the heads he could see Bobby, his face a rictus of panic, trying to protect his eyes and keep from being blinded by the waving ballpoint pens of autograph hounds. The guards were worried about hurting fans; this was drilled into them. Spandau didn't gave a shit who he hurt.

He edged close to Bobby, pushing between Bobby and a rabid fan. The fan shoved angrily back at Spandau and Spandau elbowed him in the gut and hit him in the chin with his shoulder, knocking him backwards and down. This nudged people aside as he fell and Spandau grabbed Bobby by the lapels of his Versace and pulled him forward through the open space and over the top of the prostrate fan. Spandau's two hundred and fifteen pounds had gained impetus now and he wasn't giving it up. He cut through the crowd at a run, blindly knocking people aside like bowling pins, dragging Bobby behind him. As they reached the doors guards tried to open it from the inside but couldn't push aside the fans who blocked it. Spandau solved this by simply grabbing two people blocking a door, a teenage girl and boy, then lifting them up and literally throwing them into the crowd. Lawsuits might fly, but this wasn't his problem. He opened the door and flung Bobby through, then stepped in after him.

'Shit,' said Bobby. There was a cut on his cheek where a waving pen had just missed his eye. 'Where's Irina? Did you get Irina? You have to go back out there and get Irina!'

Spandau stared at him for a second, shook his head, then

forced his way back out the door. Irina wasn't far away. The bodyguards had managed to circle her and inch forward, and the crowd was thinning now that Bobby wasn't on the menu. It was Bobby they wanted, though Irina was shaken and crying when they brought her through the door. Bobby took Irina in his arms, comforting her. Jurado was there, having miraculously skirted past it all.

'What the hell happened?' asked an outraged Jurado. 'You okay?' he said to Bobby. 'Jesus,' he said to nobody in particular, 'how the hell could this happen?'

'I'm fine,' said Bobby.

'You sure?' asked Jurado.

'I said I was fucking fine. Some professional fucking job here, Frank.'

'Where's Janine? I'll have her goddamn ass.'

'How the hell did you get in here?' Spandau said to Jurado.

'I saw the crush and had them bring me around to the back,' he said offhandedly to Spandau. Then to Bobby he said, 'At least you're okay. The bodyguards did their job.'

'Fuck the bodyguards,' said Bobby. 'If it hadn't been for Spandau I'd still be out there, being eaten alive.'

One of the doors opened and Annie staggered in, looking as if she'd done ten minutes in a clothes dryer. 'Thank you all very fucking much,' she announced. 'Now I know who my friends are.'

Janine came running up. 'Oh God, I heard! Everybody okay? Oh God, I'm so sorry! I don't know how it could have happened, these guys are the best . . .'

'We'll have a long talk about all this later,' said Jurado, 'and I assure you some fucking heads will roll. But for now, if everybody's okay, let's just get through this. The show must go on, right?'

'Kiss my ass, Frank,' said Annie.

Bobby, Irina and Jurado went into the theatre. Spandau and Annie listened to the applause as they walked in.

'I saw what you did,' said Annie. 'Thank you.'

'I'm sorry I left you but—'

'You did the right thing. You're a pro, I have to hand it to you. You did the right thing.' Annie started to go into the theatre. 'Aren't you coming?'

'I'm going to wait here for a little while,' Spandau said.

Annie shrugged and went inside. Spandau went over to one side of the lobby and waited until all the guests had come in and the film began. A few security guards remained outside, while others came inside. The security guard who'd dropped the cordon came inside. Spandau followed him into the men's room, grabbed him and slammed him hard up against the tiles.

'Hey!'

'Who gave you the order?' Spandau demanded.

'Look, I have no idea what you're talking about . . .'

'I saw you drop the cordon. Who was on the other end of that headset?'

Another guard came in, saw Spandau bang the guy a second time against the wall. He ran out and in a moment the toilet was full of security guards.

'Fucking assault, man!' said the guard as Spandau let him go. 'Your ass is going to jail!'

Spandau came out of the bathroom in handcuffs, followed by a dozen security guards. Janine was waiting and said to Spandau, 'You want to tell me what the hell is going on?'

'This bozo attacked me,' the guard said to her.

'I saw him drop the cordon,' Spandau said to her. 'He let the mob through on purpose.'

'That's not possible,' said Janine. 'Look, it was insane out there. That's what you think you saw.'

'You think the publicity is worth that much? You could have gotten him killed.'

To the guard Janine said, 'Let him go.'

'He attacked me!'

'I said, let him go. Get back to work. I'll deal with him.'

One of the guards unlocked Spandau's cuffs. The rest dispersed, grumbling.

'I don't know what you think you saw, but keep your mouth shut. Don't make an unfounded accusation like this. We'll be forced to counter it.'

'You and Jurado cook this up? It sounds like him.'

'You're mistaken. Let's leave it at that.'

'Maybe Bobby will see it differently. It was his ass you almost killed.'

'He won't believe you,' she said.

'You think so?'

'Because he can't afford to believe you,' Janine said. 'Not

at this stage of his career. You know that as well as I do. Look, you don't want to cross Frank Jurado. Or me either, for that matter. You don't need any more enemies around here than you've already got. Go home before you get hurt.'

'I'll wait for Bobby.'

'Wait for him at the restaurant. Just tell them you're with us, everything is on the house. Just go away and think this thing through. Cool down.'

They'd taken over an entire restaurant in Beverly Hills. By the time Bobby came in with Irina on his arm the place was full and Spandau had downed several free drinks. He'd also made up his mind to tell Bobby he was quitting, but he wanted to do it in person. He owed the kid at least that much. It took Bobby fifteen minutes to fight off the usual swarm of sycophants. He saw Spandau in a booth nursing a large vodka and went over.

'What happened to you? You disappeared.'

'I didn't feel like sitting for two hours,' said Spandau.

'I wanted to thank you.'

'It's what you pay me for,' Spandau said to him.

'Is that why you did it?' said Bobby. 'Is that the reason?'

'You okay?' Bobby looked tired and his jaw was tight.

'No, I'm not. I'm having a fucking meltdown but I can't do it here. I don't have that fucking luxury.'

Jurado saw them sitting together and rushed over. 'Bobby, I got some people for you to meet. They loved you, by the way. You were frigging wonderful.'

'I have to go whore,' said Bobby, and went off with Jurado.

Spandau downed part of his drink and thought about another. While he was thinking Ross Whitcomb ambled over. Whitcomb had been a famous star in the seventies and eighties, a huge box office draw, in a series of films where he played a charming redneck. He tired of the redneck role and tried his hand as the Cary Grant-type but the public refused to see him in anything other than a cowboy hat. His box office took a nosedive and a spate of bad and public marriages kept him in more courtrooms than movie theatres.

'This is the first time I've ever seen you in a suit,' Whitcomb said to him. 'You look like a housebroken mastodon.'

'Good to see you, Ross. It's been a while.'

Whitcomb sat down across from Spandau. Whitcomb had a reputation for being an asshole, but like many actors he had a soft spot for stunt men and had always been pleasant to Spandau.

'You broke your wrist. What movie was it? *A Song for the Dying*? God, that director was an asshole. What was his name?'

'I don't remember,' admitted Spandau.

'I'm fucking senile now anyway,' said Whitcomb. 'Everything runs together. I heard you got out of the trade.'

'It wasn't the same after Beau.'

'Nothing's the same anymore,' said Whitcomb. 'It's all run by limp-wristed little la-de-das with pencils up their asses. Maybe it always was. So you're with junior there?'

'Security work. You know how it is.'

'Somebody threatening to kill him?'

'I don't think so.'

'Too bad,' said Whitcomb. 'That's a bad sign. At my peak, I used to get at least half a dozen serious threats a week. I knew my ratings were slipping if it dropped much below that.' He took a hefty pull on a large scotch. 'Nobody wants to kill you, then you're not making anybody jealous. If you're not making anybody jealous, then you ain't a movie star. Of course the number of sexual propositions manages to balance it out. Nowadays nobody's looking to kill me except my ex-wives. And myself, of course. Actors should be like old Apaches. They should know when to quit hanging around, go wander off into the desert to die when the time comes.'

'You ever think about just doing something else? Hollywood isn't everything.'

Whitcomb gave him a cartoon look of astonishment. 'Of course it is. To people like us, it is. What am I going to do? Sell real estate? I was the top box office draw in this country for ten years running. Ten fucking years, straight. They'd have stopped traffic to let me crap in the middle of Sunset Boulevard, then had somebody bronze it. In one year I slept with over two hundred women, most of them actresses – my attorney actually made me keep a record, in case any of them sued. Which they did.' Whitcomb paused for breath and let out a small belch. 'When this place likes you, it's like owning the world. You can do anything. Anything. People think it's about the money. Fuck the money. You don't need money – people line up to give you anything you want. It's about the power, the sort of power you can't buy and you can't make. People just surrender it to you. It's like being elected God. I've met some of the richest people in the world – they're fans, they come up to you and say, I'd rather be you. Fuck the money. If it were about money, people'd settle for being rich instead of being famous.'

'Then there's the flip side,' said Spandau.

'What?' said Whitcomb. 'Everything that goes up must come down? Like me, you mean? Look, you ask me if I think it's worth it, if I'd do it all again, knowing what I know now, fucking-A it is. Why do you think us old has-beens make fools of ourselves, trying to hang on. Nobody wants to walk away from this. And do what? Go back to reality? Reality sucks. That's why people go to movies in the first place. Still, I've had a pretty good fucking run. I wonder if we'll be able to say the same about your friend there.'

'He's a smart kid. He'll be okay,' said Spandau, though even as he said it he didn't believe it.

'Oh sure,' Whitcomb continued. 'If he can survive the gifts of booze and drugs and sex and the fact that nobody is ever going to tell him when he's ripped his pants and his ass is hanging out. He won't even know that people are laughing at him until it's too late. All of a sudden there's just nobody there. That's how you find out. Most never survive it. They bail, they find a different line of work or they shoot themselves. The tough bastards, like me, do what they have to do and bite the bullet and hang in there. I been up, I been down. Some little pimply indie director comes and offers me a role tomorrow, I wind up winning an Oscar next March. I'm back up again. That's the way it works. Me, I'm going to die in the saddle. Your friend won't last that long.'

'What makes you say that?'

'He wants to be loved, this kid. He wants it all. You can see it all over him. Me, I never gave a shit if they loved me or not, as long as they gave me what I wanted. And, God help me, I actually like acting. But I never knew an actor who survived and ended up with any respect for the industry or the goddamn fans. But him, he needs the adulation. Look at him. That look on his face. He's eating this up. He needs it. When all the kissing stops – and it will – he's going to crumple like a Kleenex. They're going to pat him on the head and suck him dry. Like a thousand spiders liquefying his guts and sucking them out through tiny holes. And us miserable old fucks are going to sit back and watch him implode. They outlaw cockfighting, but that's like Monopoly compared to this. Great fun, as long as it's not you.'

Whitcomb stood up, his face red from alcohol and too

much talking. 'I'm too old for free booze,' he said. 'I should be home with my Ovaltine, trying to get my Guatemalan maid to give me a hummer.'

'Good seeing you again.'

'Try not to get your neck broken,' Whitcomb said to him. 'It's a rough crowd you're running with. In a town full of shits, Jurado could be elected King Turd. Watch your back, hoss.'

Spandau got up and looked around for Bobby. He spotted him and Bobby glanced back but looked nervously away. Something was wrong. Spandau made his way toward him when Jurado and two large security guards blocked his path.

'These gentlemen are going to escort you out of here,' Jurado said to him. 'I don't want any problems, so leave nicely.'

'I'm here with Bobby,' said Spandau.

'Not anymore. I've spoken to Bobby. He wants you out of here, and out of his life. In fact, if you ever try to contact him again you'll get slapped with a court order for stalking.'

'Let me talk to him.'

'You're not getting the message. You're history.'

Spandau held up his hands in a gesture of surrender. He started toward the door, flanked by the guards, when he broke and cut into the crowd toward Bobby. Bobby saw him coming but turned his back.

'Bobby?'

Bobby didn't turn around. The guards grabbed Spandau and Spandau didn't resist. Jurado said into his ear, 'You don't leave quietly and I'll personally watch these guys break your ribs. And *then* you'll spend the night in jail. Party's over, pal. I'll walk you to the door.'

Jurado walked Spandau out onto the sidewalk. It was a moment of triumph and Jurado wanted to enjoy it.

'What did you say to him?' Spandau asked.

'I explained to him how your services were no longer needed. The case is closed. Everything is taken care of. I told you I could take care of my own business, and right now Bobby is my business. Stay away from him. He doesn't want to see you again.'

Spandau looked at the guards waiting by the entrance.

'You want to do the kid a favor, don't fuck this up for him tonight. This is all for him. It's his big night.'

'And do what? And leave him to you?'

'What are you? His mother? His boyfriend? Is that what this is about, you're queer for him?'

'Something like that,' said Spandau, and hit Jurado in the stomach. Jurado doubled and the guards were all over Spandau. Jurado nodded and they dragged Spandau into the alley behind the restaurant and went to work on him.

The dark car pulled up to the curb, deposited Spandau on the sidewalk, and drove away. Spandau had sense enough to cover his face when he landed otherwise he'd have broken his nose, provided it wasn't broken already.

Actually the boys had done a pretty professional job of it, trying not to hit him in too many places that showed. Spandau rolled over and groaned and sat up in the middle of the pavement. He got most of the way to his feet except his sides hurt and he couldn't quite manage to straighten up. He eased over to a bus stop and sat down on the bench. He fished around for his cellphone to call a cab. When he found it he remembered he'd turned it off at the premiere. He turned it on and it rang before he ever had a chance to dial.

'Where the fuck are you?' Walter said. 'I've been calling for two hours!'

'I went to a premiere. I forgot my phone was off.'

'I need to see you right now.'

'I don't have my car and I'm indisposed.'

'Tell me where you are.'

Spandau got up, hobbled over and checked the street signs. 'Eighteenth and Central.'

'Don't go anywhere,' said Walter. 'I'll be right there. And stay out of sight.'

'What's going on?'

'Just do it,' said Walter. 'I'll be there as fast as I can.'

Spandau stepped into the shadows and waited. Walter was there within ten minutes. Spandau climbed into the car.

'What's happened?'

'Terry and the girl are dead. The Ventura harbor patrol found them on his boat. They'd been shot along with some other guy. Terry was fucking tied to the bed and his legs were smashed.'

At first there was the disbelief, his mind telling him he'd heard it wrong, that it was a mistake. Spandau knew it was true though. The world had taken a wrong shift, moved into darkness and an evil time, and Spandau could feel it. There was nothing to be said. The guilt and the hatred would come later, he knew.

'The cops are looking for you. I'll take you home, and we'll wait for them to come to you. Meanwhile I've got a lawyer on standby. She'll meet us at the station. Don't fucking say anything until you talk to the lawyer first.'

'It's all my fault.'

'That is the one thing you don't say. Just keep your mouth shut. But you'd better tell me the story first.'

Seven hours later Spandau, Walter and an attorney named Molly Craig walked out of the police station.

'That was good,' said Molly. 'It went well. You know how to keep your mouth shut. That's a great resource. I should have more clients like you.'

'What now?' asked Walter.

'They asked their questions. They aren't satisfied, but they can't link him to the murders and he has a solid alibi. They'll nose around but that'll be it. They know it wasn't him.' To Spandau she said, 'You going to be okay?'

'Yeah.'

'Just get some rest. If they try to question you again, call me. You have my number. Relax. They haven't got anything. They're just going through the motions.'

She got into her car and drove away. Walter said to Spandau, 'You had no control over this.'

'I brought him into it. I convinced him to use the girl. It was a stupid game.'

'Look, Terry always was a wild card. I've warned you about him. You told him to leave the girl alone and instead of that he goes out and fucking takes her on some fuckfest on his boat. God knows what he was doing out there. He didn't obey orders. That's what got him killed. He was unprofessional. He was stupid.'

They walked to Walter's car. 'I want you to drop this,' Walter said.

'Sure.'

'Take some time off. You've earned it. Go fucking break your neck at another rodeo or something. Promise me?'

'Yeah, sure, okay.'

'You feel like doing anything stupid, you call me, right?'

'You mean like killing myself?'

'I mean just stupid, you asshole. You call me, right?'

Spandau went home and did not kill himself. In fact he went inside and took a shower and climbed into bed and went immediately to sleep. He had the sort of mind that postpones grief until it can be afforded. By the time he walked into the police station and lied about what he knew, Spandau no longer felt much of anything. Later probably he would drink and break things and punish himself and rage silently at the world, but for now he knew what he had to do, finally knew the last phase in the ridiculous plan he'd set in motion that got his friend killed. Terry had given it to him. Terry had done what he was supposed to do. Terry had laid Richie Stella wide open.

The ringing phone woke Spandau late in the morning. He let the machine get it, as always.

'Mr Spandau, this is Ginger Constantine. You left your car here and we want to return it to you. Would you like us to have someone drive it there or would you like to pick it up outside the gate?'

Spandau took a cab up to the top of Wonderland Avenue. This was how fallen angels felt when they returned home. His car was sitting outside the gate, not inside where he'd left it. The keys were where Ginger said they'd be, under the seat. Before getting into the car Spandau took a long look up into the camera he knew was watching him. He wondered if Bobby felt anything, or maybe it was Bobby's gift to feel only what was convenient. You never knew with actors. Spandau got into the car and retraced his slow, winding descent into fire and brimstone. When he pulled onto Laurel Canyon he dialed Pookie at the office.

'Walter says that whatever you ask for, not to give it to you,' she said.

'It's just a phone number, Pook.'

'I'm sorry about Terry. I can't believe it. It's like . . .'
There was a long pause. 'I dated him once, you know.'

'No, I never knew that.'

'We went to some club in Venice Beach where we
wound up playing Dungeons and Dragons all night with a
bunch of other geeks. That was the sort of thing you could
find yourself doing with Terry.'

'I know,' said Spandau.

'You know who did it?' asked Pookie.

'Yes.'

'Are you going after them?'

Spandau didn't say anything.

'I give you this number,' said Pookie, 'and you won't get
hurt, will you? You'll watch yourself, right?'

'I promise.'

'Okay then,' she said. 'I want you to make the bastard
hurt. I want you to make him hurt really bad.'

Twenty-Two

It was the middle of the afternoon and Salvatore Locatelli sat at a table in the back of his restaurant in Thousand Oaks, arguing with the chef about how long you were supposed to cook the tomatoes in a marinara sauce. Normally Salvatore wasn't the sort of guy anybody would be dumb enough to argue with, but the chef was his sister's husband's nephew and Salvatore had always liked the kid. Salvatore had helped send him to a fancy assed cooking school in upstate New York, where the kid had learned to do amazing things with scungilli but still didn't know shit about marinara. He could also be very condescending in a college-boy sort of way. The kid said you didn't cook the tomatoes for very long because they'd break down and lose their identity in the rest of the sauce. Salvatore said *va fun-gool* to tomatoes and their identity, his mother and his grandmother and her fucking grandmother for that matter had cooked the tomatoes until they nearly dissolved, and

322

they made the best marinara in Europe. And unless the chef would rather end up picking tomatoes out in Bakersfield instead of cooking them in Thousand Oaks, enough with the goddamned identity crisis of fucking tomatoes and just cook them the way you're supposed to.

Salvatore Locatelli's world was a pleasant one. He had no real regrets in life. He had three kids who'd gone to college and still called him on weekends. He had a wife he still loved, and felt no guilt at the occasional indiscretion with younger women, since this was a perfectly natural thing for a man to do, and was doubtless the secret to his long marriage. Salvatore had no guilt about his business, which was mainly criminal, though not as criminal as it once was. He'd inherited the business from his father, Don Gaitano Locatelli, who ran Los Angeles the same way he ran his import–export business, his loan company, his three restaurants, his two car dealerships, his eight whorehouses, the burglary ring, and the variety of drug operations he'd lost count of. And this was only a few of his enterprises. Salvatore was educated at the Wharton School of Business, but his real education had been watching his father, a genius in his own chosen profession.

One day Don Gaitano pulled Salvatore aside and carefully explained to him his philosophy of the world. Don Gaitano said that there were two paths a man could take in life. He could withdraw from the strife and competition in this world, become a priest, surrender his balls, and worry about the fate of his fellow man. There was nothing wrong

323

with this, it was nice somebody did it, provided that you knew nobody actually gave a shit about what you were doing and you'd die poor. On the other hand, Don Gaitano went on, you could join in the fray and do the best you could do to avoid being eaten. You got to keep your balls and enjoy a family and sex and all the nice things that life had to offer. Provided you could afford them, and provided you were strong enough not to let some envious bastard take them away from you, which they would surely try to do. The key to getting by was to worry only about your family and your proven friends, to take care of them and they would take care of you. The rest of the world was on its own, and as Don Gaitano was sure that it was not the sort of world God had in mind when he set it rolling, he felt no shame that a good profit could be made by taking advantage of the confusion. At that point Don Gaitano kissed Salvatore and gave him his ring and the family business. It was a touching moment, and Salvatore could never bear telling him that the Wharton School of Business had taught him all this long before.

The restaurant was closed until six, and in the afternoons Salvatore liked to conduct business here, comforted by the smell of cooking. He owned a thirty-acre estate a couple of miles inland and an office building or three in Santa Monica but he preferred it here. Sometimes, like now, there was someone standing outside the locked restaurant door waiting to be asked in. Waiting to ask for a favor, usually. Salvatore didn't think this guy was any different, though he had balls, Salvatore had to give him that. How he got the home number was anybody's guess. Salvatore would have to find out. Anyway there comes this call right to Salvatore's personal number, which maybe three people knew, and Salvatore himself picks it up, since the caller ID says unidentified and even the Pope blocks his caller ID. And this guy, this complete stranger, announces to Salvatore that he has information about Richie Stella that Salvatore would find enlightening. That was the word he used, 'enlightening'. Salvatore said yes, he was a sucker for enlightenment, thinking that in truth there was something about this guy he liked in spite of the bastard calling him at home. Salvatore said he would send someone to meet him. The guy said no. Salvatore asked his name. And the guy told him. This set Salvatore back a little. He never expected the guy to tell him his name. Who the hell was David Spandau? And why wasn't he worried about Salvatore Locatelli dropping him some early morning head first into the La Brea Tarpits?

Spandau tried the restaurant door and it was locked. This was not surprising, since there was a big CLOSED sign hanging there. He knocked on the mirrored door, tried to peer inside. He waited. Locatelli watched him wait. It was always a good idea to keep people waiting if they were about to ask you for something. Finally Locatelli sent two men to the door. One of them frisked Spandau while the other relocked the door and checked the parking lot for surprises. They led Spandau back to the table where Locatelli sat.

Locatelli looked him up and down and said, 'I know who you are. You're the cowboy with all the dead friends.'

'That's right,' said Spandau, looking down at the small, dapper man with the impeccable moustache and the impeccable gray wavy hair. The face was hard and never changed, but the eyes switched moods like Christmas lights. Right now they seemed, fortunately, to be amused.

'Well, right off the bat we can tell you're unlucky. You got three minutes, Texas. Just like a phone call. Start talking.'

Spandau waited for a day, then three days, then a week. Nothing happened. Maybe nothing would ever happen. Spandau sat around the house and read and watched videos he'd already seen. He tried not to think about Dee or Terry. He missed them both. Only Dee was still alive. He could pick up the phone, call her, or drive out there. She hadn't heard about Terry or she would've called herself. Spandau knew he should tell her, though she hadn't known Terry very well and was one of the few women who didn't like him. Spandau came close to calling a hundred times that week, but was afraid of his own weakness, knowing that part of him saw it as an excuse to try to get her back. He worked in the garden, cleaned the pond. Discovered there were more missing fish, nearly all of them in fact, and found fins and heads in the brush. A sole fish swam in the pond, in a constant circle around the perimeter, as if looking for its own way out. Spandau knew how he felt.

They came for him early one night, about nine o'clock. Spandau was watching *Rio Bravo* for the thousandth time when he leaned back and felt the gun barrel against the back of his head. Spandau felt a little betrayed, that they'd been able to use the Duke to cover their entrance.

'Richie wants to see you,' said Martin.

'Tell Richie to go fuck himself,' said Spandau without bothering to turn around. There was more than one of them. Spandau could hear their breathing, feel their presence. One of them hit him.

Guys get knocked out in the movies all the time. In real life it isn't so simple. For instance, a single punch to the jaw is unlikely to knock a guy out unless you're a heavyweight boxer. And any blow that has sufficient force to knock you out has given you a concussion, which can be followed shortly by brain damage both long- and short-term, loss of memory, emotional shifts, violent retching, blindness, and death. And of course headaches.

Technically Spandau wasn't knocked out. Stunned is probably a better word, and the headache would not be long in coming. They hit him with something heavy but soft, with enough impact to give his brain a good rattle and scramble things for a while. Enough to make him cooperative. They bound his hands behind him. He could stand and even walk, albeit not without falling over, and the three of them helped him out into the car. They were on the 405 heading into LA when one of them put a small heavy pillowcase over Spandau's head. Spandau tried to visualize the course the car was taking, counting the curves, but now his head was hurting and he was dizzy. He wanted very much not to throw up inside the pillowcase and visualization only made it worse.

The car stopped about thirty minutes later and somebody hit Spandau again. Not as hard this time, but another pretty good rattle. They dragged him from the car with the hood still over his head, up some steps, through a couple of doors, down a hallway. They dumped him on the floor and gave him a few kicks for good measure. Spandau lay on the floor, not moving, waiting. He waited for a while for another blow, something. Then he realized they'd gone.

Spandau worked at his hands, bound by a thin rope. It wasn't much of a chore and it occurred to him they'd meant it that way. He got his hands free then pulled off the hood, sat up. He was in the office of the Voodoo Room. The place was eerily silent. Richie was sitting in the big office chair with his back to him. He stood up, swaying a little, and waited for Richie to say something. When he didn't Spandau went over and spun the chair around and saw that Richie had a small hole in his forehead and a narrow rivulet of blood trickled down the side of his face into his shirt collar. A roll of 35mm film was threaded on some string and tied like an amulet around his neck. Careful not to touch anything else, Spandau snapped the string and put the roll of film in his pocket.

He went out of the office and down into the club itself. A single overhead light was on and the place had been nearly stripped, as if the club he knew had never existed. He pushed open the side door with his elbow and stepped out onto the street. His head hurt and he wondered if it was smarter to look for a cab on Sunset or walk down to Wilshire. He'd decided on Wilshire and had turned the corner when a car behind him flashed its headlights and rolled up leisurely next to him. The back window of the Lincoln came down.

'You're out late, Texas, and very far away from home.' Locatelli motioned for him to climb in. Spandau did so and Locatelli rolled the window back up and nodded at the driver to move on. Locatelli looked out the window at the city as it passed, like taking inventory of private property. 'Well, Texas, you were right,' he said finally. 'And now I owe you a favor.'

'I don't want your favor,' said Spandau.

'Oh, you'll want this one. Because you know what it is? You get to walk away from this. You get to go on living, Texas. Provided you stay smart and keep right on walking.'

'Where are we going?'

'It's the shank of the evening,' said Locatelli. 'I thought we'd stop off for a nightcap. Sort of cement our friendship. It's been a long day. If you don't mind my saying so, Texas, for a guy who ought to be dead you don't look so happy about it.'

'It was a very funny joke.'

'Oh, gosh, the truth is that you were outclassed every step of the way. I've been watching you for weeks now, Texas.

Not much goes under my radar. You nosing around, asking questions about Richie. I knew he was selling crack, but for the life of me I didn't know where he was getting it. Turned out he was more enterprising than I thought. And using my cocaine to do it. Anyway, you did my dirty work for me. I thank you for that.'

Locatelli paused to light a cigar. He offered one to Spandau, who shook his head. The odor made him sick. Locatelli puffed happily.

'Richie was going to kill you, you know. He didn't have a choice. He'd made such a goddamn mess of things, he'd have to start cleaning up loose ends before I found out.'

'So why not let him?'

'I probably would have, if it hadn't been for that business on your friend's boat. That was ugly, messy. Richie was fucking up right and left and calling way too much attention to himself. And to me. I like things nice and quiet.'

Locatelli took a few more puffs, then looked at the cigar as if it had turned on him. He stubbed it out in the ashtray.

'Anyway, what is this, the Old West?' said Locatelli. 'You can't go around shooting people, Texas.' He stopped to think for a second. 'Well, not too many, anyhow. Guy as popular as you turns up dead and there are all kinds of problems. No real problems, mind you, but just enough to be irritating. Richie is another story. Nobody liked Richie. He will not be missed. Even his cousin sold him out. Martin's going to be managing the Voodoo Room when we open it again. We're going for a whole new look. You know, on the average, gay bars are twenty-five percent more profitable than straight ones? What is the world coming to, I ask you.'

The car stopped in front of The Ivy. Locatelli stared at him, then said, 'Well, go on.' Spandau got out. Locatelli followed, stood on the sidewalk smiling, breathing the crisp night air. In the restaurant the maître d' greeted Locatelli as an old friend.

'Good evening, Mr Locatelli. Nice to see you again.'

'Good to see you too, George. Have my friends arrived?'

'They are waiting at your table. Have a pleasant evening, Mr Locatelli.'

'Thank you, George.'

Spandau followed Locatelli toward a table at the back of the dining room, where Frank Jurado and Bobby Dye sat laughing. They looked up to see Locatelli and smiled, though it was Bobby who first saw Spandau coming up behind him. He glanced painfully at Spandau then at Locatelli and then at Jurado.

'Good evening, gentlemen. I think you all know Mr Spandau.'

'What's he doing here?' Jurado said sharply.

'Mr Spandau wanted to drop by to say hello. He can't stay long. He has something he wanted to give to Bobby.'

Spandau fished out the roll of film and tossed it across the table into Bobby Dye's lap. Bobby looked at Spandau and for a moment he thought Bobby might say something, might thank him, but he didn't. Bobby stared down at the film as he turned it over and over in his fingers.

331

'Don't you love it when everything works out nicely?' said Locatelli expansively. 'See how well things go when everybody gets into the spirit of cooperation?'

Spandau felt his stomach churn, and he couldn't tell if it was rage or hurt. Mainly he felt stupid and weak and he wanted to destroy the evidence. He couldn't look at Bobby. He wanted to shame the little son of a bitch, but it was beyond that. If Bobby couldn't tell shame now he never would, and Spandau watched his friend, his reluctant friend, drift into the darkness and out of reach. They had him now and they would keep him, and he hated Bobby more than he hated Locatelli or Jurado or Richie or any of the other million bastards who corrupted everything they touched. He hated Bobby for his weakness, for his willing-ness to be corrupted. You had to be willing, that was the key. They couldn't take your soul unless you offered it first. If he had had a gun, Spandau could have shot everyone at the table. But he knew he'd have to finish off the rest of the room as well, then down the street, block by block, all the way to the sea and probably back again. It was endless, you'd have to kill them all. And then others would come. It would always be this way. Maybe it always had been.

Spandau turned and walked away. Locatelli caught up with him on the patio. He took Spandau's upper arm in a firm but gentle grip and walked him toward the street.

'Let me tell you what my point is, Texas,' he said patiently, like a father delivering a moral lesson to his son. 'Unlike Richie, I don't have to strong-arm anybody. I've already arrived. Movies? Hell, I've made ten films. You ever heard of Collateral Pictures? That's me. That's my point. You need to know that. Collateral cleared fifty million off its last picture. We finance movies all over the world. I've got business associates in every country on the planet, the greatest source of funds to be tapped since the fucking Vatican. And everybody wants to be in the movies, Texas. That's where the real money is. Movies make cocaine and heroin look like child's play. The point is, I don't have to break into the system. I *am* the system. You're walking this time. Next time you might not be so lucky. You think about that next time you wander into my woods.'

Locatelli gave him a gentle pat on the shoulder then turned and went back into the restaurant. Spandau had forgotten where the taxi stand was in this part of the world. While he was walking around looking for one, he had ample time to think. It was over now. Richie Stella was brought down and Bobby Dye was free. Mission accomplished. Except three people were dead now, four if you counted that poor stupid girl who started it all. Four people dead but you couldn't exactly call any of them innocent. Innocence is an over-rated quality, Spandau decided. Innocence got people into trouble. Innocence got them killed. Look at me.

Twenty-Three

On a cool night in February, David Spandau sat in his house and got drunk. He'd wrapped up a case for Walter a few days before and made a point about not taking another one for a week or so. He'd planned on getting very drunk on this particular day because he knew he would need it, that getting moderately shitfaced was the only way he was going to face it and that it would be a couple of days after before he managed to shake it off. Spandau started drinking in the afternoon and kept it going until the evening. Toward the end he sat drinking in the living room in the dark in front of a blank TV. Every now and then he would take a drink and then look at his watch and then take another drink. Finally he looked at his watch and then drained his drink and poured himself another one and turned on the television. It was Oscar night.

Spandau watched with the sound off. There was no fucking point in watching any of this really, but it was some sort of conclusion and he badly needed a conclusion. Closure, Dee had called it. Spandau hated that fucking word.

He watched the pretty, happy, elegant people move around quietly on the screen. There was a knock on the door and he got up to answer it and it was Dee. He hadn't seen her for months. He'd been avoiding her. Didn't return calls. Was afraid of what she was going to tell him. Was afraid of closure. That goddamn word. Some things you never wanted closed.

'I wasn't sure you were home. The lights were off.'

'Come on in.'

He let her in and then went into the living room and Spandau dropped back down heavily onto the couch. Dee stood above him, looking down at him.

'This a bad time? I can come back . . .'

'No,' said Spandau, suddenly frightened at the thought of her leaving, even more frightened of how he'd react when she wanted to go. 'I'm glad you're here.'

Dee sat down in the chair across from him. 'We haven't seen you in a while.'

'How's your mom?'

'Same as ever. She misses you.'

Spandau nodded.

'You're watching the Oscars. I forgot they were on.'

'You want a drink?' asked Spandau. 'Or I can fix some coffee.'

'Look, I think maybe this was bad timing . . .'

335

'Stay, will you? Please?' His voice quivered and he was ashamed of it, clenched his teeth to keep it back, felt it well up in his throat.

'It's the wrong time for this,' she said.

'For what?' But he knew. Oh, he knew.

'You know what? Maybe I'll have that drink.'

Spandau got a glass and poured her a whiskey and handed it to her. She took it and rolled it between her palms and said, 'You don't answer your phone.'

There was nothing to say. Spandau nodded, took a drink. Felt himself going crazy. Felt the mad spirits jumping in his skin to be let out, wreak havoc, scream, confess their sins.

'I wanted to tell you. Before you heard it from someone else. Charlie and I . . .' She can't manage to say it. God love her, she can't.

Spandau stared at the silent TV.

'We were never going to make it work, David. It was killing both of us, just trying to hang on.'

Quiet. Let the jackals rage. Keep them on the leash, they'll quiet eventually.

'I wanted to tell you,' she said. 'I want your blessing, I guess.'

'What?' said Spandau, as if he weren't listening. Maybe he wasn't. Maybe it was that roaring in the ears. The sound life makes before it goes over Niagara Falls.

'I need to hear from you that you understand. That you don't hate me.'

336

'Sure,' said Spandau.

'I'll always be there for you.'

'Sure,' said Spandau.

'I've talked to Charlie, and if you ever—'

Spandau reached forward and grabbed the remote and turned on the sound.

GUY PRESENTER (on TV)

... And the Academy Award for Best Picture goes to ...

(to GAL PRESENTER)

... Aren't you excited?

GAL PRESENTER

(*giddy*)

Come on, come on, I'm going to have a heart attack ...

GUY PRESENTER

And the winner for Best Picture is ... *Loser's Town*! A Collateral Pictures Production, Frank Jurado producing ...

Applause, applause. We see Jurado stand up, kiss his wife, and make his way toward the stage.

ANNOUNCER (VO)

Accepting the award is producer Frank Jurado ...

Jurado takes the podium as they hand him the Oscar.

337

JURADO

You know, I'd like to thank all the little people who made this film possible.

(*laughs from the audience*)

But the fact is, there weren't any little people, only big ones. Big people with giant hearts and a giant capacity for work and dedication. It was a struggle to get this film made, but we did it. A lot of people said it would never get done, that making a movie about a racketeer trying to force his way into Hollywood was verboten, that it was professional suicide, that nobody would ever finance it. Well, we did it!

(*applause*)

First of all, I'd like to thank the one guy without whom this film couldn't have been made. And you know who he is . . . Bobby Dye!

Huge applause. The camera finds Bobby, sitting next to a new babe – who decidedly isn't Irina. She kisses him proprietorily.

JURADO

Well, Bobby's already copped his award tonight for Best Actor . . .

(*applause, whistles, whoops*)

. . . and I'm not going to give him any more publicity. I just want to say . . . thank you, Bobby! And thank you, Collateral Pictures, for the courage and the vision to allow us to make this wonderful film . . . Thank you, thank you all . . .

Spandau turned off the TV. The room fell back into a near-darkness.

'Will you stay for a little while?' Spandau said to Dee. It sounded far too much like begging, which is what it was.

'For a little while,' she said.

Outside a car went by. Somewhere in the neighborhood a dog barked, over and over again, fruitlessly, pointlessly, into the night. Dee got up and sat next to Spandau and put her arms around him. She put her head on his chest, and in a moment she could feel it making small leaps beneath her cheek. She held him tightly and allowed the man she loved the small dignity of not looking up.